JENNA COSSEY

I0737799

DUNNIGAN

Copyright © 2022 Jenna Cossey
All rights reserved.
ISBN: 978-0-578-35551-1

I dedicate this book to the sweet persevering soul whose life encourages and inspires me even today, my Ma.

Gladys Oleta Trail Jones
May 18, 1921 - September 22, 2003

1

The locomotive hoisted the line of cars forward as the train glided along the rails toward its destination. Every detail of the carefully machined beast revealed purpose, from the large driving arms on the wheels to the shiny brass bell affixed to the nose.

The train reached its stop, and plumes of steam gushed from cracks and orifices on the engine. Men leaped into action, scampering along the tops of the cars applying brakes in synchrony, as the entire assemblage ground slowly to a halt. Inside, passengers shuffled around, locating baggage, collecting personal items, and corralling small children.

The brawny mechanized beauty finally came to rest in front of a tall rectangular building with yellow wood siding and green trim. The station bore the name of its city on a hand-painted sign. Men scrambled from within the building to accommodate the rush resulting from the arrival of the train. In one nook of the neatly furnished interior, the telegraph operator laid down a faint drum line of tapping that harmonized with a strain of chimes from a cash register as the ticket agent collected fares and doled out change. A diverse chorus of voices circulated through the station. The sounds merged, and the station sang another verse of its song in predictable intervals, which became a circadian clock for the vibrant city in which it lived.

Dunnigan.

2

Dunnigan looked like an anthill.

The streets and walkways were a constant flow of people going in and out of the stores. Some entered with loads and left with empty hands, while others entered empty-handed and left with boxes.

Cars sputtered down the macadam roads until their tires found a concrete main street near the town square. The chains of horse-drawn wagons jingled in perfect time with the *clop-clop-clop* of the equine hooves.

Tempera paint decorated the storefront windows.

Skirts pleated and plain: $1.00

The ladies went in, browsed, and lingered for a bit of small talk.

One suit coat and one hat: $2.00

The men went in, eyed the merchandise, and talked about the economic boom.

A cry recognizable even to those at a distance punctuated the bustle of the anthill. The whistle of the train piped a tune that beckoned all within earshot.

"All departing to Birmingham, make ready!"

"Say your goodbyes!"

"Here they come!"

"Get your parcels!"

People gathered toward the station, venturing to see what the iron horse would bring in its wagons.

Jenna Cossey

"Look at it, Sara!" A little boy, drawn to the window by his curiosity, looked upon the scene with wonderment. He could hardly contain his excitement.

Here we are, Sara thought to herself. Her eyes followed the storefronts as they floated past her window.

Skirts pleated and plain: $1.00

Erupting steam valves punctuated the stopping of the train.

"Easton, take my hand. Come on, take it. I won't be losing you first thing."

Sara and Easton Wheeler stepped onto the platform, wide-eyed and overtaken by all of the movement.

"Baggage to the left, folks. Baggage to the left," the porter called.

"Here, let's go." Sara dragged the boy along as he pumped his short legs to stay with her. "Take your suitcase." She handed him his small case, and she took hers. Inside her case was the balance of her earthly possessions, few and precious. Tucked into the folds of her homemade dresses was a picture of a young neatly dressed couple on their wedding day. In an orderly cursive hand, the back of it read: "*Walter and Matilda.*"

Sara began to scan the swarm of people about her. She felt a familiar panic.

*   *   *

"Mama . . . Mama . . . Mama?"

"Child, I thought I'd lost you! Come on, let's find your aunt Vi."

*   *   *

"Sara! Sara! Easton, Sara!"

Jolted from the panic by the sound of her name, she saw a sleek and slender woman emerge from the host of people. The woman had a familiar look about her that made Sara feel like crying with relief.

"Aunt Vi, I'm so glad to see you," Sara said with a sigh.

Sara's aunt Violet placed one arm around her with a smile and patted Easton on the chin. "Likewise, dear!" Violet looked about for assistance. "Please, sir, can you place the bags in the car?"

A young man carried the bags and closed the door for Violet, who reached into her clutch and retrieved a nickel. Through the window, she placed the coin into the young man's palm.

"Thank you, ma'am, much obliged," he said, tipping his hat.

The car's engine turned over with ease and hummed away from the station, leaving the anthill behind.

Jenna Cossey

<u>*3*</u>

"Evenin', sir. Fill 'er up?"

"Yeah, go ahead and top me off, bud. Got cold drinks in there?"

Another out-of-town motorist. All the locals know this station has cold drinks all day long. "We sure do. About any sort ya want." He located the tank lid and turned on the pump. The liquid descended toward the bottom of the globe as the pump chimed with the passing of each gallon. *Every time that thing dings, it's another quarter in the register, and people sure don't seem to mind spending it.* He began to walk around the car, checking each tire with a gauge.

"Tires okay, boy?"

"Name's Noah. Yes sir, these tires is just fine; look new to me. Got your window glass cleaned off. Maybe you can see something now. Checked under the lid too; looks clean. Seems like you take care of your buggy."

Yes, the tires were new, he said, freshly purchased before the trip, the glass looked good, and the car better be sound because the man who sold it to him guaranteed it.

Same old. Same old.

Noah watched the man drive away without wondering where he might have been going. It was too busy at Haskins' garage for anybody to wonder what else was going on in the world.

He briskly moved around the side of the building where two large shop doors stood ajar.

A Chevrolet sedan and a Ford touring car sat idly inside, hoods open, signaling for assistance from capable hands. Two feet were protruded from beneath the Chevrolet.

"That you, Noah?"

"Yep, who else?"

"Hand me that grease gun, will ya?"

Noah located the item, and a hand appeared from under the car to take it. He turned toward the station front and cataloged the list of things that required his attention.

"Reckon them parts will make it in on the three-fifteen, Tommy? If we don't get this Ford out of here, it's gonna put down roots. I'm gonna head on down to the depot. By the time I get there, she'll be pulling in. If them parts ain't on that train, I'll be sending a right hateful wire up to Detroit. Be worth the cost to give 'em an earful."

Noah made his way through the station, removed a pair of greasy coveralls, and stopped in front of the mirror just long enough to inspect his face for smudges and tame his smooth brown hair. He gave it a quick swipe with a fine-toothed comb and moved on.

A whistle punctuated the air.

"She's beat me there!" He paced toward the service truck.

As he motored down the road, he finally wondered to himself where the man with the new tires and dirty window glass was going. *Birmingham? New Orleans? Maybe Pensacola or Miami?* A conspicuous yellow building came into view. *The depot.*

He stepped out of the old truck and found the large sliding door on the side of the depot. "FREIGHT DOOR," it read, stenciled in green. He waited as workers shuffled items around.

"Anything for Haskins?"

"Don't have anything on my list, Maclane."

 Jenna Cossey

It kindled his ire. Noah made his way around through the depot and placed a telegram to Detroit as he had threatened. It was unlike him to become agitated, but he needed the parts.

His mind wandered backward on the short drive back to the station.

*   *   *

"I told you not to come back without them parts, boy."

"But Pa, Mr. Keaton said they didn't make it. Said these McCormick pieces are hard to get parts on."

*   *   *

In his mind, there had been no arrivals for him at the depot that afternoon, but he was mistaken.

<u>**4**</u>

Sara sat with her hands folded across her lap as they motored down the road. She kept her head forward, but her eyes wandered. She had seen cars like that, but riding in one was something altogether different.

They rolled down the unpaved road, passing several houses. Sara had rarely seen them built so close together. She noticed the people on their front porches and lawns. The men sat with pipes and papers, while the women were different from house to house. Some wrangled children, some waved fans, while others gathered in clothes from the line or worked at mending.

The car slowed. Her head swiveled as she tried to take in all the details. She felt something strange in the pit of her stomach. *Is this to be our new home?*

"This is it, kids!"

Sara blinked, startled from the thought by the words of Violet. She and Easton retrieved their belongings from the car and followed her onto the porch. She opened an ornate wooden front door. Sara watched as Violet placed her automobile keys on a tiny hook beside the door. She removed her gloves and put them down next to her clutch on a long slender table in the entryway.

"I hope neither of you is opposed to staying upstairs. It does get a bit warm up there but—"

"Upstairs!" Easton bolted up the stairs. His small case collided with every third or fourth spindle on the banister railing. Violet suppressed a giggle and followed after him.

 Jenna Cossey

"I was most worried about him not liking it up there, but it looks as though he's pleased with the elevation," she spoke to Sara through a smile.

Sara loved the smile. It resembled her mother's.

Sara and Violet ascended the stairs, one after the other.

"This room is yours." Violet swept her hand toward an open door. Sara entered as her mind began to catalog again. "This is your closet. You can hang your clothes there. It's all yours," Violet explained.

Easton skipped from place to place, not knowing which one gave him the biggest thrill. "Look at the bed, Sara! Look out the window! We're up so high!"

Easton, having never been in such a place, was fascinated by every nook and cranny of the house. Violet helped him unpack his things, leaving Sara to settle in on her own. She accomplished the task in only a few moments, as she had little to unpack. She unfolded each item until she came to the photo she had swaddled in her things with such care. *Daddy and Mama. Mama…*

"Sara?"

"Yes, Aunt Vi."

"I thought you two might be hungry. I've got some things in the icebox."

Sara was distracted from her swell of emotion again. "Yes, ma'am. I do have a little hungry place, and I hate to tell you, but Easton is a bottomless pit." She waited for a reaction.

Easton burst into the room and looked at them, smiling from ear to ear.

Violet giggled again with her warm smile.

"Well, then I guess you better help me get this bottomless pit to come on downstairs and see what we can fix up!"

Her good nature was already relieving some of the apprehension Sara felt over being in a new place.

<u>**5**</u>

"No, don't send another guy. Let me handle this. I know how these people operate. I can't play it cool with a traveling circus following me around. This place isn't Chicago. Send my trunk along as soon as you can."

A man dressed in a black suit with thick shadow stripes emerged from a car in front of Union Station. He tugged his coat lapels around his neck. The crisp fall air was heavy with sounds: car horns, people talking, newsboys yelling on the street corner. A thick scent wafted past him unnoticed because he had become so accustomed to it. It was a mixture of exhaust fumes, dust, and the faint aroma of a coffee shop or cafe.

He found his way out of the way of foot traffic and set his Gladstone bag and briefcase between his feet. He reached into the inner pocket of his suit coat for a package of cigarettes. "Chesterfield smokes, won't irritate your throat." He had read it a thousand times in the paper. He smoked sparingly and was not fully sold on the habit, but the nagging advertisement stuck in his head. He shook a cigarette from the package, raised it to his lips, and removed the protruding end. He reached into his vest pocket for a book of matches, before realizing that lighting the cigarette on a sidewalk in the Windy City was a futile effort. He made his way inside. He lit the cigarette and took a moment to look up and admire the Great Hall of the station while he collected himself. Massive Corinthian columns stretched upward to meet the vaulted skylight.

The large Elgin wall clock told him that there was plenty of time to make it to his concourse. When he arrived, there was no place to sit, so he stood until his departure. He had managed to grab a newspaper as he passed through the station, and when he boarded the train, he found his way to a window seat. He unfolded the paper and skimmed the headlines with a neutral expression: "Gangster Shot; Seen as Echo Massacre."

"Sure is a sight, ain't it?"

He looked over to see that another gentleman had perched upon the seat next to him and taken the liberty of reading over his shoulder.

"Oh, this? Yeah, sure is."

"Suppose them fellas will ever leave off killin' each other?" His seat mate continued to attempt conversation.

He had learned not to be bothered by talkative types. After all, he was just a typical passenger, and typical passengers made small talk. "Not likely. I had to quit concerning myself with it. Now the sports page, that's where I'd rather be," he said as he changed the subject on his unsuspecting neighbor. They exchanged chuckles as he thumbed over to the sports section.

"Name's Harding, Rufus Harding. I'm a carpenter. Been up here from Tennessee on a job. Don't ask me how we ever come across any work up in these parts, but my boss, Mr. Moody, when he gets up the work, we go to it. Mouths to feed and feet to shoe, ya know." Rufus continued for several moments about his family and hometown until he noticed he had overlooked some details. "You from Chicago?" He lit a cigarette as he asked and offered one to his neighbor.

"The one and only. No, thank you."

"I don't reckon I caught your name," Rufus said slyly.

Jenna Cossey

"Didn't give it yet. The name's Lucas, Alfred Lucas. My friends call me Al." He took hold of the carpenter's extended hand.

As the train jerked forward, it picked up speed at a nearly imperceptible pace. He kept the paper before him, knowing it always provided the necessary inspiration for train conversations.

"What line of work you in, Al?"

"Sales," he replied, his heart rate rising.

"Sales, huh? I've heard stories about you traveling salesmen!" Rufus cackled.

"It's not exactly like that," he responded with a coy smile.

Just read the paper, Alfio. Read the paper and talk about the economy. He doesn't know anything. Alfio coached himself as the conversation carried on. After a while, he excused himself to the dining car. When he returned, Rufus Harding had fallen asleep. *You've managed again, Alfio.*

Made a bit uneasy by the crowded train, he sank into his seat and hoped to remain inconspicuous.

<u>*6*</u>

Dawn broke over the quiet streets of Dunnigan. The sunlight spilled through the trees and bathed the rooftops in a rosy golden hue. Most lay sleeping in their beds, their bodily rhythms still unaffected by the faint light slipping through their windows.

Sara was not asleep. She lay there, wide awake, in her new bed. The sheets were soft, and the pillows were fat and airy. She was convinced the bed was fit for royalty, yet she had not rested. Her eyes scanned the room as they had since she lay down the night before. Her mind was running rampant. All of her memories and thoughts of the future swirled together in her mind. She found herself unable to calm the mental turbulence.

The light coming through the windows gradually grew brighter. When the sun rose to just the right height, it shone directly into the mirror on the wall, producing a blinding glare. She turned over on her side to get relief from the intensity of it. She took a deep breath and pulled the bedclothes up around her shoulders.

"Sara? Good morning, Sara sweet!" Sara shut her eyes. She closed them so tightly that she felt the top of her cheeks pressing against her eyes. *"Get dressed. I want you to help make breakfast again this morning."* The voice from her memory was soft and sweet, but it was not real.

Tears escaped from her clenched eyes. She covered her face with the bedding. She cried silently as her shoulders convulsed inward, forcing the air from her chest. She did not make a sound.

The height of the sun told her that it was sometime later when she opened her eyes and felt the damp pillowcase against her cheek. She heard footsteps and a faint knock on the door.

"Sara." It came almost as a whisper, but this time it was real.

She turned over to see her aunt Violet standing in the doorway. She rubbed her eyes and stretched a bit, raising herself to the side of the bed.

Violet tiptoed across the room and sat on the bed beside her. She stretched an arm around Sara's thin frame and took her hand. "Good morning, beautiful child. Did you sleep well?"

Sara said nothing. She did not want to say that she had not slept, but she did not want to lie. She decided a little smile would suffice. Violet leaned against her and patted her hand with a sweetness that calmed her and renewed her tired body.

"Let's go down and get some breakfast started. I'll let you wake Easton," Violet said.

Sara nodded, and Violet left the room. She considered her nightgown. It was not like the one Violet wore, and she suddenly became ashamed of it. She rose from the bed and dressed in the clothes she had worn the day before. They were not very nice either, but she estimated them to be more presentable than the ragged nightgown.

She moved across upstairs, and her bare feet made little noise on the glossy oak floors. She crossed the hallway and came to a door that was slightly ajar. She pushed it open just far enough to pass through. Easton lay there in the middle of his bed, sound asleep. The bed matched the one in her room, and she envied the careless little boy for the night of rest she was sure he had enjoyed. A smile began to crawl across her face as she moved toward him. She had awakened him so many times and wondered if this morning would be any different. She sat on the side of his bed, reached over, and began softly scratching his back.

"Wake up, lil fella. Wake uuuup," she said it the same as always, even though they were somewhere new.

Easton turned over with his eyes still shut. His shoulders shrugged upward, his fists pulled toward his ears, and his legs stretched out stiffly as his toes pointed toward the end of the bed. He took a deep breath, and his eyes popped open. "Good morning, sis," he said with a big smile.

She could not stop herself from smiling back at him. "Aunt Vi wants you to get up. She's going to make some breakfast."

He hopped out of bed and headed down the stairs. Sara listened as his feet caught each step and drummed across the floor at the bottom.

"Well, good morning to you, sir!"

"Good morning, Aunt Vi!"

Violet and Easton chattered about good nights of sleep and silly dreams. Sara sat on the bed upstairs and listened with a little smile.

 Jenna Cossey

<u>7</u>

Noah and Thomas readied themselves for a day of work. Together they occupied a small room in the back of Haskins' Mobil station. It was not much, but they had a roof over their heads. The station was only a short distance from the town square, and when they had a good week, all of the entertainment delights Dunnigan had to offer were within a good stretch of the legs.

Almost all of them.

"You get the services today. I'll try to get these two jalopies out of the garage."

"Suits me, brother. Ain't got to twist my arm to keep me out from under them rattle traps. Half the cars we pull in ain't worth the trouble." Thomas talked with a mouthful of breakfast.

"You're right, Tom, but when the people want 'em fixed, that's what we do. If everybody went to Steel City Chevrolet and bought new cars, we'd be out of repair work, and you do like them ham and eggs on your plate, don't ya?"

He patted his stomach. "Yessiree!"

"That's what I figured, so don't be wishin' them clunkers away!" Noah grinned and ate his breakfast. He looked out the back window of their little room. The sun was still low in the sky. Thomas finished his breakfast and got up from the table. He was tall and thin like a blade of grass and moved just as quietly.

"Indians move around with soft feet. That's how your Maw sneaks around the house of the mornin' without wakin' everybody."

Noah could still hear his father say it, and he always reasoned that Thomas inherited the ability from their mother. When they played in the woods as small children, he could sneak up on Noah with ease.

Thomas went out the front door of their room, which passed into the storefront of the station. Noah finished his breakfast and followed. "Landsakes. It's already hotter than blazes, and the sun ain't even full up," Noah remarked as he opened the large doors.

"Yep, I expect we'll have a run on cold drink sales until the dog days are over. It's done got hot for good now. Won't be no better 'til September's over. Just be glad we ain't hoeing cotton, brother!"

Noah was glad. He always reserved his feelings about farm life to avoid the bitterness Thomas tended toward.

Thomas began helping him work on one of the cars. They exchanged few words while working, which was not unusual. Both had become excellent mechanics, and each of them had their own aptitude for working with mechanical things, but Noah held the credit for landing them the job.

*   *   *

"Boy, you say you want a job?" Mr. Haskins stood there with a rag wiping grease from his hands.

"Name's Maclane, Noah. Yes sir, I'd like a job. Me and my brother is both right handy fixing things."

"Well, Maclane, that heap over there needs the carburetor rebuilt. You say you can fix things, so we'll just see how you do on that. You've got 'til three. Tools are on the table." He stuffed the rag in his back pocket, spit a mouthful of tobacco juice on the ground, and strolled off to the inside of the station.

"Noah, just tell him you can't do it! You ain't never fixed one of them things before. If you cobb this up, he'll run us plum off, and by the time he gets through telling it all over town, we won't be able to get a job nowhere!" Thomas pleaded with Noah in a hushed tone while he watched Mr. Haskins through the door.

"Trust me, Tommy, I can do it. Now, are you gonna help me or stand there with your finger in your ear?"

Noah opened the hood of the car. It was a Pontiac, but it made no difference because he had never really worked on any carburetor, Pontiac or otherwise. He did, however, know what a carburetor was, so he scanned the engine compartment and studied the situation. He went to the table and chose a couple of tools and began trying his hand. Eventually, he removed the piece and examined it. He could visualize how it was supposed to work and found the issue immediately. Over the next hour, he and Thomas worked together to rejuvenate the faulty part. Thomas said very little unless Noah solicited his opinion, but he ably acted as a second pair of hands for him. When Mr. Haskins came out to survey their progress, he found them returning the tools to their original places.

"It's alright, boys. Sometimes I have trouble with the Pontiacs, too. Always been more of a Ford man myself."

"It's done, sir," Noah told him.

"Say again?"

"I'm through with it." He wiped his greasy hands on a rag.

"Well, you ain't started it up yet, so don't count your chickens before they hatch." Mr. Haskins got into the car and prepared to turn the engine over.

Thomas cut his eyes to Noah. Noah took a deep breath. The car turned over once.

Pow!

It backfired loudly, and Thomas nearly jumped out of his skin. Mr. Haskins shot them a doubtful look.

"Give it a little gas. Try again," Noah coached him.

The car turned over once, twice, then a third time, and just like a new one; it began to hum in perfect time.

Mr. Haskins got out of the car, smiling from ear to ear.

"Well, Maclane, you've done it. I'll say I had my doubts, and I didn't reckon on you being able to do it, but you've done gone and proved me wrong! Where'd you learn cars?" His demeanor improved.

"Oh, first one place and the next. We come from a farm."

"Well, I reckon if you're needing work, I've got it. I'm 'bout near too old to keep up with all of it, and truth be told, I've been looking for some good help. If your brother can do like you, we'll be sitting pretty. How 'bout I start y'all off two-and-a-half dollars a day with the prospect of a raise down the line?"

"Deal." Noah stuck out his hand, and they shook on the verbal agreement.

*　　*　　*

Locals patronized Haskins' garage, but Noah's mechanical genius also caused people to come from the whistle-stop towns up and down the line from Dunnigan. The brothers took a room at a boarding house at first, but eventually bargained for the space in the back of the station. Mr. Haskins had once stayed there himself. It was meager, but saved them the cost of letting a room.

Mr. Haskins started to tend the counter and left the car business to the Maclane boys. Then he phased himself out of the station altogether and checked in on them only from time to time. Noah wondered if in good time he might turn the business over to him and Thomas. The dream became a little more important with the passing of each day.

Jenna Cossey

8

Sara peered into the bowl as she mixed the ingredients. She had the process memorized.

"Four cups of flour, two big spoons of lard, three or four spoons of butter, take your fork and cut that in 'til it turns into crumbles."

"Yes, Mama."

"Add some milk, not too much. Spread your flour on the table."

"This much?"

"That's fine. Now pat it out. Not too much, biscuits'll be flat . . ."

"That's the way my mother used to do it," Violet remarked as Sara prepared the biscuit dough.

"Mine too," they exchanged smiles.

Violet and Sara placed the food on the table, and she reached into the oven and retrieved the beautiful tall golden brown biscuits she had made.

"Those look wonderful, Sara! I can't wait to have one!" Violet said.

They enjoyed breakfast together. Easton chattered and asked when he might be able to climb the tree in the backyard. Suddenly a loud ringing startled him and Sara. Violet left her seat and walked into the adjoining room with no particular haste. They looked at each other, both unsure what the sound was. Easton had a wide-eyed puzzled look as they listened to Violet talking.

"Hello? . . . Yes! Good morning, Mr. Farnham . . . Yes . . . Yes. Thank you very much. I'll stop in later on . . . Of course. Thank you again."

She returned to the table and found the two stunned breakfast goers staring at her. "That was Mr. Farnham calling from the general store about the radio. It had to be repaired, and he's ready for me to come and get it."

"You talked to him right here in the house?" Easton was still sorting it out.

One corner of her mouth turned up with a smile. "Yes, sir! Have you ever used a telephone?"

"No. I've seen one before, but it was in town. You have one in your house?"

"Yes. You see, the city of Dunnigan put up telephone wires out so far from Main Street, and since I live close enough, that wire goes right past this house and the other ones on this street. They put some of it right here to this wall from outside," she explained in simple terms.

"Boy! A telephone right in the house! We didn't have a telephone at our other house." He was impressed by the house telephone, but not enough to deter him from eating the rest of his food.

"So today we will ride to town and pick up the radio. How does that suit the two of you?"

"Yeah!" Easton was excited.

"I'm going to get dressed to go. Easton, what kind of dishwashing hand are you?" Violet raised an eyebrow and put her index finger to her chin.

"Oh, I'm a good one, a real good one. I help Sara all the time!"

"Well, if you do that, then we've all helped with breakfast. Does that sound like a fair deal?"

He nodded with his mouth full, "Uhm hmm."

Sara got up and helped Easton clean up the kitchen, but she was distracted by the thought of going to town. In part, she was

Jenna Cossey

thinking about what she was wearing. Violet had on a pretty little cotton house dress at breakfast. It was much nicer than any of the clothes Sara had, yet she was changing out of it to go to town. It entered her mind that what she was wearing was not fit for a trip to town. She did not even think it was good enough for Violet's house.

"Easton, you keep cleaning up. I have to ask Aunt Vi something," she passed through the sitting room and by the staircase, and then, she knocked on Violet's bedroom door.

"Yes?"

"It's Sara."

Violet came to the door. She peeked from behind it and opened it just wide enough to let Sara through. She could see that all was not right from her expression. "Is something wrong, Sara? What is it?"

Sara fought tears. She did not want to cry. She took a breath and clutched the sides of her worn-out homemade dress in each hand. "Well, um, you see . . . I was thinking that . . ." She could not get out the words. She was coming to terms with her lack of wardrobe and trying to explain it to Violet at the same time. She knew they lacked in certain ways, but it never occurred to her that her clothes were so ragged.

"Come here and sit down. You can tell me about it," Violet took her hand, and they sat down on a cedar chest at the foot of the bed.

Embarrassed, Sara looked at the floor. She tried again. "Well, I . . . I just think that you look so nice, and this . . . this is the best dress that I have, Aunt Vi." It was a relief to say it, and though she desperately tried to stop it, a lone tear escaped from her eye.

Violet hesitated for a moment, wanting to choose wise words. She knew full well how fragile self-perception could be for a girl

Sara's age. She had once been there. "Sara child, oh, but look at you! You're not a child at all. You're such a lovely young lady. I bet if you put on an old tow sack and went downtown, people would hardly even notice it because you have a kind of beauty that goes beyond any dress you could wear. I want you to know that. Do you understand?"

A few more tears came as Sara listened and nodded her head. Violet embraced her. She took another deep breath and tried to put on a smile.

"So it looks like today will be a good day to go shopping, my dear!"

Sara knew they boarded the train with hardly any money. "Me and Easton have ten dollars, Aunt Vi, that's it," she confessed.

"Well, it just so happens that I keep a bit of money set aside for times when I feel like shopping, and this is one of those times! Now, don't you worry about it! Go help Easton. I'll be right out."

Sara left the room and returned to the kitchen, where she found Easton scrubbing away. He always lifted her spirits. He was such a good boy. She tried to get her bearings in the new environment, but everything was so different. Electrified appliances and lights, a telephone in the house, store shopping nearby, and Violet was so wonderful. She wanted to feel at ease, but her sense of self-preservation was holding her back.

     Jenna Cossey

<u>*9*</u>

Noah stood over the side of an automobile. He had wrestled with it for hours. Sometimes it was just that way. Figuring out what to do with machinery came as naturally to him as breathing, but the act of doing it was not always easy. He decided to take a break from it and relieve some of the frustration that had set in. As he leaned against the side of the car, he took a rag from his back right pocket. He wiped the excess grease from his hands and replaced the rag. He then reached into his back left pocket and removed a second clean rag. In his first days at the garage, he had watched Mr. Haskins walk around with grease all over his face, so he worked out a system to keep himself from looking like he had just emerged from a coal mine. It was second nature: "Right rag for the hands, left for the face." It made perfect sense to him, but Thomas ribbed him for it.

"Well, ain't you a dainty little mechanic. Should you go powder your nose now?" Thomas thought it was so funny.

Noah stood against the car as another came rolling up. He watched Thomas stride across the empty lot toward the gasoline pumps with nothing in the background to disguise his movements. When Thomas walked, his left heel barely contacted the ground, while his other footfall was regular. He was not overly slowed by it, but he had a unique gait. *Most people would hardly even notice.*

Nonetheless, Noah noticed, and it always stirred painful memories within him.

"You're supposed to look out for Tommy. Now he's a cripple, and he ain't gonna be no help at all around here!"

The words of William Maclane stung even with time. Noah gave up getting over it. The best he could do was not to ever let anything else happen to his little brother. As they grew older, it became quite a task. Thomas was fiercely independent, a spirit which their father had fueled as he insisted on his uselessness.

"Let him say I can't do something, and I'll make him out a liar again, Noah. If I didn't know any better, I'd think he wanted me to pass a lick at him just so's he could run me off. I may save him the trouble and just leave anyhow."

When Thomas had decided to leave home, Noah went with him to ease his conscience. He needed to make sure he got along alright in the world.

He thought about it as he watched Thomas cross the lot, but the car diverted his attention. He had a habit of recognizing customers by their vehicles. *Violet Simpson.* Noah and Thomas had not been in Dunnigan for many months, but they already knew Violet Simpson.

As the car rolled to a stop and the engine died, Thomas reached the pump. Noah watched and listened. Violet was a steady customer. He generally trusted Thomas's people skills on the job, but he was a charmer, and Noah wanted to make sure he was not a nuisance. After all, she had only recently become a widow, and even with what little he knew about women, he understood that kind of situation to be treacherous water.

"Hello there, Mrs. Simpson. Fine day for a drive," Thomas flashed a wide grin.

Noah listened as best he could. Almost everybody in Dunnigan who had a car came by the gas station at one time or another, and it was enough for Noah and Thomas to observe their habits. Violet had a couple of passengers in the car. One appeared to be a small child; the other, a young woman. It was not unusual, for

           Jenna Cossey

Violet often drove the other ladies on her street since most did not drive themselves. Either they did not know how, did not own a car, or their husbands took the only family vehicle to work each day.

The interaction seemed within bounds to Noah, so he returned to the nagging situation under the hood of the car on which he was leaning.

The car left, and Thomas returned to the garage.

"Boy, I tell you that Mrs. Simpson never fails to tip me!"

"She never fails to tip anybody, Tommy," Noah reminded him of her typical generosity.

"Well, here lately she's been giving me a nickel and telling me to get myself a cola on account of it being so hot out. I think I'm winning her over, Noah." He put the nickel tip in a jar on the back of the workbench.

"You're full of it, brother. She's better than twice our age. She's nice to everybody. You know that." Noah shook his head and grinned.

"She had another gal with her this time. Never saw her before." Thomas perched on a tall seat by the bench.

"That so?"

"Yep, I didn't get a good look at her 'cause I couldn't sneak one without bending plum down and eyeing her through Mrs. Simpson's window."

"Hmm." Noah was uninterested.

"There was a little boy too. Mrs. Simpson told me their names. I didn't catch the boy's, but the gal's name was Sara."

"Sara, huh? And will you be able to try and charm her *and* Mrs. Simpson at the same time, Valentino?"

<u>*10*</u>

The 1928 Ford Sedan hummed down the road with ease. Although covered in mud and dust, it was still relatively new, and Sara recognized it to be much nicer than any vehicle in which she had ever ridden. The Model T truck her father had owned was little more than a motorized buckboard wagon. Sometimes it worked. Other times it did not. They would plan to use it only for Walter Wheeler to find that it would not start.

"That infernal pile of junk! Man that sold it to me sure pulled the wool over my eyes. Got to get to town anyways. Have to hitch up the wagon," he would say.

She had often ridden the wagon to the whistle-stop nearest their farm in Tennessee, but now cruised in a fancy Ford. She wondered if Easton was old enough to recognize the change in their situation or if he was still too enamored of in-home electricity, telephones, and indoor bathrooms.

The oblivion his youth seemed to provide made Sara glad and jealous. She was keenly aware that their new living arrangement was unusual. On the other hand, her mind never really worked in such a way that resulted in her having self-pity. It was something her mother instilled in her early on.

Matilda had repeated the sentiment so many times in various ways, *"We just have to do with what we've got, Sara sweet, and there's plenty of other folks that haven't even got as much."*

As Sara thought about Violet's home with its beautiful furnishings, and the car they were riding in, she felt something different than she had for the first fifteen years of her life. She was torn between the restlessness of being in a new place with new people and a sense of relief.

"It's hot, kiddies, but it's a lovely day for a drive."

Violet was right. The end of July brought sweltering heat, but it *was* a lovely day. They motored down a gravel road with the windows down, and the sun warmed Sara's face. She felt as though the wind against her face could blow away the cares of her past. *We just have to do with what we've got, and I've got Easton, and I've got aunt Vi, and . . .* It did not seem like much, but she loved Easton almost as a mother would love a child. She also believed that Violet really loved them. Sara had adored Violet for her entire life. How could she not be happy with a wonderful person like her looking out for the two of them?

As they continued down the road, she noticed what a task it was to drive a car. When they left the house, Sara had watched as Violet positioned different items in the car: a lever on the left of the steering wheel, a lever on the right, and a knob on the passenger side. She positioned each with no concentration and pushed the starter pedal to the floor, but that was only the beginning. When they left the driveway, another phase began. She pressed the accelerator, released it, pushed in the clutch, moved the gear shift, released the clutch, and pressed it again before moving the gear shift to its final position. She did all of it while safely piloting the car. Sara had little idea what all of the pedals and levers were, but the series of movements intrigued her. There was something about Violet doing all of that, dressed to go to town in her heeled shoes and looking like the perfect lady, that impressed her. Right then, she realized that she could see in Violet all that she hoped to be in the world: beautiful, kind, intelligent, well dressed, and capable of doing things for herself, including driving a nice big car and conducting her own business affairs.

They stopped at a filling station, and a young man attended the gasoline pumps. Sara scrunched herself against the door, hoping that she would go unnoticed. She was glad the pumps were on the side of the car opposite her. *I look dreadful next to Aunt Vi. I hope she doesn't introduce us. I don't want the first person I meet in this town to see me looking like this.*

Thankfully, Violet only mentioned that Sara and Easton were with her. She made passing conversation with the young man. He cleaned her windshield glass, scampered around the car checking the tires, and chattered like a fool when he came to the window for pay. Violet never let on that he was trying to impress her. She was good-natured and exercised her habit of giving a generous tip before they drove away.

"That was one of the Maclane boys. They both work for Mr. Haskins and are hardworking boys at that."

Sara heard her, but she was not really listening because she was so relieved to have gone unnoticed.

At least she thought she had gone unnoticed.

11

Noah bolted upright in his bed, damp with sweat. The visions were fresh, even with the passing of years. He was slightly nauseated— another potent reminder of the accident Thomas had endured. The room was dim with the light of a new day, and he looked around to find that Thomas was not there. He wondered where he might have gone so early in the morning.

*   *   *

"I can't look, Noah. Is it bad?" Thomas was clammy and pale.

"It's pretty bad, but you gonna be alright."

Noah rode next to him in the back of an old truck. It traveled down the rutted dirt roads as quickly as possible, but it did not seem fast enough. Each time it dipped into one of the ruts, Thomas winced. Noah did, too.

An Autumn chill was in the air, yet Noah wore no shirt. He had used it to staunch the bleeding.

"I'm freezin'."

"I know it. We're almost home," Noah tried to comfort him.

They hit another divot in the road, and Thomas clamped down on his hand with crushing force. Noah told himself that if he had the strength to squeeze his hand that tightly, he had the ability to pull through.

The truck approached the Maclane house, and the passengers sprang from it in a scramble to help Noah unload the mangled, wrung-out body of Thomas from the back.

"Maw! Maw! Quick! It's Tommy! He's hurt bad!"

Gertrude Maclane leaped from her chair, dropping her mending onto the porch floor. She disappeared into the house like a shot to ready a place to lay Thomas. Somehow calm and frantic, she directed the crew of helpers.

"Bring him here. Put him just there. Careful now. Jack, I need you to drive out to Doc McGee's place. Bring him back fast as you can. Tell him I said that he has to come," she ordered.

The daughter of a Cherokee native, Gertrude possessed incredible knowledge of home remedies and natural medicines passed down from many generations. It was not unusual for a neighbor to call on "Trudy" to mix a salve, recommend an herb, or help deliver a child, but the injury Thomas sustained was beyond her expertise. She knew he needed a doctor, but she was not helpless to give aid in the meantime. She tore up several pieces of a cotton sheet and retrieved a jar of poultice from the top of a cupboard. She made a mixture of the poultice and sugar and carefully removed the blood-soaked shirt from Thomas's leg. She applied a liberal amount of the concoction to the area before recovering it tightly with the cotton strips.

"That'll staunch the bleeding some till doc arrives," she was confident.

She was not afraid of blood. Though shaken by the condition of her son, she maintained her composure. Noah stood out back of the house, green with nausea and trying to get some fresh air. At the corner of the porch stood a rain barrel. He dipped his head into the water, raised it with a snap, stood up tall, and took a deep breath. As the cool water trickled down his upper body, the pit of his stomach hollowed, his heart began to race, and his ears rang. He doubled over, gagged, and retched. He regained his composure only to experience a second turn with the same outcome. The sight of the mangled leg burned in his mind.

 Jenna Cossey

After what seemed like an eternity to all who waited with Thomas, the doctor arrived. J.A. McGee was an elderly man. No one could declare his exact age, but most reckoned him to be approaching ninety. His thick hair was snow white, and he carried with him the typical leather medical bag. Although the years forced him to move at a languid pace, his mind was sharp, and he was still reliable.

He leaned over Thomas and intently examined his leg. The lower portion was barely attached, and while the good doctor was unfazed, Noah stood by, unable to look at the scene.

"Leg's got to come off," the doctor made his blunt announcement.

"No!" Thomas started to struggle, but was too weak from blood loss to put up too much of a protest.

"It's got to. Bones shattered, and it won't ever get well."

Dr. McGee took no time to mince words or dwell on the gravity of the situation. He reached into his bag and retrieved a bottle of ether. Thomas was in too much pain to appreciate the blessing of being rendered unconscious for the procedure.

"No, don't! Don't take off my leg!"

Once they wrestled him down long enough to anesthetize him, the doctor began the unsightly work of removing the leg. The operation required several trade tools with which he had become quite familiar. He had started practicing medicine during the Civil War and was no stranger to amputations. It would be one of many he performed, and the repetition rendered him just as skillful as he had been in his prime.

Noah removed himself to the backyard and suffered another bout of sickness. He passed out and was lying flat on his back in the yard when a nearby scratching on the ground roused him. He raised himself and saw his mother there, shovel in hand, digging a hole.

"Maw, what are ya doin' out here?"

"Got to bury this leg and bury it good. If we don't, the ants'll get on it, and poor Tommy will itch himself crazy," she said.

Gertrude had several superstitions in which she firmly believed, and she coupled them with her knowledge of natural remedies. Noah peeled himself off the ground long enough to help her finish digging the hole. She placed the limb in the pit, and Noah began to cover it. He almost finished the task before he became sick again.

By the time Noah felt well enough to come back into the house, Thomas was awakening. He went to his side and blotted his forehead with a damp rag.

"Is it bad, Noah? I still can't look." Thomas was weak and exhausted.

"Guess there ain't no point beatin' around the bush about it now. It's pretty bad, little brother, but now that doc cleaned it up, it'll get better," he tried to be positive.

"Well, my leg ain't gonna grow back," Tears welled in his eyes.

"Naw, 'fraid you're right, Tommy."

"I'm gonna be a sight now, going around with one leg all over the place."

"Goin' around with one leg is better than not goin' around at all," Noah told him.

"Yeah, reckon it is." Thomas drifted off again.

     Jenna Cossey

<u>**12**</u>

On the trip to town, Sara thought about the first time she had seen Dunnigan. Some of it was familiar, but a few of her memories were vague. Life had changed so drastically since then.

"Here we are, kids! Let's see if we can find some bargains today!" Violet seemed so excited to be taking them shopping.

They had arrived at their destination. Sara looked up at the building and saw a familiar name, a concrete memory from her previous trip. The sign on the back of the building simply read "Stillman's."

*　　*　　*

Sara took a small bundle of mail from the postman. "Thank you, Mr. Carrol," she said, smiling.

"Welcome, Ms. Sara. Tell your folks I asked after 'em!"

She skipped toward the house with the treasures. She loved it when the mail came so she could find out what was going on outside of Holley Creek, Tennessee. Relatives and acquaintances would write to her mother and father from time to time. Walter seldom replied. He mostly had Matilda pen his returns for him, but on rare occasions, he would receive a letter from old hunting or army friends and respond for himself. He had little education and needed assistance.

"Tildy, how do ya spell fertilize? With an 'a' or an 'e'? I forget."

"F-e-r-t-i-l-i-z-e," Matilda answered.

"Oh."

Matilda Wheeler had received a better education with eight years of school. She loved to read and did so by the coal-oil light each night for a short time after everyone had gone to bed. There were only a few readily available selections in their home: The Bible and the Sears and Roebuck Catalog. More often than not, she read from the former. Reading letters from friends and family was a pleasure to her.

Sara sorted through the mail upon entering the kitchen. One by one, she eyed the return addresses.

LaPorte, Indiana.

Summitville, Tennessee.

Dunnigan, Alabama.

Dunnigan.

"It's a letter from Aunt Vi, Mama!"

Matilda smiled. "Open it!"

Sara carefully opened it, making sure not to tear the contents of the small white envelope. She removed a few small pieces of folded lined paper.

"Here," she surrendered the letter to her mother.

"No, you read it aloud to me. My hands are full."

Matilda had begun teaching her to read early. Though slow, Sara read aloud in her best voice, just as she did in school when called upon and asked for help with words as needed.

January 21, 1920

Dear Sister,

I will write you a few lines at this time. How are you? How is little Sara? I am getting on quite good here. The room I have taken in Dunnigan suits me just fine. I think it's fitting enough. Each day I take the train into the city for my schooling. The fare is reasonable, and there's a daily local that runs at just the right times. I've taken on mending for some in the building, and on the weekends I work in a clothing store called Stillman's. Getting the job was dumb luck because one of the county girls had just quit and gotten married when I arrived. Sometimes, they let me buy things wholesale and my, they have

                    Jenna Cossey

beautiful things! I don't dare shop in Birmingham. My purse would suffer awful if I did. I want you and Sara to come and visit for a few days if you can! I'm on friendly terms with the building manager and am of the understanding that it would be fine to have some visitors, seeing as how you're my sister and all. Well, I will close for now. Do write and tell me how you are getting along.

Love from your sis,

Violet Rose Stratton

"Mama, are we gonna go visit Aunt Violet?" Sara bubbled over.

"Well, I don't know, dear."

Matilda wished she had read the letter for herself after all because she knew that Sara would surely fix her mind on a trip to Alabama. It would be difficult to explain to her that they did not have the money for the fare. In addition to her household duties, Matilda often helped Walter on the farm when he got behind on his work, and behind on work was something Walter seemed increasingly to be.

The US government had banned the sale, production, and transport of alcohol by its passage of the Volstead Act, but it was no magic wand for the Wheeler household. Walter always knew where to come up with a jar or bottle, even if Matilda was unaware of the source. Still, she silently battled his growing habit. A nearby sawmill served as his place of employment, and he farmed otherwise to help them manage. She woke him each morning, made him eat a hearty breakfast, and urged him out to his work.

"Walt, I had a letter from Violet yesterday," Matilda told him.

"Yeah?"

"Yes, she wants Sara and I to come and visit her," she braced herself for the response.

None came.

Walter sat in his porch chair, looking across their property and smoking his pipe. He was sober. Matilda would not have bothered to ask him had he been drunk.

"She allows we can stay with her in the room she's taken." She waited. "Sara read the letter. She's fit to be tied. You know how she takes on about Violet." Matilda was making her case.

He took the pipe from his mouth and leaned forward, still not making eye contact with her.

"How you figure on affording the fare?" he finally gave a low and monotone reply.

"Well, next Saturday when we go into town, I'll have to ask about the fare. I don't even know how much it'd be to—"

"Too much," his tone changed.

"Well, I'll be asking."

She was not going to argue with him, she did not think it was proper, but she did let him know, in her way, that she was going to figure out how to make the trip. If he could find money to waste on the drink, she could find some to take Sara to Dunnigan.

On their next trip to town, she did as she planned. She discovered that her fare was less than two dollars, and Sara could travel for half that amount. She did not know how long it would take her, but she was determined to save the money before Sara's birthday.

"Mama, are we gonna get to go see Aunt Violet?" Sara asked every day after reading the letter.

"Yes, yes, we're going to go," Matilda tried to speak it into existence.

"When?"

"I'm not sure yet. We're going to go visit Violet, but you'll have to be patient, dear," she challenged Sara.

 Jenna Cossey

Matilda quietly stowed away money for the trip in a little black coin purse that she kept in the kitchen. She never let anyone see her place her earnings in it, especially Walter, for she knew that, if he obtained the purse, he would squander the money on corn liquor. Difficult though it was, she scraped up enough money to take Sara to visit Violet in Dunnigan for her birthday.

<u>13</u>

Noah was making breakfast as he usually did. Since he and Thomas had hearty appetites, he made sure they stayed fed. At times, he wondered whether his cooking tasted as good as he thought or if he had just forgotten what good food was. There were days when he missed being able to walk into the kitchen and take leftovers out of the warming closet to temper his hunger.

He wondered what his mother might have been cooking that very morning for the others. Missing home was something he did from time to time, but when thoughts of returning crossed his mind, they were found wanting in the balance with reasons he and Thomas had found to leave.

"Mornin', brother," Noah said as Thomas walked into their living quarters.

"Mornin'."

Noah refrained from asking him where he had been. "Here, eat this while it's hot. I'll have this other when it's done." Noah put a plate down in front of Thomas and continued cooking.

Thomas started eating and did not say much. Some mornings they said very little, but Noah found him a bit too reserved. When the silence extended beyond normalcy, he posed a question. "Where were ya so early this morning?"

Thomas kept his eyes on his plate. "Ah, just couldn't sleep. Went out and walked around. Got some fresh air. You know, sometimes a fella wakes up and can't go back to sleep."

"Oh," Noah let the explanation suffice for the moment.

Nobody knew Thomas better than he did. Something about his manner said that he was not forthcoming. Noah tried not to be overly concerned about it, but on the other hand, he knew how reactive he was. He had seen it over and over again from the time they were schoolboys. A particular incident came to mind.

*   *   *

"I ain't goin' up there no more, Noah."

"What do you mean you ain't goin'?" Noah was surprised at Thomas, ever the social butterfly, not wanting to go to school.

"I mean I ain't goin'."

"Now, Tommy, this don't make no sense. Somebody pickin' on you?" Noah was determined to get to the bottom of it.

"Ain't nobody pickin' on me. I just ain't goin'."

The two of them sat astride of a fallen log on the side of the road.

"Is it that old Mrs. Jenson? 'Cause if it is, you ain't got but this one year left with her, and then you'll be up in Ms. McCurry's class with me and—"

"It ain't Mrs. Jenson neither!"

"Well, then what in the hog hair is it? A body don't just up and quit the school year when it's just started."

They sat there in silence for several moments. Noah tried to think of every possibility as he tried to pry an answer from his brother. He knew that Thomas sometimes found mischief during the school day. At the end of the previous year, he and three other boys had gotten in trouble for smoking "rabbit tobacco" from a pipe they made out of a walnut hull. The principal discovered it and punished all of them with the standard three licks of the paddle.

"It's Mr. Bradford, ain't it? What'd you do this time? You might as well just go take your licks and get on with your day. It won't be the first time," Noah tried to appeal to reason.

"I didn't do nothin'! For the last time, I ain't in trouble!" Thomas was clamming up.

"Well, if you're not gonna tell me why you ain't aiming to go, I reckon I'll just have to sit right here with you on this log 'til you do," Noah tried a different approach.

"Then you'll be late, and it'll be you that's gettin' the licks." Thomas leaned over and planted his elbows on his knees.

"You mean to sit there and tell me that you ain't never going back to school? You know there ain't nothing waiting for ya at home but work, Tommy. Why, we're lucky we even get to come what times we do! You stay home, and Pa'll work you like a borrowed mule."

Thomas knew it was true, but whatever stole his desire to go to school was bigger to him than any work he envisioned their father having in store.

"Well, you've hemmed and hawed around long enough. If I stay here any longer, I'm gonna be late myself. I don't want to get my britches dusted this morning. So you sit here if you want to, but I'm goin' up there and ask Mrs. Jenson and Mr. Bradford if you're in trouble. I'm gonna find out what's holdin' you, so you might as well go ahead and tell me!"

Thomas looked at him and relented. "Them vax-nations," he said matter-of-factly.

"Huh?" Noah was even more confused than before.

"You know, where they line us all up and stick us with them needles, vax-nate us," he said it like any fool would know what he meant. "Mrs. Jenson told us yesterday that that old nurse lady

     Jenna Cossey

from town was comin' out today to shoot everybody with them shots, and she ain't shootin' me again!" Thomas crossed his arms.

Finally, Noah understood that he referred to the time of the year when the nurse from the health department came around. He also vaguely remembered the tantrum Thomas had thrown at the last inoculation, and the subsequent punishment he received for it.

"Look, Tommy. Vaccinations ain't so bad. You made a big fuss about nothing last time. It's over real fast; plus it's for your own good."

"Nope, I ain't doin' it, and I told that heifer Mrs. Jenson that I wasn't doin' it, too. She said I had to if I was at school today. I just told her I wouldn't be comin' today, and she said I might as well because if I came back the next day, they'd just send that lady out to our house, so I thought about it Noah, and I ain't going back no more." Thomas was out of breath from explaining the scenario.

Noah was sure of a few things. When Thomas went home without him, he would get a whipping from their father, and if he was not there with him, it would be much worse. He knew that Thomas had made up his mind. Most of all, he knew what a miserable time Thomas would have every day if he was not there to act as a buffer between him and their father.

So in a few brief moments, when Thomas was beginning the fourth grade and Noah the sixth, they both quit school over a triviality. Thomas quit because he was stubborn, but Noah quit to look out for him.

*   *   *

"You gonna eat, brother?" Thomas stared across the table at him.

Noah's food was nearly cold. "Yeah. I was just thinking about something."

<u>**14**</u>

The heavy wooden door swung open. Its hinges croaked as light from the hallway invaded the room. Clothes and shoes were strewn about the space. There was a summer hat, which had missed its mark when tossed aside, wedged between the top of the bureau mirror and the wall.

"Mr. Ransom?"

The drapes were pulled shut, and their opacity forbade any sunlight to enter the room. The call of the visitor came louder through the stillness.

"Mr. Ransom?"

A heap of bedding began to stir as a sigh came from beneath it.

"Mr. Ransom, it's time you be gettin' up 'fore noon, Mrs. Cahill said," a small thin senior man beckoned. "Mr. Ransom?"

One arm emerged, and then a second. The movement increased until, finally, a man appeared from beneath his cover. He sat up, rubbed his eyes, and groaned as his head fell against the headboard. "What time is it?"

"Eleven, right near it." The visitor pulled the drapes to the side of a large window, creating a tidal wave of light.

"Agh! Was that necessary, Cephas?" He squinted at the sunlight.

"Yessir, Mrs. Cahill say you got to get up and make yourself presentable and ready to receive company this evenin'." The old man seemed unconcerned about the tired state of the younger.

"Company? What company? Please don't tell me there's *another* ridiculous dinner party."

"Yessir, your paw having some more of them folk from Birmingham up here. So you got to get up outta that bed and get ready. You look like you been drug down the road behind a runaway team," Cephas told him.

"I *feel* like it too, Cephas. Draw me a bath, and would you get Zennia to make up one of those drinks she does?" He had managed by that time to get his feet onto the floor.

"Yes sir, you sure do need it, Mr. Ransom." Cephas shook his head as he eased into the bathroom to start the bathwater.

Ransom stood up from the bed and stretched, reaching toward the high ceiling in the room. He had no recollection of making his way there that morning. His head pounded. Each step he took across the floor sounded like a drum inside his skull. When he reached the bathroom, he opened the medicine cabinet and found a bottle of aspirin. He rattled a few from the bottle, placed them in his mouth, and lowered his head to the faucet for a sip of water. When he raised up, he closed the cabinet and looked at himself in the mirror. His thick wavy hair stuck straight up in the air from hard sleep, and puffy skin encircled his tired eyes. Cephas came back to the room bearing a glass filled with a concoction resembling the color of Alabama clay.

"You were right, Cephas. I look like a corpse," Ransom conceded.

"Well, sir, Mr. Ransom, I didn't quite say them words, but I reckon that's about what I was gettin' at. Now you get yourself quickened up, sir. Which suit'll you be wantin'? Looks like you pretty well wrecked the one from last night."

"Lay out the gray three-piece."

"You sure, Mr. Ransom? That be your least favorite suit is what ya always tell me." Cephas wanted to make double sure.

     Jenna Cossey

"Right. I don't like it very well, but I'll be hanged if I waste my favorite suit on another one of the mayor's dinner parties." He upturned his chin and started to shave.

"Gray one it is, then! I know ya don't like it so much, but I still think it's a fine suit, sir. I surely do."

At twelve thirty in the afternoon, Ransom left his room and descended the large flight of stairs. He found his mother in the dining room, directing those preparing it for the dinner party.

"Ah, Mrs. Cahill, lovely as ever!" He took her hands into his.

"Good afternoon, Rans. What time did you come in last night? You've slept the day away," she chided him.

"Now, is that any way to greet your favorite son? Come now, mother, did you miss me all that bad last night? Is that what it is? Or perhaps you're vexed because your handsome son was not present for coffee with you this morning?" He flashed his best smile.

The scowl on her face faded into a smile, "Oh, you!"

He kissed her on the cheek and continued pouring on the charm, "So tell me, what has Mrs. Cahill planned to have set before us at supper tonight? Something fit for the finest dignitaries in the South, I'm sure."

"Roast beef, with all of the trimmings. Zennia has outdone herself. The kitchen smells wonderful!" She was anxious to extend some of her famous Southern hospitality.

Ransom, still not feeling his best, had no desire to smell the scent of food that wafted through the house, but he humored her and pretended to take in a deep breath through his nose.

"Smells wonderful, mother. I'm sure the guests will love it." He headed toward the back door of the house as he left off talking with his mother, "I'll be back!"

He could hear her calling out to ask where he was going as he exited. He climbed into his Chevrolet coupe and headed toward downtown Dunnigan. He had nowhere to be, but he knew that the mayor would want him there well before the guests. It was an unspoken request that Ransom was not willing to grant.

"The mayor," he said aloud to himself with a chuckle as he drove down the road.

Edward Cahill wanted everything done his way in Dunnigan, including the affairs of his own family, but by the time Ransom reached manhood, he had grown weary of being governed by him. It was a constant source of angst for the entire household.

"Something has to be done about the boy, Charlotte. He's rebellious, proud, and lazy. You don't know how close I am to putting him out."

"You will not put him out of this house, Edward Cahill. He is my son," Charlotte said.

"Will you ever shrink from propping him up? He should be at the college still. We paid good money, and I had to call in several favors to get him there. He's making nothing of himself!" Edward slapped the arm of his chair.

"It makes him no less my son and no less welcome here," Charlotte Cahill continued, unfazed by the increasing agitation of her husband.

Several shades of red flushed across his face. Edward finally made eye contact with her. Charlotte Palmer and Edward Cahill had each entered the marriage with property and wealth. He spent his early life using the family name and money for influence and married only when he encountered a woman that could not be bought. The very thing that endeared him to Charlotte Palmer Cahill in the outset came to present frequent turbulence. She had no real dependence upon him. He loved and hated it.

     Jenna Cossey

"Very well, then. If that's the way you want it, that's the way you can have it, but I will not be a party to Ransom's self-destruction. He will have no more allowances from me to spend on his frivolities!"

"And if that's the way you want it, Mr. Cahill, then that's the way *you* can have it as well. No Palmer ever needed a Cahill to support him financially," Charlotte made the final dig of the spur.

There were a number of hired servants in the Cahill house and few secrets to be had. It was not long before the conversation between Edward and Charlotte Cahill found its way back to Ransom.

"Was that all, Cephas?" he queried.

"Yessir, that was about the size of it. I really shouldn't ought to be tellin' you all of this, sir." He stood there with downcast eyes.

"Cephas, how long have you been working for this family?"

"Nigh on forty years, Mr. Ransom. You know I come from Birmingham at your granddaddy Palmer's when the Mr. and the Mrs. married."

"Yes, and who pays to retain you here?"

"Mrs. Cahill. She been paying Zennia and me both good cash money every week since the day we come to Dunnigan," he made the record clear.

"Don't you forget it either, Cephas. The only loyalty you have in this house is to mother," he paused and took a long drag from a cigarette, "and of course to her favorite son."

Ransom continued down the road, and a wide sheepish grin crept across his face. He recalled his secret conversation with Cephas; sure he had the advantage over Edward Cahill.

That was just the way he wanted it.

<u>*15*</u>

Sara looked over at Violet, unsure of what the store shopping experience would bring. More than anything, her shame and anxiety began to return. Easton had no reservations. He was too young to understand that his appearance was not very good, and Sara envied his naïveté again. She anticipated a long day, and her shame turned to dread as she sat paralyzed by the emotional frenzy.

"Sara? Come on. It's alright." Violet opened the door for her.

They had come to the same door nearly a decade ago during her first and only other visit to Dunnigan. The store had an entrance facing downtown Main Street, but this was not it. Violet had parked her car in the back, and they were at the rear entrance. Sara assumed it was a special privilege to enter through the back, which was not altogether untrue. What she did not realize was that Violet understood her feelings. She was attempting to spare Sara any embarrassment that she could.

Violet had a naturally kind disposition that was cultured further by her job as a school teacher. She taught lower grades at a county school on the outskirts of town. It gave her a first-hand look at the varying economic situations of the people in Dunnigan. She often witnessed in her students the very thing she saw in Sara: the sudden awareness of lack and plenty. Because of past experiences and her general good nature, she was determined to help Sara leave town walking a little taller.

They entered the store, the inside of which had changed no more than the outside. It was one four-story section of a row building on Main Street. The Stillman family had lived on the fourth floor for several years when the business was budding, but now used it for storage along with the basement. The footprint was long and rectangular, with the short walls containing the entrances or windows on the upper floors.

Violet called out, "Hello! Is there anything on sale today?"

The sound of two pairs of feet came tapping across the floor toward the sound of her voice. "Violet! How lovely to see you! I wondered who I heard coming through back there!"

A neatly put-together woman with a touch of silver in her hair greeted Violet with a casual hug, followed by a medium-height man, who was somewhat round in the middle.

"Mrs. Violet, how are you? How are you?" He grabbed her hand and shook with a smile that sparkled.

They exchanged pleasantries, and introductions soon followed. Sara wanted a place to hide, but she soon felt the soft grasp of a hand on each of her arms. They were the hands of Mrs. Stillman, and she searched Sara's eyes in a warm, motherly way.

"As I live and breathe, Vi! What a lovely young lady! She's come to favor you very much since I saw her last!"

She caught Sara's attention. *Lovely? Favoring Violet?* She thought perhaps that Mrs. Stillman was trying to make her feel better because she looked so ragged.

"Yes, Florence, she is all grown up, isn't she?" Violet patted Sara on the back.

"We want to do a bit of shopping today. Sara has grown up so that I don't feel her wardrobe befits a girl her age. Do you think we could do something about that?" Violet waved her hand in the direction of the ground floor merchandise for women and girls.

"No place in town could do it better!" Mrs. Stillman said.

"Pardon me, ladies, pardon me, but what about this fine lad here? Will he be needing some new duds, too?"

"You know, Jacob, it's true. He's a fine lad indeed, and he could probably use some clothing more suited to a young man about town!" Violet placed a hand to her chin as she cut her eyes toward the upstairs.

"I know just the thing! Jacob, you take the young man upstairs and see what you can find for him, and I'll get Sara started with some things to try. One of us will be up shortly to check on the gentlemen's meeting!" Mrs. Stillman tousled Easton's sandy blonde hair.

"Come with me, sir!"

Easton took the stairs two at a time, and Mr. Stillman followed. Mrs. Stillman turned to Violet and Sara and started inquiring about the types of wardrobe items they were seeking.

"You know, Florence, I suppose we should begin at the beginning."

Violet took off her hat and placed it and her clutch behind a counter.

Mrs. Stillman knew what it meant to "begin at the beginning." She and Violet had learned to speak the same language over the years as Violet first worked there and then became a loyal customer. They moved toward the back corner of the first floor where there was all manner of undergarments for women. Sara never knew they could be so fancy, but it did not take her long to accumulate an entire line of them. They moved on to dresses, and Sara was in awe of the variety. She was thankful Violet stepped in to give her fashion advice.

"I think she should have a pair of plain skirts," Violet said.

"What about the length? Will you be wanting her to show her knees?"

Jenna Cossey

Mrs. Stillman knew the right questions to ask. The fashions had become increasingly shorter, and while many made no bones about the emergence of their knees from time to time, others still considered it a breach of good taste.

"I trust your judgment," Violet said with a smile.

"In addition to the plain ones, maybe we could find one of those coin dot dresses to fit her. And what about a pleated skirt or two? Of course, she'll need some blouses."

Sara could not believe what was happening.

They settled on several different items before moving on to the shoe department. "How about a low heel in black and a pair of sport oxfords?"

"That sounds practical," Mrs. Stillman concurred.

They looked at hats, handkerchiefs, and scarves. Florence and Violet teamed carefully to make selections that paired with multiple dresses. After the passing of several hours, they amassed quite a mound of items.

"Sara, if you'd like, you and Mrs. Stillman could choose some of your new things, and you could wear them home. I'm going upstairs to see what kind of damage the gentlemen have done. I'll be right back!" Violet made her way up the stairs, calling to them as she ascended.

"What's it going to be, Sara girl? You look lovely in everything. I think you should just take your pick. You can't go wrong!" Mrs. Stillman was pleased with the fitting they had accomplished.

Sara made a selection, and emerged from the fitting room wearing new clothes. As she headed back toward the counter, she caught a glimpse of herself in a full-length mirror. She recognized herself, yet she saw someone very different. Violet reappeared behind her.

"Sara, dear. You're the very image of your mother. She was beautiful, and so are you," Violet said.

All of the anxiety that had engulfed Sara that morning was gone. She almost felt like a new person, not the common girl from Tennessee. She did not quite know what to think of herself.

"Mrs. Stillman, let's add all of this up and box it. I believe our work here is through!"

All of the new clothes for Sara and Easton were boxed and stacked on the counter. The boy came bounding down the steps, also wearing new things.

"I'm going to take a few of these things out to the car," Violet said.

"Let me help you, Mrs. Violet." Jacob Stillman took several boxes in his arms and followed after her.

"Look, Sara! Ain't I dapper? Mr. Stillman says I'm dapper!" Easton wore a newsboy cap pulled down in the front so far that he had to tilt his head way up to see.

Sara straightened his cap. "Excuse me, sir, do I know you?"

"Course ya do, Sara, it's me!"

"*Oh!*" She put a hand to her chest. "I'll say, for a minute, I didn't know who the handsome young man talking to me was!"

They both giggled. It was one of the happiest moments they had experienced in some time.

Sara heard the bell at the front entrance of the store. A tall young man emerged from the glare of the sunlight coming through the storefront windows.

"Hello? Mr. Stillman? Mrs. Stillman?"

"Hello there!" Mrs. Stillman looked up from the sales slip she was working on.

He strode up to the counter and leaned against it in a purposeful, imitable pose as if to impress.

 Jenna Cossey

"Give me just a minute here," she continued with her sales slip.

He took inventory, but not of the store merchandise. He eyed Sara while her attention was on Easton.

Mrs. Stillman finished with her sales slip and let out a sigh of relief "Whew! Now, what can I do for you today, Ransom?"

"For a start, who is—"

Loud laughter interrupted him as Violet and Mr. Stillman reentered through the back of the store.

"I think we've almost got it all, Florence. Oh, hello, Ransom!" Mr. Stillman extended a hand.

"Good afternoon, Mr. Stillman, and to you also, Mrs. Simpson." He seemed to be familiar with them both.

Sara paid more attention once she realized that he appeared to know Violet. Her curiosity nudged her toward the small huddle of adults at the counter. He turned his eyes again to her.

"Oh, I've forgotten my manners," Mrs. Stillman said. "This is Sara Wheeler. She is Mrs. Simpson's niece from Tennessee. They've only just arrived, and I failed to make introductions."

The young man extended a hand to Sara. "Hello. Ransom, Ransom Cahill."

"Pleased to meet you," Sara responded.

He held onto her hand a little bit longer than she expected and stared into her eyes as a slight grin crept over his face. He looked at her as if he knew something about her that she did not even know herself. It gave her a strange feeling.

He finally let go of her hand and bent himself slightly at the waist. "The pleasure was entirely mine, Ms. Wheeler."

"I'm Easton!" Feeling left out, he attempted to jump into the conversation.

It amused everyone, but the attention of the man mostly remained on Sara. It did not go unnoticed.

"We should be going. We have a few other stops to make. Florence, Jacob, thank you ever so much!" Violet said as she tucked her clutch beneath her arm. She motioned them in the direction of the rear entrance. Sara could hear the man talking as they made their way out.

"What can I get for you today, Ransom?"

"Mr. Stillman, I hate to admit it, but I've ruined another hat . . ."

The odd feeling he gave her was short-lived. When they left the store, Violet raised a question.

"Who's hungry?

Jenna Cossey

<u>*16*</u>

In Nashville, Tennessee, a southbound train approached Union Station. Heavy steam billowed from the engine into the chilly autumn air. Passengers prepared to disembark from the railcars.

Whirling masses of people moved about in the station, just as they had in Chicago. Alfio gathered his things, also. He had another train to catch.

"Well, Al, it was nice to meet you. I hope business is booming wherever you're headed."

Rufus Harding seemed to have become an attachment, and it was getting harder to avoid more detailed personal conversations. Alfio was accustomed to dealing with these situations, but it was not effortless.

"My business is always booming, friend," Alfio responded with a coy smile.

"Mine too. I don't know where we'll be headed next, but as I said, Mr. Moody seems to find us work in places I never even thought about going to." He shook his head as he pulled out a handkerchief and wiped his nose.

"Funny, my boss tends to do the same," Alfio said.

"Well, I reckon I better catch my ride before I miss it. You take care of yourself, Al. If you're ever in Woodbury, Tennessee, you look me up now, ya hear?"

"I'll do that, Mr. Harding."

"Safe travels to ya, Mr. Lucas!"

With that, he was gone, and Alfio Colucci proceeded to his next train. He would also reach his destination that evening. He boarded and settled into his seat once again. The seat next to him was one of few that remained empty, and a lady took it. She perched beside him with noticeable timidity and removed from her handbag an Agatha Christie novel. To his relief, she did not say a word to him during that leg of the trip. He was happy to sit quietly and admire the serene southern landscapes passing across his window.

17

"How would you like to get to know some of the neighbors?" Violet looked across the table at Sara.

In a single morning, she had taken a trip to town, been treated to a new wardrobe, and ended up in a cafe eating food she did not cook. She had never eaten a meal that was not home-cooked. It was quite a novelty to her and Easton to sit there in the bustling establishment and have hot soup and sandwiches. All of the excitement of her newly discovered self made her more talkative.

"You mean the people on your street?"

Back in Tennessee, neighbors could have meant people from miles around. Sara anticipated a redefinition of the term.

"Yes, some of them, but others live close by," Violet answered.

"I think that'd be alright."

She could hardly believe what she was saying, but she could not seem to stop herself. They had pulled into the back of Stillman's store that morning, and she was glad, but afterward, she felt like she could walk down the street without casting her eyes at the sidewalk. She had no explanation for the change, but Violet recognized it.

"Good! We'll have a get-together. I've got to pick up the radio from Mr. Farnham's down the street, and we can get some little invitations to mail. It'll be like a welcome party!"

"I love parties!" Easton said with a mouthful of sandwich.

They finished their meal and walked toward the car. Sara caught a glimpse of herself in one of the storefront windows. Never had she worn so much store-bought clothing. Their outfits were not overly fancy, but it made little difference to Sara at that moment. To her, they all looked like they had walked straight out of a newspaper advertisement. Sara was unaware of her beauty, but she and Violet did make a lovely pair that day. She was only thinking of her beautiful new clothes, and assumed that the slightly prolonged glances of bystanders were because of Violet's appeal rather than her own.

They went to Farnham's to retrieve Violet's radio, and Mr. Farnham, ever the salesman, welcomed them each with a piece of stick candy. The real winner of the trip to Farnham's Five and Ten was Easton. While Violet completed her transaction, he managed to fall in love with a toy car. He meandered around the store, but he made several passes by the little red car. Violet watched his movements.

"Do you see anything interesting over here, Easton?"

"Mmmmm . . . well, yes'm . . . lots of things. I never been to a place with all of this!" His eyes danced with excitement.

"Anything in particular?" She casually moved toward the little red car.

"Well, that car. It looks real neat! I bet it goes fast!" He already had a passion for it.

"Hmmm, I bet if I spoke to Mr. Farnhum, he would let us buy it. A young man such as yourself, smart and handsome, should have a nice car. Don't you think?"

His eyes widened. "You think we could buy it?"

"We shall see." Violet picked up the car and headed to the counter.

The prices were marked, but Easton did not have enough shopping experience to realize it. As she conversed with Mr. Farnham, she gave him a look that let him know to play along.

Jenna Cossey

"Now, Mr. Farnham, young Master Wheeler here is looking to buy this car, but we need to make the best deal possible. What is your price?"

"For you, Mrs. Simpson, twenty cents."

"Oh my, that is a little much," she said with a look of disappointment.

She bent down and whispered in Easton's ear to tell him she was willing to give fifteen cents for the car and that she was going to make another offer. Easton nodded.

"I'll give you ten cents for the car. It's a fair price." She reached into her coin purse.

"Oh no, Mrs. Simpson. I can't possibly let the car go for ten cents," he countered. "How about right in the middle at fifteen?"

Violet looked down at Easton, making him think that she was seeking his input. He motioned her to bend down to him again.

"Do you have fifteen cents? Is fifteen cents a good price?" He was on edge.

"Yes, I think fifteen cents is a fair price. Shall we get it?" She placed her hand to her chin as she questioned him.

He nodded again.

"Mr. Farnham, you've got a deal. The young man will buy the car for fifteen cents."

He reached down over the counter and shook Easton's hand to seal the deal before walking around from behind it to place the toy into his hands. Easton received the car gently as if it were a newborn kitten, and a smile covered his entire face.

Sara was in awe of Violet's generosity. She did not know how much money Violet had, but assumed that she must have been well off. She had already spent more money than Sara had ever seen, and she freely did so. As they traveled home, they continued discussing their party plans. That night they sat down and wrote out invitations together after Easton had gone to bed. Sara attempted to express her gratitude, even though it felt awkward.

"Aunt Vi, today was so wonderful."

"Wasn't it, though? I had a great deal of fun!" Violet continued writing.

"I just . . ." Sara looked around the room as she searched for words. "I guess I just don't know what to say. You've been so kind." Tears began to well up in her eyes, but they were tears of joy and relief. Her arrival in Dunnigan had propelled her out of darkness and into a bright and unexpected light. She knew what a lovely person Violet was, but she never realized the magnitude of her kindness.

Violet put down her pen, looked at Sara, and placed a hand on hers. "Sara, I have loved you since the day you came into this world. You've always been special to me, just as your mother was. It makes me so happy to have you here, and Easton too. Everything is going to be alright. You don't have to worry. I'm going to take care of you both in the very best way that I can."

Violet showed signs of tears. Though they were partly happy ones, they were also ones of grief. She and Matilda had always been close in heart, and when the opportunity came for Violet to take the children into her care, there had been no hesitation. However, she was sure that the loss was felt even more intensely by Sara. She worried about giving her the emotional support she needed.

Sara hugged her tightly, and they cried together. Neither of them had the strength at that moment to hold back their tears. Eventually, they returned to their invitations and talked way into the night. Sara did not mind. She was so overloaded with joy and happiness that she was not tired anyway. Life in Dunnigan began to seem like it would be a good thing.

<u>18</u>

Noah made his way out to the garage and surveyed the tasks that lay before him and Thomas. A practically new Chevrolet coupe sat inside, and he had somehow missed its arrival. He got inside and attempted to start it. It turned over and ran without any noticeable issues, so he killed the engine and got out to look around the car. He glanced at all the wheels and tires, and then checked the undercarriage looking for anything that seemed out of place. He opened the hood, and the engine bay was as clean and new as the rest of the car. He was puzzled.

"Tommy, what's wrong with the Chevy?"

"Ain't nothing wrong with it. Fella wants us to see if we can make it run better."

"Better than what? She runs perfect."

Thomas peered into the engine compartment. "You know, he kinda wants it sweetened up some. We can figure it out."

"It looks like a fairly new buggy to me. I don't see a reason to tinker with it."

"Wasn't it you that said the other day we just do what people want when they bring 'em in?"

"Yeah, yeah, I did, but that was a clunker. This ain't no clunker." Noah lowered the hood panel. "Who's it belong to?" He had to know which fool brought a perfectly running car to the shop.

"Ransom Cahill brought it in. You know, the mayor's boy."

"I know of him," Noah said.

Noah was easygoing and seemed to be liked by most who knew him. He had few hard feelings toward anybody, least of all in Dunnigan, but for some reason, Ransom Cahill struck a chord within him that he could not quite explain. Their social positions limited their interactions, but Noah had gotten a sense of Ransom's attitude from afar on a few occasions. He had a feeling that he was not the Southern gentleman he claimed. He rarely shared his negative opinions with others, especially Thomas. The last thing he needed was for Thomas to have a scrap with one of the best-known young men in the county.

He decided Ransom's money was as good as that of the next person, even if it was foolish to tamper with a car that was running fine.

"Well, what is it? Is he just wanting her to top out a little faster?"

"Yep, something like that," Thomas said.

"We'll see what we can do, but I'm still learning about these new sixes, and you ain't worked on 'em much either. How long did he give us?" Noah started to examine the car in the other bay.

"Day after tomorrow."

"Oh, sure." Noah kept working, taking it as a joke.

"No, really. He wants it back the day after tomorrow," Thomas said.

"You're crazy. We'd end up working around the clock the next few days if we did that!"

"True, but he said he would make it worth our while," Thomas tried to make a case.

"Oh, is that right? How's he gonna do that? It'll take some more deal to get me to spend two nights in here working on a perfectly good car!"

Noah made a point not to argue with customers unless they were wasting money and time, and this, he felt, was a complete waste of time. An added detraction was that it was Ransom Cahill who was asking them to waste money and time. He changed his mind.

"Go put a call in to him. Tell him to come by here today when he can. It's foolishness, and we ain't got the time for it this week. Just look at that list over there. We've got steady repair work, and I don't wanta put any of it off to fiddle with a new car."

The warmth of the morning gave way to the stagnant heat of high noon. That day, like many others, had been filled with steady work and a frequent flow of customers. The people came and went, and there was never too great a lapse in time without someone stopping for gasoline.

A car pulled up to the garage. Ransom Cahill got out and made his way inside, where Noah was completing one of his repairs.

"Thomas here says you want to see me about the car?" Ransom was hoping for good news.

"Yeah. Look, I checked the car over. It runs fine. There ain't a need in the world to do anything to it. It would be—"

"I know there's nothing *wrong* with it. I just want it to run better," Ransom explained.

"If it ran any better, it'd drive itself."

"I need it to run faster. I know you can make that happen. I've heard the talk around town. You're the best mechanic anyone here has ever seen," Ransom tried appealing to his ego.

"Well, thank you, Mr. Cahill, but we've got steady repair work coming in. I can't stop what I'm doin' for two days to work on a car that ain't busted."

"Maybe I can persuade you." Ransom reached into his pocket and produced two fifty-dollar National banknotes. "You say it will take you two days. How does fifty dollars for each day strike you? I see you're busy for the day, but if you work on it tonight and tomorrow night, you won't have to push aside a single repair job. You'll bring in your pay as well as this hundred." He pulled the two notes taut so that they made a popping sound.

Thomas had an expression on his face that would have appeared calm to most, but Noah recognized the excitement in his eyes. They both knew it was more money than they could make together in weeks. Before he knew it, he was accepting the job.

"Alright. I'll see what I can do."

"I want the two of you to fix this car so that every other will take its dust." His intensity grew.

Thomas jumped in unexpectedly, "If anybody can, we can!"

Noah shot him a look that let him know not to say anything else and took one of the notes from Ransom.

"Here's fifty now. Get the job done, and I'll pay the other fifty."

They shook hands, and Ransom left the station.

The brothers stood there speechless for several minutes before Thomas broke the silence.

"A hundred dollars. He's gonna pay us a hundred dollars to soup up that car."

"Yeah, I don't like it much, but I guess we'd be fools not to make the extra money. When we finish up this evening, pull that thing back in, and we'll get started. It may be a long couple of days."

Noah looked at the crisp new banknote and wondered if it was the right choice, but there was no time to waste. They had work to do.

 Jenna Cossey

___19___

With his car at Haskins' garage, Ransom puttered down the road in a shiny wine-colored Buick sedan that belonged to the family. He did not usually drive so slow, but he was in no hurry. Another dinner party required his presence. He had to offset his disgust for boring political events somehow, and stealing some of the attention from Mayor Cahill by showing up fashionably late always seemed like an easy way to even the balances.

He stopped at Stillman's on his way back. Jacob and Florence had an established reputation for keeping inventory that rivaled the shops in Birmingham. He frequented the store to keep up with the latest fashions and dressed as sharply as possible. Though he fussed over his appearance, it did not keep him from losing accessories during his adventures. At least once a week, he seemed to lose a hat, a handkerchief, or ruin a necktie.

"Good afternoon, Mr. and Mrs. Stillman." He entered the store with a swagger. "I've come to patronize your most excellent establishment once more!"

They returned welcomes and friendly smiles to their recurrent customer. Ever sharp business people, they recognized the steady flow of income he provided. He had the option of traveling to Birmingham to make his purchases, so they always humored his attempts to pour on the charm, even though they found him disingenuous.

"What is it that I can do for you today, Ransom?" Mr. Stillman placed his hands upon the front counter.

"You see this necktie?"

"Yes indeed. I believe I sold you that tie not too long ago!"

"Well, I had a pocket square that matched it just perfectly, and I seem to have misplaced it." He pulled his breast pocket open and drew attention to the loss.

"Ah yes, I believe we can find one that will look just as well. Let's go up and have a look!"

As they made their way up the stairs, Mr. Stillman continued conversation with him, "I see you've kept your hat!"

"Oh yes, this one I've grown to like. We've been together for days now—it could be a new record. Say that reminds me, what of the girl with Mrs. Simpson the other week when I came to buy this hat? I've never seen her before. What was her name? I—"

"Sara Wheeler. She's Violet—" Mr. Stillman corrected himself, "Mrs. Simpson's niece."

"Niece?"

Mr. Stillman deflected, "Yes. Now here, let's hold up these two squares."

He stood to the side of Ransom in a mirror, holding up two squares to his tie. They examined the squares together, determining that neither was just right.

"Alright then, let's look at these," he held up two more.

"So what brings Mrs. Simpson's niece to—"

"Her niece *and* her nephew," Mr. Stillman interjected.

Ransom shook his head in disapproval of the two pocket squares. "Yes, what brings them to live with an aunt?"

"Can't say as I know fully. Here. What about this one?" He held up a final square.

"Interesting, interesting . . ." Ransom examined the lone square. "I believe that's the one after all. I'll take it."

He had come in to purchase a new pocket square, but the talk of the new girl in town diverted his attention. Whether they dared say it or not, most of the men in town thought Violet Simpson to be quite a lovely woman, and Ransom could see the resemblance. Sara was slender, not very tall, and only a trace of her girlishness remained. Her name had escaped him, but he remembered her large cerulean eyes. Now they went with a name. *Sara.*

Ransom made small talk as he paid for his pocket square. He wished them both a pleasant evening in his typical unctuous way and left the store for another dreaded appointment with the political socialites of Central Alabama.

<u>**20**</u>

The day for the welcome party had arrived. Violet and Sara bustled around the house and prepared for the guests. Easton was out in the backyard by the porch, and from the dining room, they could hear him playing with his little red car.

"Vrrrrrrrrooooom!" he raced it across the porch floor.

"That boy has gone hundreds of miles on his hands and knees since we brought that toy home," Violet said.

"Yeah, and almost every mile has been in the dirt. He looks like he's been wallowin' with the sows."

Sara had not thought much about farm life since arriving in Dunnigan, but the comparisons still came naturally to her most of the time. As she watched him play, she could not help but think of the many evenings he had come in covered in filth and the battles that would ensue between him and their mother.

*   *   *

"I don't wanta bathe!"

"Son, you've got to. You're filthy as a hog. You'll not be getting in any bed of ours looking like that." Matilda continued her work as she reasoned with her son.

Easton had conjured a long list of different places to sleep, which he would offer just about every time she brought up the bed, but none of them ever sufficed.

"You will not sleep in the hayloft, you will get in this tub, and you will wash, and you will sleep in the house." Matilda Wheeler rarely raised her voice.

Jenna Cossey

Without fail, he would eventually stick his lip out, peel off his dirt and sweat-laden clothes, and climb into the big metal washtub, but that night he argued too long.

"Mama, do I have to? I don't like it. Can't I just do it tomorrow? I played in the crick today!"

The sound of the back screen door slamming caused everyone to jump. It was Walter. Already dark outside, it was well past the time that he should have been home. Sara recognized the look in his eyes.

He attempted to hang his hat by the door, but missed the hook. "Boy, I'm getting sick and tired of hearing you whinge and cry about a little bath once in a while. Should've already been done. How many times did your mama already tell you?" his voice boomed.

"Well, she—"

"Don't sass me, boy!"

Walter took him up by the arms; his large and powerful fingers touched around his tiny biceps. He gave Easton a shake as his voice became louder. "I don't want to hear you fuss about a bath nary another time! Now get in that tub and wash!"

He shoved Easton backward into the tub of water, clothes and all. It was a stroke of luck that he hung onto him just long enough to keep his head from hitting the back of it. Shocked, Easton started to cry violently as soon as he found himself in the water. "Hush up, boy!"

"Walter! Please," said Matilda over the cries.

"You hush it up, or I'll give you something to really cry about!" Walter began to unbuckle his belt just as Matilda stepped in.

"Stop! Walter, please stop. Please leave him be." She begged, and for reasons unknown, Walter relented.

Sara stood there frozen in disbelief that her father had become physical with small Easton. When the screen door slammed shut again, she exhaled.

"Sara, get me that towel . . . Sara?"

*   *   *

"Sara?"

"Yes, Aunt Vi?" The voice summoned her back to the present.

"It looks like we'll have to ride into town. We need to get a few more things," she spoke softly, unlike the voices in Sara's reminisces.

"Want me to stay here with Easton and just you go?" Sara assumed he was not presentable for town at that point.

"No! I'll need your help! After all, it is your party. Well, Easton's party too, but . . ." She gave Sara a wink. "Let's go ahead and go. We'll need time to finish getting things ready when we get back." Violet grabbed her clutch and put on her hat.

Sara went to the back door and beckoned Easton away from his imaginary racetrack. They all climbed into the car and headed downtown.

"Remind me to fill up with gasoline on the way back home," Violet said.

They picked up a few items in town, first from the grocer, and then from the dime store.

"Can we get a cone?" Easton, though new to city life, had already taken a shine to the soda fountain.

"Well, don't let's get one today, Easton. Remember, we are having the party tonight, and there will be lots of goodies," Violet convinced him.

They headed back home, and when they reached the station, Sara remembered. "Gasoline for the car, Aunt Vi!"

     Jenna Cossey

She slowed quickly and pulled up to the pump. A young man met them there.

"Hello, Mrs. Simpson. Fill the tank for ya?" he asked.

"Yes, please. We're going to go inside for a moment. I've talked the boy out of an ice cream cone, but it's so hot I think I've talked myself into an orange crush!" He opened the door for her, and she got out, "Come on. Let's go get a cold soda pop!" She motioned Sara and Easton out of the car.

Easton spent several minutes debating which flavor he wanted. By the time he made his selection, Noah Maclane had come in from the gas pumps. "Is that gonna be all for ya today, Mrs. Simpson?"

"Yes, the gasoline and these drinks."

"Can you look at my car?" Easton raised his little red car to Noah.

"Well, now. This looks like a nice one. Let me have a look." Noah set the car on the counter and pretended to check it over carefully. He looked underneath, spun each wheel, and took a rag from his back pocket to wipe the dust and dirt from the car. "I believe she's in perfect working order, sir. Should be good for miles!" He handed the car back to Easton.

Sara noticed his gentle way. She watched the strong-looking young man with smooth brown hair handle the car as though it were an expensive item. The station was always busy, and she thought it especially kind of him to take time to humor Easton.

"You know, I don't believe I've properly introduced us all yet. This is my nephew, Easton Wheeler, and this is my niece, Sara Wheeler. They've come from Tennessee to live here in Dunnigan with me."

"Ah, Tennessee, nice," he replied.

"Easton, Sara, this is Noah Maclane. He helps keep me on the road!"

Noah bent down to look the boy in the eye and extended a hand to him. "Pleased to meet you, Easton. Fine car ya've got there!" He returned to full height and nodded at Sara with a half-smile. "Pleased, ma'am."

Sara returned the nod and the smile.

"Well, you have a nice afternoon, Noah. Don't work too hard. It's mighty hot out today," Violet cautioned.

"Yes, ma'am. You take care."

Easton held his prized toy automobile with both hands, and Violet carried his drink and hers.

Noah had impressed Sara with his kindness. There was something different about him, and it stuck with her as they drove away.

_21_

Two gatherings commenced that Friday evening: one at Violet Simpson's home on Ketcherside Drive, and the other on the far side of town in the stately retrofitted antebellum home of the Cahill family.

One by one, Violet welcomed guests into her home. Some presented dishes of food for the occasion, and Violet met them all with her warmest welcome. She planned to begin the party with an announcement, but deciding what to say had been quite a challenge. The unexpected passing of Joseph Simpson earlier that year left her wondering if their house would ever reclaim any of the joy it had once contained. The death of her only sister brought an equal heartache, but the arrival of Sara and Easton filled part of the void on both counts. She needed them as much as they needed her. When she welcomed the whole group, she tried not to say too much.

"I want to thank all of you for coming this evening. I'm happy that everyone could be here to welcome these two. Sara and Easton have come from Holley Creek, Tennessee. I couldn't be more thrilled to have them here with me. With that, I hope that you'll all be able to get acquainted this evening. I'm sure you'll be charmed."

Everyone applauded softly, and soon Sara and Easton were mingling with their new friends and neighbors.

After dinner, Sara began fielding the carousel of questions from the visitors. She found herself a little uncomfortable and running out of answers.

"How do you like it here?"

"What year are you going to be in school?"

"What kinds of recreation do you like?"

"What of your father? Will he be coming to Dunnigan?"

The last question surprised Sara. Her mother was constantly on her mind, but she had not spoken of her father since her arrival.

"I . . . I don't rightly know," she managed to get out the words.

After a time, almost everyone had their chance to talk with her, and things settled down. Violet turned on the radio, and the low smooth strains of jazz that drifted over the room seemed to have a calmative effect. Some of the men stood and talked, or retreated to the kitchen for a lively game of Rook. The others sat around the house chatting and tapping an occasional toe when a familiar tune came over the airwaves. It was a peaceful gathering.

Suddenly there was a knock at the door. Everyone in the room turned to Violet, who was eating a large piece of apple pie.

She quickly swallowed the bite and wiped her mouth. "I wonder who that could be. Perhaps the Carsons? They are about the only ones I expected who haven't made it yet. Why don't you get it, Sara?"

Sara preferred that Violet answer it, but she went into the short hall that led to the front door. She opened it and found Noah Maclane standing on the front steps.

She was not alarmed, but was baffled by his presence. *Did Violet invite him? Why is he here?*

Jenna Cossey

The Cahills began receiving their guests that evening, and Ransom was not present. Edward Cahill fumed. He leaned into Charlotte's ear and inquired as to his whereabouts. Just as he began to express further discontentment, Ransom, well put together, appeared in the room of people.

"Ah, Ransom! Looking sharp as ever, my boy!"

The guests heaped praise on him as he made his way across the room, shaking the hands of the men, kissing the hands of the ladies, and spewing out Southern charm.

"You have to admit, Mr. Mayor, that he can win over a room," Charlotte Cahill simpered.

Edward gave no response.

Ransom fulfilled his duty by playing his part as a gracious host. One woman, a mother of one of the young ladies, remarked on his tie and pocket square, "What a lovely tie, Mr. Cahill. And the square! It just goes marvelously with that tie!"

He gave credit to Jacob Stillman for choosing the pair and remembered their conversation. *Sara.*

None of the girls he saw there that night looked quite like Sara. They were all predictable, calculated society maidens. Most young men would have jumped at the chance to mingle among them, but to Ransom, the whole scene was dull. He was part of the Cahill illusion. He hated that his life seemed manufactured. Everything appeared to be decided, from the career he should pursue, the type of girl he should marry, even the places he should go. The expectations were constrictive to him. Even Mr. Stillman appeared to recognize the standing social order when he curbed the inquiries about Sara.

Ransom was beginning to feel more and more rebellious toward the hierarchy of the upper crust.

Dunnigan

"Tommy, do you know where Violet Simpson's house is?"

"Huh?" Thomas had been puzzled.

"Violet Simpson, do you know where she lives?"

"Why?" Thomas asked.

"She left her handbag on the counter when she was here this afternoon. She bought gas, and she came in for cold drinks." Noah continued, "The little boy asked me to look at his toy car, so I just flat didn't notice when she walked off and left it. She must not have missed it yet, but she will soon. Thought I'd take it to her. She's such a good customer."

"Let me take it! I'll be happy to go see Mrs. Simpson. She might even kiss little brother on the cheek for returning her personal belongings!" Thomas had a sheepish look on his face.

"Shut your gap." Noah became impatient. "That right there is the exact reason why you *won't* be going. Get over there and make a plum fool of yourself and stand there and talk half the night. Now, do you know where she lives or not?"

Thomas reeled himself in, sensing that Noah was not kidding. "Yeah, I think she lives over past Archie Duncan on Ketcherside, you know that little area down the way here."

"Good, then. I'll just take this over there before it gets too late. You stay here and keep working on Cahill's car. I'll be back in just a minute."

With that, Noah had gotten into the service truck and made his way to Ketcherside Drive. He rolled down the street trying to spot the Ford sedan that he knew belonged to Violet Simpson. Much to his dislike, it appeared that a gathering was going on at the house. He decided that Mrs. Simpson would be missing her clutch and opted to knock on the door anyway.

He peered at the young girl standing in the doorway, holding the clutch in his hands.

"Oh, hello. Mr. Maclane, was it?" Sara was terrible with names and hoped she guessed the right one.

"Yes'm. Noah Maclane."

She spotted the clutch in his hands and recognized it. "Do you generally carry a woman's clutch?" She giggled.

He blushed and smiled. "Oh! No, ma'am. That's what I've come for. Mrs. Simpson left this at the filling station this afternoon. I didn't notice until I was closing up for the evening, and I brought it over soon as I got a chance."

His kindness impressed her again.

"That's very good of you. Let me get Aunt Violet." Sara knew she would also want to thank him.

Violet came to the door and, seeing her purse, threw her hands across her chest. "My purse! Oh, aren't you just a dear! I can be so absentminded! Thank you so much for bringing it to me, Noah." She collected the purse from him. "Do come in for a bite to eat. We were just having a little gathering, and there's plenty!"

Sara looked at him standing there. His frame was thick and muscled. His face had boyish quality, but his jaw, nose, and brow were chiseled and perfectly set. A smooth mass of sandy brown hair dashed against his dark complexion, creating a perfect landscape for his blue-gray eyes.

"No, ma'am, I can't stay. I've got some work waiting for me. It's special for a customer, and me and Tommy are working nights to get it done, so I better head on back. I thank you for the asking, though."

"No, no, thank you, Noah Maclane! You're sure you won't come in?"

"No, ma'am, I better be going. I'll be seeing you. Good evening, Mrs. Simpson," he nodded his head to Violet and again looked at Sara, "and good evening to you too, Ms. Wheeler."

Sara could not believe that he remembered her name amidst the clamor of their stop at the filling station. She thought of him often throughout the remainder of the evening.

Noah could not help but notice the beautiful young girl who greeted him at the door. He had felt her looking at him as he talked with Violet, but his mind quickly turned again to the deal he had made with Ransom Cahill and the work that was still left to do.

The Cahills ushered the final guests out of their dinner party later that night. Ransom's growing sense of entrapment distracted him from the drawn-out affair, but no one noticed. If only for a short time, Ransom redeemed himself from the ire of Edward Cahill with his superb performance for the dignified guests of the evening.

<u>22</u>

Sara and Easton sauntered down the roadside. They were used to walking barefooted, and shoes were not needed where they were going. The loose dust on the road, cool and fine like powder, pressed between their toes with each step. Violet had told them of a path in the wooded area that lay at the end of the road, and as they reached it, Sara began to scan the edge of the woods for it.

"It's just off to the left. You'll see it. Joseph and I used to walk down there, and I've kept the path worn down," she had said.

She frequently spoke about Joseph, and it was apparent to Sara that she missed him a great deal. She was intrigued by the way Violet was dealing with her losses. Sara tried not to think of missing people because it hurt too badly. However, Violet seemed to speak often about the people she missed. Maybe it eased the pain of their absence, but Sara struggled to understand it and preferred not to spend too much time in such conversations.

"There's the path!" Easton let go of her hand and bolted into the woods.

She watched him running down the path, and her thoughts turned to their old home. Opposing feelings seemed to meet her at every turn. She was happy to see him bounding through the woods so carefree. She so desired the innocence he had yet to lose, his lack of understanding about the gravity of their loss, and the freedom that it seemed to give him. *Oh, if I had the same power to forget!*

The wooded area opened into a small clearing bounded by a creek on one side. Just as Violet described, there was a path on the edge of the meadow alongside it. Easton enjoyed the adventure in the woods, a frequent pastime for him back in Tennessee, but Sara became uneasy.

The quiet and picturesque creek-side meadow felt too much like home, which no longer carried feelings of contentment and peace. Her stomach knotted, and she began to feel sick.

"Sara! Look at this crawdad! It's a big 'un! Sara! Come look at ___"

"Let's go." She sounded sharp, almost hateful.

"Why? I want to play in the creek." His mouth sank into an emergent frown.

"Maybe another day. Come on."

He pouted as they made the half-mile trek back to the house. Sara did not blame him. She felt terrible about spoiling the adventure, but the feeling that overcame her snatched the wind from her sail. She had battled her emotions since their arrival. Sometimes she feared that they would slowly overtake her, and she did not know what to do about it.

Back at the house, Easton went to the yard to go about the games he had developed for himself. Sara followed him and claimed a chair on the back porch. Before too many minutes passed, Violet appeared at the door.

"I thought I heard you two. Back so soon?"

"Yes, ma'am."

"Couldn't you find the path?"

"We found it." Sara looked across the yard, with her eyes fixed on nothing in particular.

"I see." Violet came over and took a chair beside her.

They watched Easton as he darted back and forth. He found little sticks, rocks, and dirt clods to build towns with, and then raced his toy car through them. He was in a world of his own.

"The boy just has fun no matter what, doesn't he?"

"Mm hmm," Sara said with a nod.

Violet sensed the disruption in her tenor. "Supper will be ready in just a little while," she offered as if to test.

"I don't think I'll have anything. I don't much feel like it. I must've gotten too hot. If it's all the same to you, I think I'll go and wash up. Maybe I'll rest a little." Sara hoped to escape to the privacy of her room before her emotions boiled over.

Violet reached out and patted her hand. "Alright. You go rest, and maybe you'll feel better in a little while."

Sara got out of the chair and disappeared into the house. Violet knew full well that she was not suffering from the heat. Sara was sick, but the sickness was one recognized easiest by those who had suffered it: grief. She was well acquainted with the silent demon called grief. She understood the potential power it held. She was a fully grown woman, but her battle with grief had been considerable. Helping Sara without rekindling her own grief added to the task, but her instincts drove her to tackle the problem.

As daylight gave way to darkness, Violet ascended the stairs and softly knocked on Sara's door. "Sara? It's your aunt Vi."

"Come in." She had been lying down and began to rise when Violet entered. It was evident that she had been crying.

Violet perched on the end of the bed, unsure of how best to calm the torrent. She started small. "Are you feeling any better?"

The right corner of Sara's mouth upturned, and she shrugged. Violet took a deep breath and proceeded in the best way she knew how. "Sara, I know that things have been difficult and that coming here may have made certain things even harder, but you have to believe me when I tell you that it will get better with time." She paused. "I also want you to know that I think I can understand how you feel."

Sara looked at Violet. She was so composed. *How could she know how I feel?* "You can?" Sara asked sincerely.

"Yes. At least I think that I can. I know how much it hurts to lose someone when they are the most important person in your life. For you to lose your mother and be so young, it must be hard."

Unable to disagree, Sara nodded.

"My heart has been where yours is. You probably feel that you have fallen deep into a pit and that you will never be able to find happiness again, but you will, Sara. *You will.*"

"I just don't know how, Aunt Vi. I keep thinking of Mama. I see her face in my mind, in my dreams, all of the time, and I don't . . ." Sara hesitated, fighting tears.

"It's ok, Sara. Tell me what's on your mind."

"I don't want to forget her." The tears came freely. "When I think about her, I miss her so badly, but when I don't think about her, I feel . . ."

"Guilty?" Violet completed her sentence.

Sara shook her head. "Yes. Guilty is it, I guess."

Violet slid over and wrapped her arms around Sara. Sara felt familiarity in the embrace. Even a simple hug reminded her of her mother.

"Let me tell you some things, Sara. Your mother . . . she was wonderful. I miss her, too. She was my only sister. No one in the world could take her place. She loved you and Easton so much. She would not want you to be sad, but I have to be truthful with you. You're never going to stop missing her. Somehow, if we

     Jenna Cossey

remember the good things about the people we love, we learn how to miss them, remember them, and find a new kind of happiness. For me, all of the places that made me miss Joseph the most after he was gone are now the places where I feel closest to the memories I have of him. I know it's all very hard to understand, but what you mustn't do is feel guilty when you find yourself happy and living your life because that is the very thing that your mother would have wanted you to be doing."

A bit of weight was lifted from Sara's conscience. Violet hugged her tightly, and then left her in the solitude of her room. Maybe her aunt was right, but Sara wondered if new happiness was truly possible.

<u>**23**</u>

Noah and Thomas finished working on the coupe in time. As promised, Ransom Cahill gave them the additional fifty dollars.

"What you gonna do with that fifty dollars, Noah? I've been trying to decide what it is I'd like to buy most, but I can't hardly make up my mind." It was the expertise of Noah that afforded them the opportunity, but Thomas had been an invaluable help. He thought it only fair to split the bonus with him. "We got that thing roaring just like I told him we could," Thomas said.

"When exactly did you tell him that anyway?"

"Oh, you know, when he first brought it over. He didn't know if we could do it and—"

"You mean he didn't know if we *would* do it."

"What do you mean?" Thomas came back.

"What I mean is the man stood right there and said I was the best mechanic around. He wasn't asking if I *could* do it. He was asking if I *would*."

Thomas, still unsure, asked him outright, "What are you getting at, Noah?"

"One's just led to wonder how it is that Ransom Cahill would get the idea that I might be able to soup up his car for him. That's what I'm getting at, Tommy."

It did not take long for Noah to realize that it was a bit of a setup. Ransom left the car at the garage without his knowledge, an unusual occurrence that took some coordination. He had been so sure they could do it. Noah knew his brother. He sometimes talked a little too much, and his fear was that Thomas would someday go too far.

"Well," Thomas searched, "people around here know you're good with automobiles."

"Come on, Tommy, you talked to him before that morning. This is me you're talking to. On the level, what made Ransom Cahill bring his car down here?"

Thomas sighed, knowing that his brother was onto him. "Ok, ok. I was downtown one day, had stopped in the drugstore fountain, and Cahill was standing out front with some guys ogling this car. I overheard 'em talking, and I stopped and looked at the car myself. He started talking about how it drove and how some fella had one that would outrun it. He told those guys how much it chapped his hide to have that there new car and get outrun in it. So I told him I was sure you could make it do a little more."

Noah listened to what Thomas was saying. It was just like him to make such a bold claim. He was always so cocksure. "Why did you tell him that, Tommy?"

"His daddy is the mayor. You saw how he dressed and the way he fanned out the greenbacks. Handed 'em over no problem. I figured we could make a quick buck."

"That's just the trouble, Tommy. If we hadn't got that done, we woulda wasted a lot of time for nothing, and there was always the possibility that I coulda messed something up."

"I knew you weren't gonna mess it up." Thomas was still trying to make his case. "You *are* the best around here. What you did was help us make this easy money, brother! Don't you get it?"

Noah tried to guide him to think more maturely, "I just need you not to make assurances that we might not be able to come through on. A side job like that goes awry, and it cuts into our regular business. You have to look at the everyday bread and butter, Tommy. We don't make a living souping up cars. We make a living repairing cars."

"A living?" Thomas shot back. "How long do you think we'll have to keep doing this to make a go of it?"

They were making enough money to be comfortable for the most part. It cost little to live in the back of the station, and they always had food on the table. They had the money for an evening in town when they were inclined, which was more than some could say.

"I'm not sure what you expected, brother. We ain't back home anymore. We're on our own and fending for ourselves. This is what you wanted, ain't it?"

It was true that Thomas had wanted to leave home. His father continually patronized him over his physical disability. He did not feel that he was disabled in any manner. It had been difficult when he lost his leg, but he was young and quickly adapted. He found a way to do just about anything. He plowed mules, rode bicycles, drove vehicles, and whatever else stood between him and a task. William Maclane constantly goaded his son and made him feel inferior.

"Let Zeke take care of that. You can't do that with a bum leg," he would say.

It was an insult to Thomas when his father suggested that his brother Ezekiel, four years his junior, take on his work for him. It was enough to weary anyone, and as he often did when he reached a breaking point, he decided that escape was the best plan.

"I think we've done well, Tommy. We haven't even been here a year, and we practically run the place to ourselves. It ain't gonna happen overnight. Besides that, what we do is honest," Noah said.

"What do you mean, honest?"

 Jenna Cossey

"Have you ever thought about why it is that some of these fellas are interested in having such fast cars and how it is that they carry all that cash on 'em?"

"The Cahills are loaded. They ain't gotta do any dirty dealings if that's what you mean," Thomas said.

"Maybe not, but I don't want to get it going around that we are in the business of doing that kind of thing here. It might draw the wrong kind of business and the wrong kind of attention. You *have* to think about these things, Tom."

The transformation that the Chevrolet coupe underwent at the hands of the Maclane brothers met with the approval of Ransom Cahill, but it was the beginning of something much bigger.

_24_

In the August heat of 1928, Sara had turned fifteen. She had finished the eighth grade that spring, which was exciting for some of her classmates because they would go on to high school. For others, it marked the effective end of their childhood. Only a few would continue beyond grade school. Sara was not one of them.

"I do wish I could go to year nine, Mama." She had never been one to complain, but in that instance, she could not help sharing her disappointment.

"I know it, Sara sweet, but it's just too far. There's no way to get you there."

School was a predictable place, and Sara was comfortable there. Every day the routine was the same: "*I pledge allegiance to the flag of the United States of America . . .*" the class would recite in perfect unison.

Some thought it was monotonous, but not Sara. She liked the rhythm of each school day. Maybe it was because such order was not present elsewhere in her life, especially as she got older. In the evenings, she never knew which version of her father would return home. Sometimes it was the quiet Walter; other times, the agitated and gruff Walter. It was apt to be the slightly or the completely inebriated, belligerent Walter. Every evening was a spin of the wheel, but at nine in the morning each weekday, the bell would ring, and things would be in order. It helped bring her down from whatever she might have experienced the evening before.

Her disappointment was soon forced aside by other emotions. After Thanksgiving that fall, her mother shared surprising news as they worked on a Christmas quilt together.

"Sara sweet?"

"Yes, Mama?"

"I'm going to have another baby." The words fell from her lips.

Sara stopped sewing. She looked at her mother, who appeared nonchalant, and finally landed on something to say. "Are you happy about it?" she asked before she could stop herself.

"Of course, Sara. The birth of a child is a blessed event."

"But Mama, how will we—"

"We'll do the best we can with what we've got. You needn't worry. We always manage somehow. Maybe this house could use a lively little one."

Sara was awed by her positivity. *How could she be so calm and happy about bringing another child into this? What will we do with another mouth to feed?* Without question, Matilda was not ignorant of the ever-increasing challenges in the Wheeler household. Despite the circumstances, she never wavered from the persistence that it would be a "blessed event."

Matilda Wheeler experienced intense sickness in the months that followed. At times the pregnancy enfeebled her and left Sara with most of the household responsibilities. Easton was still small and required looking after when he was not in school. The tasks Sara took on in her place consumed her. Her duties kept her busy all day, and at night she crumpled into a tired heap on her bed only to wake up and repeat the cycle. She accepted the lot with dignity and never shrank from doing what was needed day to day. She never complained, but it was an extreme form of education that paled in comparison to whatever she was missing at school.

*   *   *

The experiences that shaped Sara's life were never too distant in her thoughts. The past year had rendered untold devastation, and her breakdown the night before reminded her that the wounds were still fresh. After her talk with Violet, she fell into a heavy sleep of emotional exhaustion. She awoke the next morning knowing that the only thing she could do was get up and take on another day. If she had learned anything from her trials, it was that she had to keep charging ahead.

She helped cook breakfast and listened to Easton chatter, but her mind was on something else. *Today I'm going back down to the meadow. I'm going to make myself. It's what Mama would do. It's what she would want me to do.*

She was trying to leverage her inner strength and will herself through the moment, but Violet posed an unexpected question.

"Sara, I've been meaning to ask you if you'll be wanting to go to school this fall."

Sara was so surprised by the proposition that she could not answer.

"So, will you?"

She knew the education she had received over the past year would not suffice. "Well, I didn't go to school last year. I really didn't expect to go back."

Violet half-smiled at her. "I think it's safe to say that we aren't strangers to the unexpected, but that didn't answer my question. Would you want to go to school this fall?"

The question gave Sara instant hope of regaining something she truly enjoyed and missed. She thought her aunt Violet would surely know if it was possible and not give her false hope. "Well, yes. If I can, I'd like to." Her answer came a little easier then.

"Of course you can! I think it would be a wonderful thing for you to do. We have a fine high school. The principal there is an

 Jenna Cossey

acquaintance of mine. I'll call him today and make the necessary arrangements. It won't be long before school is in session—two weeks from today, in fact." Her excitement for the opportunity was apparent.

"Do you think I'll be able to catch up?" Sara had reservations.

"I have a feeling you will," Violet said with a smile. "I'm going to take Easton with me to Pine Ridge. I go through to the other side of town on my way there and pass very near Dunnigan High. I think it will work out just right."

The troubles of the previous evening seemed to dwindle as Sara considered a new possibility. Violet had a knack for knowing when she needed the encouragement. Sara was not sure how she knew, but she was thankful just the same.

After breakfast, Easton excused himself to the backyard to play. When Sara put the final dish in the cupboard, she had come to another decision.

"Aunt Vi, if it's alright with you, I'm going to take a walk down to the meadow this afternoon."

"Shall we come with you?"

"No. I mean . . . if it's all the same to you, I think I'd like to go by myself."

Violet smiled. "You go ahead, Sara. I understand."

<u>**25**</u>

Ransom drove away from Dunnigan. The road wrapped around the Alabama terrain and wound through the edge of the Appalachian Mountains. He had driven it many times. He knew every curve and straight way.

Some landmarks served as navigational aids. In the distance was a turn-off to a provincial town through which the railroad failed to pass. Since the people there often made the journey to Dunnigan for their store-bought goods, Mayor Edward Cahill saw that the road between them was well maintained. Ransom rounded a curve, and a straight, smooth stretch came into view.

He shifted gears and pressed his foot steadily to the floor. A few seconds later, he felt himself gliding across the road as never before. He fixed his hands on the wheel and prepared to maintain control of the vehicle as he took a long gradual curve to the left. Flickering lights danced on the grill of the Chevrolet coupe as the sun occasionally found its way through the treetops. The speedometer topped out, having surpassed its maximum readout. He had no idea how fast he was traveling. His eyes darted from the road to the rearview mirror, and a sizable cloud of dust billowed up behind the speeding car. He released the throttle.

As he returned to a more casual speed, a grin expanded across his face. "Maclane, you really did it," he said aloud.

He cruised until he came to an old log cabin, which he knew marked a lane that lay just beyond it. A skinny stand of grass grew between the red clay tire paths. Ransom eased down the lane, and the mountains rose before him. They dotted the region and often served as barriers to automobile travel, but the road he had been on, like many others, ran parallel with them. The lane terminated in a clearing where there was another automobile. A man leaned against it and waited while Ransom parked and walked over to him.

"Cahill," said the man as he outstretched his hand.

"Haynes," Ransom shook his hand and surveyed the land.

"This way," Haynes motioned.

Ransom followed Haynes into a sparsely wooded area on a wide well-traveled footpath. They continued into the woods until they approached a large outcropping of rock.

"Right through here."

They walked between two large rocks that formed a natural corridor. Ransom outstretched his arms, noting the breadth of the passageway. His arms barely touched either side. Finally, it narrowed and adjoined itself to an overhang. As they walked underneath, they left the light of day, and the path darkened. Haynes stopped and ran his left hand over the wall of the dark crevice. His hand found a lantern on an oddly placed hook.

"Here, hold this," he said to Ransom. Haynes took a book of matches from his pocket and lit the lantern. Light flooded the darkened stone hallway, and he reclaimed the lantern. At the end, they came to an out-of-place large, heavy ornate wooden door. It was solid, windowless, and equipped with sturdy brass hardware. Haynes removed a stringer of keys from his pocket affixed to his belt with a chain. The door opened and revealed a well-lit area.

The large cavernous room was illuminated by several coal oil lamps. As Ransom surveyed it, he noticed that the light revealed adjoining rooms. He had heard about caverns buried within the mountains, but had never seen one.

"This way." He continued to follow Haynes as they crossed the stone floor.

In another room, Ransom could see a makeshift office. Behind a simple wooden table sat a man sharply dressed in a summer suit.

"This is Ransom Cahill," Haynes introduced him.

Ransom extended his hand, but the man did not reciprocate. He glared at Ransom, who was not used to being uneasy. He knew that he was outside of his territory of meeting people who were indebted to his father or somehow wanted to take advantage of his mayoral privileges. Haynes sat down, and he followed suit. A long silence ensued as the man removed a cigar from the front pocket of his suit coat and lit it. Everything seemed to move slowly, and Ransom became more and more nervous.

"Ransom Cahill, I understand you to be a man who can assist me with something." He rocked back in his chair with his left arm across his body and rested his right elbow on it as he took a long draw from the cigar.

"I suppose it depends on what that something is. I do know people," Ransom replied with a self-important smile.

The man remained expressionless. Ransom cleared his throat and abolished his smile.

"Look here, fella. This thing, it ain't exactly legal eagle. I need to know that you ain't gonna be letting your family affairs interfere. You should know that I've already looked you over. I know everything. I know about your family, your status, and your indiscretions. Now Haynes here says he gambles with you. Says you and your pals enjoy the drink too, so I know that you're one of the scofflaws, but what I've got to know is whether you're a stupid college boy looking for a good time or a man with guts. This is big."

          Jenna Cossey

"My father's affairs are of little concern to me," Ransom said smugly.

"Well, they need to be of concern to you because your name carries a great deal of importance in these parts. I know of the New Orleans Palmers and the Birmingham Cahills. I think you're the man we need."

The gravity of the moment suddenly seized him. He glanced at Haynes and posed a question. "Why did you not go to my father? He's the mayor. Nothing goes on here without his say-so."

"Or *does* it?" The man behind the table finally allowed his expressionless face to creep into a smile. "Cahill, your old man would lie about his own mother if it would win him a vote. I've made my inquiries."

The words struck Ransom. Edward Cahill was a professional politician. The family money purchased his influence, which outreached Dunnigan and extended into and beyond Birmingham boardrooms. He would stop at nothing to keep his name untarnished, but Ransom believed him to be a duplicitous man, and he despised him for it.

"Let me be sure I understand. You want whatever this is to go on here, in Dunnigan, right under my father's nose, without him being involved in it?"

"That is *exactly* the case."

Ransom looked at Haynes, and fixed his eyes on the man with a steely gaze. "Then tell me what I can do for you."

26

Noah walked the two miles to Sharp's Creek that evening. He seldom allowed himself the time to make the journey, but the day was not so dreadfully hot as the ones before it, and work at the garage was unusually slow. It was nearing three in the afternoon when Thomas agreed to stay and close down the station and give him an afternoon to go fishing. He had only one condition.

"Bring us back a good supper, Noah! I've got my mind on some fried fish now!"

Noah was confident enough to agree and gathered his meager tackle.

It was the time of year when rain was sparse, but the creek rushed through the forest with vigor. Noah sat on the bank and tidily arranged his socks and dust-caked boots. Red clay was a substance cotton farmers coveted, but everyone else fussed or cussed about it. Whether it took the wet, muddy form or the dry, powdery form, it clung to everything it touched as tightly as the Virginia Creeper on the trees.

He sat on the bank and listened to the moving water and wildlife around him. Not long after he arrived in Dunnigan, someone told him about Sharp's Creek when he asked around for a fishing spot.

"It's just down the way. Nice little spot. Been there a few times myself. They's always fish in there! They'll just about bite a bare hook! Sharp's hardly ever gets dry. She's more like a little river, but all us around here call it Sharp's Creek. I reckon mostly because that's what our daddys and granddaddys called it."

Noah had taken the suggestion and made the jaunt down to the little river at the first opportunity. It did not disappoint and became his favorite place. He tried not to go too long without a visit. It was somewhere he could sit down and think, but home was never far from his thoughts there. He could hardly help thinking of the complicated road between their old home and Dunnigan.

*　　*　　*

"You could go back and work without me, you know. No sense in us both being no 'count."

"Ain't neither of us no 'counts, Tommy. You're gonna be fine. Before long, you'll be back at it," Noah had tried to reassure him.

In the weeks after the injury, Thomas had considerable pain and despair. To keep his spirits up, Noah carried him to their favorite fishing spot as often as he could convince him to take a "piggy-back ride" to get there. He had natural brute strength that made it easy for him to carry Thomas. It benefited them both in the end.

"Besides, the mill wasn't paying us what we was worth. We worked like two borrowed mules, while them others set there like knots on a log for full wages. Nah, I'm gonna find me something else to get at. Maybe I can just help Pa pick up some slack around here. It's about time to harvest. I'd be one less picker to hire."

They had been hired at the heading mill where Thomas was injured because they were a pair. Between them, they earned the wages of one adult each day even though they outworked most of the grown men. Noah jested about it to make Thomas feel better.

They bonded strongly during their fishing trips and Thomas's recovery. They talked about everything in their world. It was crucial to Noah that they share their dreams. He thought that, if Thomas entertained his ambitions, it would keep him moving forward and save him from falling prey to his disability. He felt responsible for what had happened and made it his duty to always look out for Thomas from that time forward.

*   *   *

He sat with his fishing pole in hand, buried in his thoughts and enjoying the calm that he had come to expect there. Amid all the life and activity, a stillness remained. Suddenly Noah heard movement behind him. Someone was approaching. His head snapped around toward the disturbance, and he sprang to his feet, surprised to see her standing there.

"Oh, hi. Sorry. I didn't mean to startle you. I didn't think anyone else would be down here."

<u>27</u>

Sara had spent the day envisioning herself back in school. Daydreaming distracted her from confronting her emotions. When she came down from the crest of her anxieties the night before, she tried to soak in Violet's words and see if they could bring order to her inner turmoil. The things she said began to make a great deal of sense. Her aunt was right. She did so often feel that she was at the bottom of a deep pit. Sara also knew that she was right about what her mother would have wanted for her. Without a doubt, she would have wanted her to be happy.

Feeling encouraged by the good news of the morning, Sara began her journey back to the meadow. Barefooted as before, she ambled down the road. There was something she had been trying to remember. It was a poem her mother had recited to her thousands of times. In her moments of gloom, she clamored so desperately to recall it. When she felt the most alone, and when her tears flowed so freely in the still hours of the night, she would shut her eyes as tightly as she could, clench her teeth, and try to force the recollection. In the end, no matter how hard she tried, she could only remember in part.

Her mother had memorized from a reader she had used in school.

"Sara sweet, I think that I recited that poem to you so much when I carried you that I was gifted with a beautiful baby to match the poem I so loved," Matilda told her.

Sara was unsure of when she first heard it. She only wished that she had written it down or memorized it, so she could imagine the sound of her mother's voice speaking it.

She continued toward the end of the road, where the trees rose tall into the sky, confronting the pale blue vault with variant shades of green foliage. Reaching the edge of the woods where the path began, she slowed her walk, breathing deeply and taking in the scenery. Eventually, she came to the clearing and stopped, taking time to consider the beauty of the place where she had felt so uneasy the day before. She raised her arms and folded them across her body, grasping her elbows to pull them in close. She continued walking as if entranced. Sara was headed to no spot in particular as she eased through the clearing with her mind far away. She closed her eyes and listened to the sound of the gentle breeze moving through the trees and grass. It did feel like home. It sounded like home. It was not home, but her mind was home, and somehow this time it did not hurt so bad.

She took a deep breath and opened her eyes. The tears that blinded her were not the same as the ones she cried alone at night. Miles away from her old home and still trying to grasp the permanence of her mother's absence, Sara felt close to her again. It was hard to describe, but it was a nearness that she longed for and never believed she would find again. Violet was wise in her counsel, and Sara felt at ease knowing that someone had answers for her. Perhaps she was overlooking the advantage of being with her mother's only sister. They shared some things in their personalities; she had already begun to see that. While there was no way to fill the void her mother left, maybe, Sara thought, she could learn a new kind of happiness with Violet's help.

At least something was falling into place for her inside. She walked along the meadow and scanned the ground for wildflowers

     Jenna Cossey

and things. She neared the creek, and was startled when she saw someone. Unbeknownst to her, he had been sitting there, pondering life in much the same way as she was. After a moment, she realized that she knew the man standing before her.

Noah Maclane.

<u>28</u>

Charlotte Cahill mingled amongst society ladies in the large sitting room of her home. Each of the ladies was well dressed. They executed their movements in the unaltered way to which they had made themselves accustomed over time. Most were the wives of Alabama politicians, some more prominent than others, but all occupied an elevated place in their respective communities and social circles. They held to the rapidly vanishing notion that it was not proper for women to discuss politics, but since their husbands occupied public offices and it was a gathering of women, they seemed to make exceptions.

Zennia and Cephas worked tediously in the background to sustain the fluidity of Charlotte's event. Zennia had been laboring in the kitchen as she usually did, this time producing sweet confections for the women to enjoy with their afternoon tea. Cephas went about his usual tasks, but he also considered it his business to see that Zennia could accomplish hers. He stood over a large pot and stirred it steadily. He hummed a tune and stirred to the rhythm. He thought the sound was faint and perceptible only to himself, but Zennia recognized it as "Hard Hearted Hannah" and began to giggle.

"Cephas, I see you still singing about that Hannah!"

"Awe, you know it's them mean ones that get my attention!" They laughed.

The two of them had worked together for so many years that their relationship became a familial one. They treated each other as siblings, with mutual respect and watchcare. There was hardly anything that went on under the roof of the Cahill mansion that one or the other did not know. Between them, they seemed to be everywhere, and they kept little from each other.

As Cephas hummed and stirred, he heard the telephone ring. He left the kitchen and entered a small corridor where the phone hung on the wall and picked up the earpiece.

He spoke into the receiver, "Cahill residence . . . Yes, I'll take a message. Who shall I tell him called? . . . Uh huh. I'll make sure he knows . . . Yessir, thank you. Good day to ya," he said as he replaced the earpiece.

The conversation was momentary and left him puzzled as he returned to the kitchen.

"Who rang?" Zennia inquired.

"Don't know."

"Oh?"

"But it wasn't no message for Mr. Cahill or Mrs. Charlotte."

He had her full attention. "No?"

"Nope. Say they had a message for Mr. Ransom."

"What'd it say?"

"Just said he needed to come downtown to the office for a meetin'," he raised one suspicious eyebrow.

"What's that mean?" Zennia was unsure, but she knew Ransom did not have an office in town.

"Sounds awful peculiar to me, don't it you? Reckon what they mean 'bout goin' to a meetin'? They didn't say what day, or what time, just that he needed to come downtown to the office."

Zennia agreed with him—the request was unusual. Cephas knew that Ransom had been somewhere out of the ordinary a few days before. He made no motions about where he was the way he usually did. It troubled Cephas because it was hard for him to fulfill Mrs. Cahill's request to help keep him out of trouble when he did not know where he was.

Not long after the mysterious phone call, Ransom breezed in through the back of the house. He had been out driving, and his dark brown waves and curls were windswept. Cephas intercepted him at the bottom of the staircase. He kept his voice in a low whisper, taking care not to be heard by anyone else.

"Mr. Ransom, a phone call came."

"Yes? Who was it?"

"Don't know, sir. Didn't say."

"Was there a message?"

"Yes. Said to tell you that your presence was requested for a meetin' in the office downtown."

"I see." Ransom found a wall mirror and tried to tame his thick mass of hair. Once finished, he stood in front of the mirror a moment longer and took a deep breath. "I'll be back."

"Want me to go along?" Cephas asked, hoping for a chance to obtain more information.

"No need. I'll be back shortly." He moved toward the rear entrance as he spoke in a hushed way, "Don't worry, Cephas."

Cephas returned a diffident smile to him, knowing he had overplayed his hand. He was hopeful that Ransom would make his usual full disclosure later.

<u>29</u>

Noah stood with his back to the creek. He still held the cane fishing pole in his hand, but was unaware of any activity on the line. The person before him was none other than Sara Wheeler. He captured her unique image. She looked like a grown woman, tallish and slender, but there was a youthfulness in her face. The sun touched her dark brown hair, exposing a tawny cast. Her large blue eyes had widened, indicating that she was just as startled as him. He had rarely encountered any other people during his visits to Sharp's Creek. He always reckoned that there were much better fishing spots that the locals kept to themselves. Sara quickly apologized for alarming him, but Noah wanted to set her at ease.

"Oh, don't worry 'bout that. It's just that I never have run into anybody else out here. Sara, right? Sara Wheeler?" He knew her name, but wanted to make conversation.

"Yes." Her heartbeat slowed from the fright. "Noah Maclane, is that right?" She returned the formality.

After all, they were virtually strangers. In confirming their names, they listed most of what they knew about each other. Noah suddenly realized he was standing there with his back to the creek while his hook bobbed helplessly in the water behind him.

"Oh my, look at this, I nearly plum forgot about my line." He made a half turn toward the creek and tried to recover the situation. "So, Ms. Wheeler, what's brought you to Sharp's Creek?"

"Is that what this place is called? My aunt Violet just calls it 'the meadow.' She sometimes takes a walks down here," Sara continued. "I wouldn't have found it otherwise."

"Yes ma'am, Sharp's Creek, but Mrs. Simpson's right. It does lay next to a meadow, don't it?"

He smiled almost imperceptibly, glancing at her as he posed the question.

"Yes, it's a pretty place. Kind of reminds me of home." The words passed her lips before she could stop them.

"Yes'm, does me too. Reckon that's what I like about it. Reminds me of home."

Sara had assumed that Noah was from Dunnigan. She did not know enough about the town or the people in it to question who was native. She was intrigued by the idea that she was not the only foreigner, so she continued the conversation. "You're not from Alabama?"

"Oh yes, ma'am, I'm from Alabama, just ain't from Dunnigan."

"I see."

She waited a few seconds before she continued the line of questioning. "So how long have you lived here?"

Noah reset his line. "Well, let me see here. It's almost August . . . I reckon that makes us being here about eight months or so."

"Oh, is that all?" It made her feel better to know he was new, too.

"Yes, ma'am—Ms. Wheeler, me—"

"Sara. You can call me Sara."

"Yes'm, me and Tommy, my little brother, we lit here not long ago."

There was a long silence this time. Sara had surprised even herself by carrying on any conversation with him, but her mind was drawing comparisons and connecting dots. It seemed like the two of them were not so very different. She was not sure what to say next. She did not want to pry, so she decided to prepare for a departure instead. "Well, Mr. Maclane, I—"

"Noah. You can call me Noah," he mimicked her directive with a smile.

"Well, Noah, I'm sorry I disturbed you. I guess I should be going."

"Oh, not at all, Ms. Whee—" he stopped himself. "Sara. Why don't you sit a spell? I ain't no booger man!" He reclaimed his seat in the grass.

"I'm sure you're not."

He noticed that she was not wearing any shoes, and he knew about how far the walk was for her. He wagered to himself that she was probably used to walking barefooted, having come such a distance without shoes.

"Pull up some grass. Have a seat."

He displayed a quiet brand of congeniality. Sara sat down in the grass several feet away from him, and he continued the conversation.

"So where is it that you've come from?"

"I'm from Tennessee," Sara told him as she tucked her knees beneath her.

"Tennessee. Hmm. How come you to move to Alabama?"

"Well, I guess mainly because my aunt lives here. The rest is a long story."

He sensed her reluctance to continue about her previous home and decided to withhold his questions for the moment. The atmosphere of the meadow rose around them. Tranquility and vitality existed in perfect balance there. It was something they both seemed to understand and appreciate. They sat there quietly for a good while, and occasionally Noah would catch a keeper. They exchanged a few innocent words about the trees or a bird they saw.

The sun began to disappear below the tree line, signaling that the daylight would shortly slip away. Noah decided that it was time for him to get back to the station so that he and Thomas could prepare the fish he caught, which he was looking forward to eating. He brought in his line and began putting his shoes back on.

"Well, Sara, I reckon I ought to be gettin' back. Thomas'll be expecting me," he said as he held up the stringer of fish.

"Yeah, I guess I should be heading back, too. Aunt Violet will be looking for me." She got up and straightened her dress.

Noah gathered his tackle. "We'll head toward the road, then?"

He made his way through the woods, down the path, and she followed behind him until they reached the road. It was there that Sara was to cross and make her way up Ketcherside Drive, and Noah was to make his walk back toward the station. They each started on their way without stopping to say any goodbyes, but Noah halted.

"Should I walk you home, Sara?"

"Oh no, don't worry about me. I'll be fine, Noah, but thank you just the same," she said.

They exchanged smiles and commenced walking on their separate roads.

30

"Before you say you're in, you better think about it, fella. We ain't some two-bit operation. It's dangerous, and we've got power. If you throw in with us, Daddy can't help you anymore. His little ivory tower here in podunk doesn't mean much to me. Do you understand what I'm telling you?"

"I understand."

Ransom had rehashed the events of his clandestine mountain meeting over and over. It was still heavy on his mind as he drove into town.

Haynes gave him little information beforehand, and became even more cryptic afterward. Ransom held off on his usual twilight antics as he tried to sort through it. He found himself wondering what he really knew about Haynes. He did not even know his first name. He had only heard him referred to as "Haynes" and was never inclined to wonder beyond that. He did not live in Dunnigan, but he always seemed to be there for every soiree, seemingly partaking, yet never overtaken by vice as the other attendees. Ransom was also trying to make sense of the mysterious man from the cave meeting. He made no introduction, gave no name, and it was clear that he made a quick study of him.

"I know everything. I know about your family, your status, and your indiscretions."

The statement had hit a nerve although Ransom was sure he had not let it show. How did this man, of whom he knew so little, know so much about him? The entire thing was like a dream, but reliving the moment, he understood full well that it could not be one.

"You decide, Ransom Cahill."

The man consistently used his full name during the encounter.

"You decide whether you want to ride your mother's skirt tail or be a man in a man's world. You can do something really big here. In a few days, you'll get word. Haynes here will give you the details. I'm just giving you fair warning, that whatever you decide is final, whether it's in or out, it's all or nothing."

Ransom struggled for clarity. He knew so little, but he knew a few things about himself. His relationship with his father was fast deteriorating. Cephas had told him enough for him to know that. He was not going back to college. He found it a complete annoyance and was fairly certain that there was no thrill there that could not be found elsewhere without the sidecar of academic drudgery. The downside was the boredom, and he knew that, if he did not take up some seemingly productive activity soon, his father would have him ramrodded into the endless balderdash of politics. If this escapade was to hurl him into independent manhood, he decided after a couple of sleepless nights that he better capitalize on it before the opportunity passed.

Haynes had escorted Ransom out of the cavern that afternoon with few words. When they made it back to the clearing, there was a brief exchange.

"I'll leave word in a few days."

"Will we meet back here?" Ransom had no idea what to expect.

"No, no. Just like he said, say nothing about this place and don't come back here anytime soon."

"What was his name again?"

"Don't worry about that. Look here. When I send word, I won't give any details so you better remember all this. The alley down by the side of the hardware store in town, there's a room beneath one of the buildings. It has a side door into the alley. The door is painted red. Four o'clock in the afternoon will be the time, four knocks, and of course, come alone."

"What if I miss the word?" Ransom asked.

"Don't miss the word, Cahill."

Ransom did not miss the word.

He headed into town; he wanted to be prompt. He parked his car near Stillman's store, thinking to himself that it would not look suspicious there. Four in the afternoon on a weekday was a well-chosen time to be in town. A steady flow of people moved along the street, but it was not overly crowded. He would be able to disappear with ease. It was still early, just after three o'clock, so he went into the drugstore and made his usual request for a creme de menthe. The soda jerk disfavored the drink himself, but honored his wishes nonetheless. Ransom was surprised to find himself able to calmly enjoy his beverage, despite the unknown chasm he was about to traverse. At five minutes to four, he casually walked out of the drugstore. He stopped as he stepped onto the sidewalk, looked both ways, and saw no one who seemed to be paying him any attention. With liquid movement, he covered the yardage between the drugstore entrance and the alley. He turned the corner. Just as Haynes had instructed, he found the red door and knocked four times. With no sound perceptible to the human ear, it opened, and Ransom vanished from the alley.

_31_

The walk back to the garage from Sharp's Creek was slightly uphill. A person in good physical condition would have found themselves winded, but Noah was unaffected by the trip. He was not one to be overt in matters of the heart, and Sara Wheeler parted ways with him not knowing how captivated he was. He walked along the road with his usual expression, part serious and part serene. When men of lesser self-control would have added an extra bounce to their step or whistled a tune after a chance meeting with a pretty young lady, it was like him to continue unchanged.

When he arrived at the station with his catch, the sun had all but disappeared over the horizon. Thomas kept his word to gather the other items needed for their meal and was waiting on him.

"Musta been good fishin' today! I figured on you bein' back before now. Boy, I can't wait to get my claws into some of these! Looks like you got some good'ns!" He was impressed by the string of fish Noah returned with.

"I never have had as good a luck there as all this! It's a good thing too. I'm so hungry! How 'bout you?"

"I could sure eat a bite. Let's get it goin', or we're gonna starve ourselves to death talking about it!"

They talked about the memories of bringing their catches home and how their mother always managed to give the food that special "something" they seemed unable to replicate. For the first time in a long time, they found themselves openly reminiscing about home while they prepared the food. Noah rarely let Thomas know, but he did so often.

"Remember that time we caught all them dozens of fish and brought 'em home? Paw nearly fainted when he seen us coming up the lane. I can just hear him hollerin' at Maw now. 'Trudy, look at all these fish! What on earth are we gonna do with 'em all? We can't waste 'em; it'd be downright sinful!' and Maw comin' out there with her hands on her hips and that look on her face! Don't you remember?" Thomas chuckled at the thought.

"'Course I remember it! I thought Paw was gonna beat us half to death. Good thing Maw come to the rescue," Noah added.

The evening in question was hardly forgettable. There had been heavy rains and the waterways around their former home overflowed with wildlife. They caught fish with such ease on that Saturday afternoon that they became carried away. They came home with enough fish to feed four families. They were big enough to know they needed only to keep what they could eat, and their father had been very displeased with them. At the behest of their mother, they went to the nearest neighbors and told them of an impromptu fish fry that was to occur at the Maclane place. It was her solution to prevent the waste of food and stem the tide of William Maclane's wrath.

"Hurry now. Tell 'em to bring fixin's if they take a notion, but mostly just tell 'em to come hungry!"

The two boys decided they would deliver their message faster if they took their favored molly mule. With only a halter and a piece of thin rope for a bridle, the two of them climbed a fence, jumped astride, and took off as fast as her legs could carry them. They whooped and shouted as they screeched down the roads to make their invitations.

The neighbors gradually arrived, and all had a great time. In the years that followed, Gertrude Maclane joked about "the time we fed the few with five thousand fishes."

The evening at the creek, the tastes of home, and the stroll down memory lane with Thomas set Noah's mind aswirl with thoughts of the life they left behind. Sara Wheeler was also in his thoughts. He had no idea why he felt such an affinity toward her. Their stay at the creek consisted of long periods of silence punctuated by small talk. He hardly knew anything substantial about her, only that she was from Tennessee and now lived with her aunt in Dunnigan. He could not explain it yet, but he knew that she was different.

Though he was not fully aware, the girls in his hometown had thought him very handsome. They swooned amongst themselves over his sharp facial features and stout figure. There were a few with whom he had fleeting childish romances, but none of them ever really moved him. He found himself thinking that, had it been any of them with him at Sharp's Creek that day, it would have only been an annoyance.

Why is she so different? Perhaps it was because she was something of a mystery. Maybe it was because she had been so deliberate in her choice of words rather than babbling. It could have been that the sight of her bare-footedness gave him the impression that she was like him, just another simple, countryside soul. He wondered how he could see her again. Violet Simpson was not likely to leave her handbag at the station again. Maybe when Sara returned to the station with Violet, he could ask her if she would see him again, but there was no way to determine how long that would be. He stayed awake until late in the night and finally determined that if he wanted to see her, he would just have to pay her a visit.

          Jenna Cossey

<u>32</u>

Violet milled about the house taking care of various chores. She could hear Easton playing around the back porch, and if she listened long enough, a smile was inevitable. He was a lively and funny little fellow, and she could not help but think about the first time she ever saw him.

*　　　*　　　*

January 20, 1922

My Dearest Sister,

We welcomed a baby boy on the 13th, Easton Walter Wheeler. He seems to be perfectly healthy and is mostly content. Vi, I'm writing you now, dear sister, to ask for your help. I am still very weak. My sweet Sara helps me in anything I ask of her, but I'm afraid that Walter is proving quite difficult. I need your help. I know this might interrupt your work and studies, and I ask only as a last resort. Please come if you can, and do please write and tell me of your intentions.

Love,

Tildy

Upon receipt of the letter, Violet Stratton promptly spoke with her instructors at the school and made the necessary arrangements concerning her studies. She asked her employers, the Stillmans, for a few days' leave so that she could go. Always kind and understanding people, they insisted that she go and even made double sure that she could afford it. On a Thursday morning, Violet caught a train to Tennessee.

When she arrived at the Wheeler home place, she found that Matilda had weakened even further since penning the letter. Sara was small, only eight years of age, and though she tried to help as much as possible, she was not big enough to cook and help care for a newborn on her own. Violet was shocked by the condition in which she found her sister.

"Sara, dear, you run out and play awhile," Violet kindly issued the directive to her niece, and Sara obeyed. "Has the doctor been here?" Violet took a seat next to the bed.

"Not since last week. He says everything is fine, but I can't do this on my own, Vi." Weakness forced Matilda to speak softly.

"Where is Walter?"

"I don't know. He was here the day Easton came. Since then, he's been in and out. Most nights, he finds his way home, but not always." A tear fell from her eye, and her pale lips quivered, "I don't know what I'm going to do."

"Don't worry, Tildy. I'm here, and I'm going to get you back on your feet." Violet stroked her soft brown hair and spoke softly. "You just rest now."

Violet went to the kitchen and took stock of what they had on hand. She began preparing food for Matilda and tidying up. Sara came in and immediately wished to help, so Violet seized the opportunity to question her.

"What do you think of your little brother, Sara?"

"He's pretty!" Sara beamed.

"Yes, you're right. He's a very pretty child."

"When he got here, he cried and cried, but he don't cry much now."

"No, he doesn't. He's hardly made a sound." Violet casually continued, "What does your daddy think of him?"

"I don't know. I think he likes him. He thanked Mama for the baby being a boy, said he was happy he was a boy. Are boy babies better than girl ones?"

 Jenna Cossey

"No, dear, all babies are wonderful, but most fathers like to have at least one son. Where is your father now?"

"Don't know. He said he was going to work," Sara shrugged.

"I see. Where does he go to do that?"

"Where they cut logs," Sara said.

"A sawmill?"

"Uh huh, that's what it is. A sawing mill," Sara mispronounced.

"Does he work there every day?"

"I think so. He is there a lot, and sometimes he comes home way after dark." Sara went on, "And he is very grumpy and tired when he gets home. Sometimes he hollers, and sometimes he just goes to sleep."

Violet's temper flared. She knew exactly what Walter Wheeler was doing. His drinking had become progressively worse. It went in cycles, and there were times when Matilda revealed her concerns. She knew that Matilda's greatest strength was her greatest weakness. Unfortunately, she could not love Walter enough to make him sober. She tried to adapt to his habit. She stopped him when she could, and she tried to shield Sara from it however possible, never remarking about him being "drunk," but always telling young Sara that he was tired or not feeling well. It seemed to have worked until then, but Violet knew the ruse would not last forever. Moreover, Matilda needed his help.

Violet slept little that night. By the next morning, she developed the only plan of action that she thought would work with a stubborn drunk. It required an equal stubbornness that Matilda, even at full physical strength, did not have the inner strength to employ, but that was where she and her sister differed.

A shotgun hung over the fireplace, and Walter, like most men, used it for hunting various game on occasion. Violet suspected it was nearly time for him to make one of his grand appearances. So that night, she helped herself to the shotgun, loaded it, and waited on the porch for Walter to come home. Just as she predicted, he came unsteadily down the lane leading to the house. She was not sure how he made the journey, but it made no difference. The moment his foot fell on the bottom porch step, her voice came crisply through the air.

"That's far enough, Walter."

Startled by her voice, he attempted to focus by the dim light of the coal oil lamp that shone through the front window. "Violet? What are you doing here? Did you—"

"I said that's far enough." She stood to block him from resuming his ascent. "Don't take another step."

Walter slurred when he spoke, "I don't know if you forgot, but this is my house and my porch you're standing on. I'll come in when I please," he raised his voice.

"No, Walter. No, you won't." She descended onto the top step and pressed the barrel of the shotgun into his chest. "I've been here for a couple of days now, nursing my sister, trying to get her back on her feet. So, while you stand there talking about your house and your porch, let me just remind you that your wife and your children are in your house, and they need your help, but you haven't been here to give it." Her voice was heavy and calm. "You're a low-down, sorry excuse for a husband and father. I ought to blow you away from this porch right now, but I know it would break Tildy's heart, so I'm trying to exercise my patience. You better listen when I tell you that's about the only thing saving you from a hide full of buckshot right now, you miserable sot. So, I'll thank you to lower your voice and take your foot off these steps before I give you a little help."

Walter backed away from the wooden steps. "What do you want me to do, Violet?" He knew he was in no position to argue any further.

"You're not coming in this house until you're sober. That's it, and that's all."

"What?" His voice rose again.

"Shhh." She took a step down and bumped him lightly in the chest once more with the gun barrel. "I won't tell you again to lower your voice. I've made you a straw tick in the barn. You'll sleep there. I'll see you in the morning."

He snatched his hat from his head, but kept his voice low, knowing Violet's patience was thin, "You want me to sleep in the barn, like an animal? You're cracked!"

"Look at yourself, Walter. You smell like an animal, and you're as filthy as a hog. Seems to me it's the best place for you. Now, are you going, or am I gonna have to corral you like the rest of the stock around here?"

He made his way toward the barn, muttering to himself all the way, but he did indeed find the bed Violet had made for him in a small interior feed room of the barn by the base of the loft stairs. The room had a wooden floor, so he was off the ground, but it also had a door with an exterior latch.

The following morning, Violet tended to Matilda and the children. She decided it was best to tell her sister before she found out on her own.

"Tildy, you're not going to like this, but Walter is in the barn."

Matilda looked at her sister and raised an eyebrow. "In the barn?"

"Yes, in the barn. Neither of you can go on like this. It's got to stop."

"I'm in no shape to argue with you." Matilda, though improving, was still weak.

"Good, then." Violet smiled at her sister, hoping that she understood.

When Violet determined Walter had slept long enough, she woke him with the shotgun in the crook of her arm. He had slept in his clothes, looked like a terrible mess, and was still partially drunk. She presented him with a cloth full of freshly cooked food and a small bucket of water with a dipper in it.

"Walter, what have you got in your pockets? I know you're hiding something."

With shame and defeat on his face, he reached into his inner pocket and produced a glass vessel that she assumed was filled with moonshine.

"Give it here. You won't be needing that for sure. I've brought you food, and there's water. I'll be back later."

"What do you mean?"

"You're staying right here, Walter. Like it or not, I'm going to dry you out."

She shut the door behind her and closed a series of hasps and latches. For the rest of that day, and the next, the locks and hasps designed to keep critters out kept Walter Wheeler inside.

<u>**33**</u>

Near the main thoroughfare of Dunnigan sat a large two-story brick building. The street facing side boasted of several large white columns that provided the regality of a Greek revival structure. The facade had the year "1922" embossed in the mortar along with the name "Dunnigan High School." Sara followed Violet toward the building, and as she reached the bottom of the concrete steps, she looked straight up to the top of the columns. The building was even more imposing from that angle. She wondered how many students attended there, but stopped herself, hoping not to fuel any nervous energy.

There were three pairs of large wooden doors beneath the massive portico. Violet chose the door farthest to the right. After a series of turns, she and Sara arrived at a door with a large glass window on which was painted "Office." They entered, and Violet rang the brass call bell on the counter. A man appeared from somewhere within the office.

"Ah, good morning, Mrs. Simpson. So good to see you again!"

She shook his hand and made an introduction. "This is my niece, Sara. Sara, this is Mr. Davis Winton. He is the principal here at Dunnigan High."

"Nice to meet you, Mr. Winton," Sara said.

"Nice to meet you as well." He outstretched his hand and smiled as he shook hers. "You all just come on back. Sara, if you don't mind, I'd like to speak with Mrs. Simpson for just a moment."

Sara thought it a bit silly for her to have come along only to end up sitting in a chair outside the office door, but she patiently waited during their conversation. Since school was not in session, the place was quiet. As she sat there waiting, she could hardly help overhearing most of what was said. She was amused at the two of them not accounting for the silence when they began their closed-door meeting behind such thin walls. It seemed Violet was doing most of the talking, punctuated by questions from Mr. Winton.

"It is a slightly unusual circumstance, but I don't see any reason she can't be enrolled here."

"I felt sure you would agree. She did not attend last year, but her mother contended that she was very bright, and I tend to agree. She made excellent marks in her last year of grade school."

Violet had done as she promised. After gauging Sara's willingness to attend school, she had phoned Mr. Winton. He felt that a meeting was necessary to discuss the prospective pupil and give him an opportunity to meet her.

"I'm sure that she will be a good addition to our incoming class here," Mr. Winton maintained an optimistic trust in Violet's judgments.

"I think that she needs this. She lit up when I mentioned the possibility to her. This past year was very difficult for her—"

"For all of you, I dare say," Mr. Winton interjected.

"Yes, indeed, for all of us, but particularly for her. Their situation was less than desirable even before her mother's passing. I never dreamed that it would come to this end, but it seems as though this was the most appropriate place for them to be, all things considered."

"Yes, yes." Mr. Winton removed a pair of wireframe glasses and leaned forward as he asked, "What of the children's father?"

Outside, Sara heard: *What of the children's father?*

 Jenna Cossey

The question ricocheted in her mind so vehemently that she stopped listening. It was a fair question for a man in his position to ask. She wondered what had become of him by then. There had been times when he was gone so long, she had felt sure he was lying dead somewhere. Even worse, there were times when she wished him dead, but seeing the way her mother continued to love him despite his faults made her feel guilty for it. She wondered how a sweet soul like her mother could love a man who behaved like her father. While Matilda held out hope for Walter to be as he had once been, their children grew up living with his insobriety and unpredictability. In the end, they all suffered together. Sara came to understand that her mother must have seen something in her father at some point that was no longer apparent to everyone else. After one flurry of outbursts from him, Sara began to ask natural and logical questions of her mother.

"Mama, why does he do these things? Can't you and me and Easton just go away so he can't hurt us?"

Sara's tolerance of his behavior diminished as she entered her teenage years. She became old enough to do more work and help Matilda keep food on the table. Walter worked when he was sober, but Matilda knew that he was not dependable. They were able to sustain, but Sara wondered what it would take to put a stop to the absurdity. That summer, before she and Easton came to live with Violet, she finally got the answer to that question. With the passing of Matilda Wheeler, and their move to Dunnigan, Walter Wheeler's maltreatment of his family came to a halt.

"What of the children's father?" Sara was still embattled by the question when the door of the office swung open.

"Come in. There are some things Mr. Winton would like to discuss with you," Violet said.

Sara felt herself shutting down. It was her default reaction. She did not want to discuss her life with a perfect stranger. She took a seat in the office and stared at the floor.

"Well, Ms. Wheeler, if you're going to be joining us here at Dunnigan High this year, I'd like to make sure that we get you into the right courses," Mr. Winton still spoke with the same kind expression. "If you'd be agreeable, I'd like to have you come back in a day or so and complete a few examinations to determine the best placement for you."

Relief washed over Sara. She had avoided the subject of her past again.

<u>34</u>

"Your ticket, please, sir."

Ransom reached into his coat pocket and produced his ticket. The conductor punched it as he seized the opportunity to converse. "New Orleans, eh?" There was a coy look on his face that implied mischief.

Ransom looked at him with a condescending expression. "Yes. Family there. I don't suppose you know of the New Orleans Palmers."

"Never heard of 'em." Unimpressed by the self-important air, the conductor returned the ticket and continued his tour down the aisle.

Later on, Ransom found his way to the dining car. The time of day was such that it was not overly populated there. Train cars were never very quiet, and he found himself thankful for that, unsure that his nerves could handle silence. Part of him wished that Cephas were along with him, but bringing him would have necessitated explanations that he was not yet willing to give. Cephas had been part of the family for decades, and Ransom was well aware of his uncanny knack for knowing almost everything while pretending ignorance. Not taking him along to New Orleans would at least allow time to collect his thoughts and decide what to reveal and keep to himself.

"What can I get for ya, sir?" The waiter approached the table so inaudibly that it startled Ransom. "S'cuse me, sir. Didn't mean to give you a start."

"Cup of coffee, please."

He had always been able to manage situations so that the upper hand was his. He disliked being at a disadvantage in any affair, yet there he was, headed to make arrangements he did not fully understand, in a town to which he was not native, with people he did not know. He questioned his wisdom.

Get a hold of yourself, Rans. He tried to calm down, knowing that if he did not regain some self-confidence before stepping off the train in New Orleans, he was likely to be eaten alive.

"Hot coffee for ya, sir. Can I get ya somethin' to eat? Club sandwich is the special."

"No. This will be all."

As the waiter disappeared again, Ransom slid the cup and saucer nearer to him. Out of the corner of his eye, he scanned the dining car, and then slipped a small metal flask from the inside of his coat and added a bit of liquor to the cup. He needed to be sharp when he got there, but being too edgy could be disastrous. He sat for some time and sipped the concoction. He remained still a little longer when the waiter came by and warmed the cup. He then returned to his seat and watched sedately as the train sailed over the diverse Southern landscape and eased into the Canal Street Depot. They would be waiting for him there, and he would be easy to identify. There was no turning back.

He stepped off the train with only a single small suitcase in his possession. He was to be back home in two days. As if from the shadows, a large man with dark hair and eyes appeared beside him.

"You Cahill?"

"Yes."

"Come with me."

Ransom followed him to a shiny black Stutz car. It looked brand new. He was rarely impressed by fineries having come from a family of means, but it caught his attention in a sea of Buicks, Fords, and Chevrolets. He got into the car with the large man, and they proceeded along the route. Before long, they ventured beyond the familiar part of the city. The car stopped in front of a tall brick building that he thought to be some type of warehouse. He was escorted through a side door, and when they entered, there were two other men in an outer office.

"He's here to see Mr. Messina."

One man took his case. "I'll hang on to this for you, pal."

Another patted him down, finding only a silver cigarette case, a book of matches, his wallet, and his flask. The man gave him a sly grin when he discovered the flask and kept none of his personal effects.

The man with his suitcase knocked on a door twice. "Mr. Messina, a Mr. . . . eh, what's your name, kid?"

"Cahill."

"Mr. Cahill here to see ya."

"Send him in."

When he entered, he found that Mr. Messina was the man from the cave meeting. This time it was no makeshift office. He sat behind an ornate wooden desk topped with a fancy cigar box and a silver ashtray and lighter.

"Have a seat, Ransom Cahill. I'm glad you could make it. It seems like you're up to the task if you've come this far."

"Yes, sir, I am." Ransom came back confidently, but inside his nerves were on fire. "I do hope you'll tell me now exactly what it is that I can do for you."

Mr. Messina stared at him with a serious look, yet he smiled at the same time. It heightened Ransom's anxiety. He could feel himself breaking into a nervous sweat and hoped the meeting would end before it soaked through his coat and gave him away.

Mr. Messina leaned forward and retrieved a cigar from the decorative box. As he lit it, he fixed his eyes on Ransom again.

"I'm not going to waste a lot of breath trying to explain this to you. Plain and simple, this is part of a big operation. We've got men and clientele scattered from here to Canada. Not twenty miles from here, there's liquor waiting to come ashore, and when it gets here, there'll be more, and more still after that. We're trying to cut in on our rival operation. We've got warehouses in Birmingham, and we are looking to move some to Dunnigan."

Ransom was not yet clear, but he listened and tried to ask direct questions, "Why Dunnigan?"

"A large portion of our stuff is sent North. We can supply either one of the outfits in Chicago, but it is becoming more and more difficult."

"Why the difficulty?"

"If either of them had their way, the other would be choked off from our supply, but if Carollo had his way, we'd work out something exclusive and quit trying to play both sides. In the end, it's one big game of sabotage, and it's a loss for us." Messina shook his head in disappointment.

"So why not work out something exclusive, then?" Ransom asked carefully, knowing that there were likely limits to what Mr. Messina was willing to share.

"Funny you should ask. That's kind of where you come in. Some time ago, we became aware of the large cavern outside of Dunnigan. What you saw was only part of it. Rather than trying to move goods to supply two competing outfits, we are looking to satisfy the demands of only one and make up the difference in other ways." Messina leaned back in his chair and puffed his cigar.

"I'm supposing these other ways are the ones that concern me, correct?"

"Correct."

"So, what are these other means?"

"A combination of warehousing, gambling, and entertainment. We're getting ready to establish a destination that will be known all over the South, yet stay a secret in all the right ways. We've done this in other places, but we believe that this particular location will be a great success *if* we can make it happen."

"So, what is my part to play?"

"Haynes has been in and around the area for some time. He wears a lot of hats for us, but he's made a study of the logistics, and you will deal directly with him. He'll figure out what we need to get this thing going. Your job is to make sure that the right people are looking the other way when we need them to. Money is no object. You'll have more than you need, but I'm making it your business to see to that detail. Of course, if you encounter resistance, there are other methods. We operate by any means necessary. Do you understand what I'm saying?" His countenance was icy.

"By any means necessary." Ransom contemplated the gravity of the phrase. It was a much bigger situation than he first estimated, but backing out would endanger him. He had been ushered into the bowels of an operation that spanned from the Gulf of Mexico to Canada. If he failed to commit, anything could happen to him. He already knew too much.

"By any means necessary." The words rang in his ears, over and over. Sweat gathered on his forehead.

"Do you understand, Cahill?"

He felt like he was watching himself from the outside. "Yes, Mr. Messina. I understand."

35

Noah recalled with bittersweetness a conversation with his father. He had been younger then, thirteen or fourteen years old as best as he could recollect. A number of the local girls took interest in him as he changed from boy to man. Likewise, he and his friends began to take interest in the girls, but he found the territory most awkward. Courtship, love, and marriage were not regular points of conversation between he and his father. To make matters worse, speaking with William Maclane about it provided precious little insight.

"Paw, how'd you know you were gonna marry Maw?"

"Don't know, boy. Reckon I just asked her, and her paw agreed to it, and that was it."

Noah was inexperienced, but knew that there was surely a great deal more to it than that. Being the firstborn, he was not the most outgoing of the lot. Everything he encountered in life was new in so many ways. If a situation arose, it was not only he who was navigating it for the first time but also his parents. They had lived their young lives and could speak from experience, but as mother and father, their solutions to the trials of life changed. William Maclane decided early on that his approach would be one of least intervention. When his son questioned him about girls, he adhered to his usual method.

"How'd you know she was the one you wanted to ask, though?"

"Been too long. Guess I've forgot. Somebody you're sweet on?"

"Maybe."

"Hmm."

The conversation fell flat, and the advice Noah hoped for never came. He decided that it was in his interest to be observant rather than overt in the company of females. It won him the admiration of many young ladies, but none ever compelled him like Sara Wheeler.

He let the next day after the encounter at Sharp's Creek pass without action. He did not want to seem overeager, but when the second day came, he could not wait any longer. He dreaded the moment when he would have to tell Thomas. He knew he would tease him mercilessly, but when they finished the work of the day to begin cleaning and shutting down the garage, Noah got a chance to break the news.

"What we gonna have for supper tonight, brother?"

"Well, I was gonna tell you earlier, but you're gonna be on your own this evening."

"What are you talking about?" Thomas asked in disbelief.

"I mean I'm going somewhere when we're done here. Don't know what time I'll be back, so make your own plans."

"Where you goin', Noah? You *never* go anywhere."

He made a snap judgment on how best to answer. "Well, if you have to know, I'm going to Violet Simpson's to call on her niece."

"You're what?"

"You heard me."

Thomas grinned and began to laugh. "Mrs. Simpson's niece, huh? Boy, I knew I shouldn't have let you go over there with that purse the other night! Shoulda known you'd go over there and find you a gal!" He was enjoying the laughter at Noah's expense. He loved to kid him about those kinds of things and watch his face bloom into various shades of red. "I tell you what, Noah, I never did figure you for the kind of fella that had the nerve to go call on a girl he hardly ever met before!"

"I did meet her."

"Sure, sure you did, but that's about all you had time to do. Did she make eyes at you or something?" Thomas clamored for details.

"No, I just—she seemed awful nice and I'd like to call on her. I ain't sayin' nothing else about it. I'm going over there, and I hope Mrs. Simpson don't shut the door in my face."

"Oh, I don't expect she'll do that, brother! I think she favors us, Noah. I do!"

"I hope you're right."

Noah downplayed his anxiety. He did hope Violet favored them. He knew that he would not be able to visit Sara if she did not approve, and unlike Thomas, he was not a very persuasive person. If she turned him away, he would have little recourse.

After work, he cleaned up and put on his best pair of slacks, a dress shirt, and a tie. He did not own a suit. He had scoffed at Thomas for wanting to buy one out of his fifty-dollar bonus from the Cahill job, but owning one did not seem like such a bad idea after all. All he could do was put on his best and hope that it was enough. Noah took the keys to the service truck as he prepared to leave. The seat was dirty, but not wanting to soil his best clothes on the dusty road, he decided that driving it was better than walking and sweating. He made a few passes over the seat with a damp shop rag before getting in and hoped it was enough to save his clothes from ruination.

He drove slowly toward Ketcherside Drive, fearful that he would not say and do the right things when he got there. When he stopped the truck in front of the house, he ran his fingers through his wind-tousled hair and straightened his tie. He reached the door and took a deep breath before knocking. He heard footsteps, the door began to swing open, and he wished for Sara herself to answer it.

"Well, hello, Mr. Maclane, what a pleasant surprise."

36

The smell of fried foods wafted through the house as Sara and Violet worked together in the kitchen. Cookware occupied every burner on the stovetop. The two complimented each other in their efforts, making it easier for both.

"You needn't help me unless you really want to, Sara."

"Oh, I want to help!"

Violet was continually amazed by her good nature. There were so many reasons for Sara to be bitter, yet she was not. Violet knew that she struggled at unpredictable times. However, she believed her ability to cope was growing. Sara underestimated the knack Violet had for sensing when she was having a tough day. She wanted, more than anything, to be a helpful and pleasant addition. If she did not manage her struggles, she believed she would only be a bother to her aunt. She even entertained the thought that things might become quite normal with time. After finding out that she would return to school, her meeting with the school principal, and her important lone journey to the meadow at Sharp's Creek, Sara felt like she was finding her feet.

There was an unexpected knock at the door.

"Who on earth could that be?" Violet wiped her hands and untied her apron. "Wasn't expecting anyone."

Sara continued her task, but tried to listen in the direction of the door. She could barely make out the words, but she was surprised when she recognized the name and voice of Noah Maclane.

Jenna Cossey

"Evenin', Mrs. Simpson." His hands were behind his back, one loosely grasping the other. "I'm sorry to drop by unexpected like but—"

"Not at all! What a pleasant surprise! Now I haven't been by the station, so I know you don't have my purse. What brings you this evening? Do come in!" Violet exercised her habit of smothering visitors with hospitality.

Noah entered with subdued confidence and concealed apprehension. "Mrs. Simpson, I know this might seem mighty forward of me, but I've come with hopes to visit with Ms. Wheeler."

Hearing this, Sara froze in place. *Noah Maclane is here to see me?* She moved to the other side of the kitchen to ensure that she was not visible to them as they stood near the landing and listened.

"Sara? I see. Have a seat, Noah. Give me just a moment."

Violet reentered the kitchen and found Sara standing near the far wall with a look of surprise. She knew that Sara had overheard and had to ask a few questions.

"Sara, Noah Maclane is here. You know, from the station?" she spoke in a low whisper.

Sara nodded. "Yes, I know him, well, kind of. Aunt Vi, I was going to tell you but—"

"What, Sara? What is it?"

"Well, the other day—"

"When he came to the house with my clutch?"

"No, after that. The other day, when I went to the meadow by myself. He was there."

"Yes, and?" Violet needed to hear more, but Sara did not take the cue immediately. "Don't tell me he was forward with you."

"No!" Sara's voice rose, and she caught herself. "No. He was very nice. He was there fishing. We talked a little, useless chatter mostly."

"Uh huh, well, he's here to see you. What shall I tell him?" Violet put her hands on her hips and smiled.

Sara did not know what to do. She had not entertained any thoughts of being called upon, especially being new to Dunnigan, but she and Noah had already broken the ice. She wondered how bad it could be if he was there to see her. In her hesitance to answer, Violet interceded.

"If you want me to send him away, I will, but he must be sweet on you, Sara. I think he's a nice young man. Why don't we ask him to stay for dinner? It won't be so bad that way, and I'll be right here with you." She wanted to leave it in Sara's hands. "So what will it be?"

All of the interaction with Noah Maclane went through Sara's mind. She thought of his patience with Easton, the way he remembered her name, their peaceful evening at Sharp's Creek, and he was decidedly handsome. "You can ask him to stay."

"Alright, then. He's sitting out there waiting to see you, so you better come with me." Violet moved back toward the living room.

They entered the room, and Noah got up from his seat.

"Sorry to keep you waiting, Noah. Sara and I were finishing up some things. We'd love for you to stay and eat with us."

"Oh, no'm. I'd hate to impose."

"It's no imposition at all. We always have plenty," Violet assured him. "Sara and I get together in the kitchen, and we almost always end up overdoing it, right, Sara?"

"She's right, Noah. Do stay and eat with us." Sara smiled faintly with her head tilted downward.

"Well," Noah hesitated, "as long as you're sure it's no trouble."

 Jenna Cossey

"Not in the least! So it's settled? You'll join us for supper?"

"Yes'm, I'd love to." He gave a thankful nod as he accepted.

"Good, then. I'll finish up and call you all in a minute." Violet disappeared into the kitchen.

Sara and Noah stood there in the living room and looked at each other for a moment. She sat down in the chair adjacent to the settee on which Noah had been sitting, and he followed suit.

"Evening, Sara."

"I'm kind of surprised to see you," she paused, "but I'm glad too."

It was unusual for his emotions to show, but Noah could not stop himself from smiling. "Well, you see, I was thinking about the other day when we was at Sharp's."

"Yes?"

"I was figuring on that part you said about you coming to Alabama being a long story."

"It is."

"Well, I kinda like to hear me a long story every now and then." His sweet solemnity caught her off guard.

Violet reappeared from the kitchen, before Sara could generate a response. "Everything is ready! Come on, and eat!"

Violet opened the back door and summoned Easton in from the yard. As usual, he was dirty, and she sent him straight to the washroom to tidy himself.

"The car man!" Easton exclaimed.

Violet intercepted him, "Yes, yes, he is the car man, and *you* are the dirt man! Now go wash up! Hurry now!" Easton bolted down the hallway to clean himself up.

"I declare, that boy finds more dirt than just about any creature in the world could hope to. He's an expert."

When Easton returned, he had a series of questions for Noah. He chose the chair next to him and peppered him with conversation. He had a way of bringing a certain childish levity to every situation. The four of them had a pleasant meal over small talk.

When dinner was over, Violet volunteered Easton to help her clear the dishes. Noah and Sara retired to the living room again. He was so easy to be around. Occasionally Sara worried about what she said or did, but she found him to be so unassuming. Her worries quickly disappeared. She had spent most of her life believing that men were like her father, but his disposition so contradicted that of Walter Wheeler, she knew almost immediately that he could be nothing like her father. They bantered for a time as they had at Sharp's Creek, talking of inconsequential things.

"I've enjoyed y'all's company. I really get a kick out of that Easton. He puts me in mind of Tommy when we were kids," Noah said.

"Oh, he's a mess. Tommy, he's your little brother, right, the one that works at the station with you?"

"Yes'm, only he ain't so little anymore. He reminds me all the time."

"What's the difference in your ages?"

"Two years. Almost on the nose. Our birthdays are real close. July nine for me and July eighteen for him. I just turned eighteen, and Tom sixteen."

"Is there only the two of you?"

"Oh no, there's a whole mess of us still back home. Five others."

"Brothers?" Sara asked.

"Some, but sisters too. Zeke and Teddy are a few years behind Tommy, twelve and ten, I think. Then there's Kate and Anna. They are about nine and seven. Then little Patrick, he's about five."

"That's a lot. What about your mother and father?" Sara had fallen headlong into her curiosity.

"Oh, they're there with the brothers and the sisters. Alright, to my knowledge. I try to write Mama ever so often, but I'm not much of a hand to write," Noah patiently answered her questions before inserting some of his own. "How about you?"

"Me?"

"Yes'm what about your family?"

There was a long pause, and then came the answer, "I guess this is my family now."

He noted a change in her countenance. He tried to recover the conversation, "It's a long story, right?"

"It is. My mother . . . she died not long ago."

Noah had not been prepared, and it struck him hard. There he sat, talking about how scarcely he wrote to his mother when Sara no longer had a mother to write to. He felt terrible. "I'm sorry, Sara. I didn't know."

"Of course not. You couldn't have."

He sat there, lost for words. He frantically tried to think of something to say. Violet had a penchant for appearing when the conversation wore thin, and she did not disappoint.

"I am so happy that you decided to stay and join us for supper, Noah. I hope you won't mind, but it's about time for us to settle in for the night." She had been cautiously nearby and felt that Noah had enjoyed a reasonable amount of time with her niece.

"Thank you for asking me to supper, ma'am. It's the finest meal I've had since I last had my maw's cooking." He patted his stomach as he commented.

"It was nice to have you with us," Sara told him. "I hope you'll come again." Sara really meant it. She did hope to see him again. Most of all, she hoped that she had not scared him away with the disclosure of her mother's death. She did not want pity.

"Mrs. Simpson, with your permission, I'd like to call on Sara again."

"Here," Violet took a pad and wrote down a telephone number. "This way, you can call when you'd like to visit."

He accepted the small piece of paper, smiled, and held it up in the air. "Thank you ever so much, Mrs. Simpson."

"Sara, you see our guest out. I've got to check on Easton. Good night, Noah," Violet bid him a kind farewell.

Sara saw him to the door. Before he descended the few steps, he turned around and extended his hand. "Good night, Sara," he said with a smile.

At that moment, she saw him just as she had the night he first came to the house. His blue-gray eyes glistened beneath the dim porch light, and this time his magnificent facial features were improved by a smile. As she shook hands with him, she felt him restraining his strength to gently grasp her smaller hand.

"Good night, Noah."

He headed toward the old service truck he had driven, but halfway there, he stopped and made a half turn. "Sara?"

"Yes?"

"I'll see you soon."

 Jenna Cossey

<u>*37*</u>

A line of large rolling boxes moved over the contours of the land. Brightly colored skins of wood masked the steel skeletons. One dark and powerful force led them all.

The beast motivated through the wilderness, and occasionally revealed itself to civilization with the long scream of a whistle. It traversed the peaks and valleys of the land as it inhaled the steady coal heat and exhaled plumes of steam and smoke.

Bound to the path that men had carved out, the iron horse followed the carefully marked way.

The beast was only tame to the degree that something of such immense strength and power could be, for it was not of flesh but steel. When it was appointed to go one place or another, it went without care for what was in its way.

The iron horse.

38

"Mama, does Daddy love you?"

Sara had turned into a young woman, and she had started to notice things. She was in the upper half of the grade school with the teenagers, where talk of "love" and "sweethearts" became a regular part of the day. She was thirteen and did not have the faintest idea what constituted love. From all that she gathered, if two people were "in love," they spent time talking and laughing with each other, and her mother and father never did that. She rarely hesitated to question her mother about things she did not understand, so it seemed only fitting that she ask.

"Sara Angeline! Of course, Daddy loves us."

Her mother had a way of being right about things, but something did not add up. She pressed her mother no further on the subject, but it did not stop her from wondering how much her father loved her mother. She was old enough to recognize that Walter Wheeler was not a wonderful husband. The excuses her mother offered no longer sufficed or made sense to Sara. Her mother must have realized it, because when Sara began to question his devotion to the family, she stopped offering them.

*   *   *

Sara did not know whether to be sad or angry that her mother had tried to conceal her father's true nature. She was always honest with her mother, something her mother taught her to be, yet her mother was not totally honest with her.

With those things in mind, Sara sat in her room, contemplating her relationship to Noah Maclane. Sure, he had been friendly, but that did not mean that he loved her. It was true that he had gone out of his way to make his visit that night, but she wondered why. Violet assumed aloud to Sara that he must have been "sweet on her," but how was she supposed to know? Her inexperience in matters of the heart left her anxious. She could talk to Violet about it. *What would she think?* She knew that Violet had a protective streak. *How will she react?*

She could hear Violet reading to Easton in the next room. He begged her to read to him each night when she put him to bed, and Violet never turned him down. She was reading *Winnie the Pooh* to him, and each night he awaited the next part of the story with excitement that endeared Violet to the reading time. Sara heard him giggle.

"A Heffalump? What's that, Aunt Vi?"

"Just wait and see. 'What was it doing? asked Piglet,'" Violet read.

Violet did not know it, but on most nights, Sara also listened to her read. The walls were thin, and the sound of her voice easily carried down the short hallway. Sara never let on, as she was too old for bedtime stories, but sometimes she closed her eyes and let her mind drift. Violet sounded so much like her mother. It was almost as if Matilda Wheeler herself was there reading. It was no small comfort to Sara. It was at night when everything fell quiet that she missed her mother the most.

After a time, Easton would fall asleep. Violet would mark the page for a later continuation and silently make her way out of his room. That night was no different than the others, except Violet stopped and softly knocked on Sara's partially open door.

"Come in," said Sara.

"I'm glad you're still awake."

"What is it?" Sara was sitting up in her bed.

"Well, I thought we better talk about this thing with Noah."

Sara was a little nervous, but in a way, she was glad that Violet brought it up so that she did not have to. "I guess so."

"What's on your mind?" Violet asked her.

It was a complex question. Everything was on Sara's mind, but she knew Violet was referring to Noah. "I don't know. Why do you think he came here?"

Violet smiled. "Well, I think he came because he likes you."

"Me? But why?"

"For one thing, my dear, you're a very pretty young lady!" Violet patted her on the leg.

"What should I do?"

"Ah, this is the hard part. There are no instructions for it, sweetheart. I suppose the first thing would be to consider what you think of him."

"I think he's very nice. He was nice to Easton, he brought your purse to you, and he offered to walk home with me the day I saw him at the meadow. He's very nice," Sara repeated.

"I agree. He's a nice young man. I don't know very much about him, though, and that bothers me a bit."

"Well, I know he's not from Dunnigan," Sara said.

"No, he's not. I know that Mr. Haskins took the boys on back in the winter. They've been doing a good job running the station, but where did he come from? Do you know?"

"Not really. I only know that he is from Alabama. He has five other brothers and sisters back home and a mother and father."

"I see. Well, that's more than I knew. Besides his being nice, what else do you think of him?"

Sara's cheeks reddened, and she cast her eyes down. "I do think he's handsome."

"Yes, he is a nice-looking young man," Violet said.

 Jenna Cossey

"Do you think that he is in love with me? Do you think that's why he came?" It was an innocent question.

"He may very well think that he loves you. Sometimes you love someone right away. Joseph—rest him—he always told me he loved me right away." Violet shook her head in disbelief as she reminisced.

"Did you love him right away?"

"No, I don't suppose I did." Violet's eyes narrowed. "It took a bit of convincing on his part, but he was devilishly handsome and wonderfully kind hearted. I couldn't have resisted for too long."

"What if he calls again, Aunt Vi?" Sara needed a plan.

Violet was smiling, but her expression became a little more serious as she considered the question. "Sara, I hope you will understand my responsibility for you and for Easton. I believe this young man is very nice, but that's not enough for me. I have to *know* it." Violet took her hand. "I'm not your mother or father, but I have to do what I believe is best for you."

"So you'll send him away?"

"Of course not, but I'd like to have him here so that I'll get to know him. If he is truly a nice young man, he will understand this."

Sara was surprised at the sensibility of the plan, and it removed some of her concerns. In a few short weeks, she would turn sixteen, and she had not faced the possibility of courtship back in Tennessee. Overcome with relief, she hugged Violet. "Thank you, Aunt Violet. Thank you for everything."

"You're welcome, Sara dear. I'm always here for you. You can always talk to your aunt Violet. Just remember that."

"I will."

Violet got up and started out of the room. Before she reached the door, Sara asked her something else.

"Aunt Vi?"

"Yes."

"How did you really know that Uncle Joseph loved you?"

Violet raised one shoulder. "He just showed me. Every day he showed me. It's not what people say, Sara. It's what they do that really tells the story. If Noah loves you, he will show you. You'll know."

"I will?"

"You will."

_39_

"Whatcha figure that boy up to?" Zennia was hanging laundry on a line to dry while Cephas helped her.

"Don't know. Ain't like him to go down to N' Orleans on a whim, least of all to see his kinfolk." His eyes narrowed in thought. "He don't care for them Palmers much no how. Something's afoot. Can't say as I know what just yet, but sure as I stand here right now, Zennia, that boy up to no good."

"He ain't no boy. He's a man, Cephas." She lowered her voice as if the laundry had ears, "You best watch yourself. Mr. Cahill catch you skirtin' around trying to cover for that boy, and he'll bring down the roof a that house on you. Don't make no matter what Mrs. Charlotte say."

"What you mean, Zennia? You and me both know that Mrs. Charlotte's got the final say-so around here. Mr. Cahill can say what he want 'bout Mr. Ransom needin' to do this and that. If it don't agree with Mr. Ransom, you know he ain't gonna do it, and Mrs. Charlotte ain't gonna make him," he said with a confident nod.

"And you think you helping matters by goin' around sweepin' up behind him when he get out and act foolish?"

"Yes'm, it's a sight better than having Mr. Cahill find out about some a them things and raising a ruckus."

"Maybe Mr. Ransom need a ruckus," Zennia quipped.

"Naw, naw, Zennia. I think Mr. Cahill done 'bout gone his limit with him."

"Well, sure he has. Any ordinary man would've by now," she replied.

"I know you're thinking it be a good thing that Mr. Cahill tired of his restlessness, but Zennia, this ain't about Mr. Ransom." Cephas became solemn.

"What you mean it ain't about Mr. Ransom?"

"I mean it ain't about Mr. Ransom, Zennia. They's some things you don't know. I been with Mrs. Charlotte's family since she was just a tot." He put his hand down by his knee.

"Fine, so you beholden to Mrs. Charlotte."

"More than that. Mrs. Charlotte's daddy was good to me. Always treated me better than I ever expected, and I've kept a many of his secrets, but another thing I've kept all these years is a promise I made Mr. Palmer before he died."

"So what the promise got to do with Mr. Ransom?" Zennia picked up her basket.

"Well, it got some to do with Mr. Ransom, but it got more to do with Mrs. Charlotte than anything, and so do this other business. Why, if Mr. Cahill ever finally gets fed up with it, he liable to—" Cephas stopped himself.

"He liable to what?" Her left eye narrowed.

"I can't explain it, Zennia, but you got to trust ol' Cephas when I tell you that it's best if I help keep Mr. Ransom's britches out the fire."

Zennia sighed and started toward the house. "Whatever you say. Ain't in no position to argue with you. I got too much to do."

"And I've got to get down to the depot and fetch Mr. Ransom off that evening train."

Cephas took the key to the family car from the house and began the short drive into town. He was in a hurry to get there and see what he could find out. He was not used to Ransom hiding anything from him, and he was sure that it was an ominous sign of things to come.

Cephas and the train neared the depot at about the same time. Ransom sat in the railcar with a steely look about him. The remainder of his brief visit to New Orleans had been dreadful. After meeting with Mr. Messina, he spent the evening and the next day visiting with some of the Palmer family. They could not have cared less whether he was there or not. Pretending to enjoy himself in their company was far more difficult than pretending confidence among gangsters. All they talked about were stocks, bonds, and country club social gatherings. He found them unimaginative and boring, and they unexpectedly solidified his decision to do the adventurous thing.

He was to meet with Haynes immediately upon his return. It required some finesse on his part because Cephas was to take him home from the station. When he disembarked from the train, Cephas was waiting for him as expected.

"Welcome back, Mr. Ransom. Good to see you. Let me get that bag for you," he greeted him with a smile.

He got into the car, allowing Cephas to drive him. On his way back from New Orleans, he had devised a way to get to his meeting with Haynes on time without Cephas knowing. When they pulled away from the depot and made their way down Main Street, he began to work his plan.

"Cephas, I need to make a stop here in town," he said nonchalantly.

"Yessir, where to?"

"Stillman's."

"Stillman's? I say, Mr. Ransom! You keep them in business all by yourself!" Cephas parked along the street side near the storefront.

"I need for you to go down to the drugstore and get me a tin of pomade. You know the kind I use," Ransom requested. It was not unusual for him to ask him to do an errand for him. He felt sure Cephas was unperturbed by it.

"Yessir, I know the kind. Just one tin?"

"Better make it two," Ransom said. "I'll meet you back here in a minute."

With that, they both got out of the car. Cephas headed toward the drugstore, and Ransom ambled toward Stillman's, straightening his tie as he watched out of the corner of his eye. The moment Cephas disappeared into the drugstore, he moved calmly past Stillman's and into the alley that lay between it and the hardware store. He strode up to the red door and rapped four times just as he had before. The door swung open, and he entered.

Beneath the hardware store, he stood there with Haynes. "Hey, let's make this quick as we can. I barely made it back in time. The houseman will be waiting on me out there." He noticed that Haynes' lip was split open. "What happened to you?"

"Never mind that. It's time to get to work. There's some things that have to be smoothed over before we can get started. Here. Take this bag." He shoved a black leather bag into Ransom's hands.

It was full of large and small bills. "I can't take this bag right now, Haynes."

"What are you talking about? You getting jittery?"

"No, no, that's not it. Listen, the houseman is waiting for me. I told him I was going into Stillman's. I can't come back carrying this beat-up bag. Maybe he isn't as smart as I think he is, but I think he knows they don't sell used bags." He handed the bag back over to Haynes, and they stood there looking at each other. Ransom knew that his time was nearly up.

"Alright, alright. Listen, tomorrow evening, meet me down at the depot when the train comes in from Birmingham. It'll be so busy no one will notice. Be there, and don't get out of your car. I'll come to you."

"Ok, the train from Birmingham. You know my car."

He exited the building and went cautiously to the corner of the alley. Carefully he glanced around the corner. Cephas was standing by the car waiting for him. *Did he go into Stillman's looking for me? Or did he wait by the car?*

Ransom thought quickly. He waited until Cephas turned his back and darted out onto the sidewalk to appear as if he had just exited Stillman's. He called out to him. "Did they have it?"

"Yessir, got it right here for ya!" Cephas held up a small brown paper bag.

They got into the car and headed out of town. Ransom felt good about the ruse he had executed until Cephas posed a simple question.

"What you buy in Stillman's today, Mr. Ransom?"

"Nothing. Went in for a new necktie, but I already had all the ones on the rack."

The lie slipped off his lips so easily that he almost believed it himself.

40

When Noah returned from his visit with Sara, he found Thomas standing over their basin sink. He rinsed his face and tended to some scrapes on his knuckles.

"What happened to you?" Noah asked.

"Nothin'," his reply was short.

Noah walked over and grabbed his hand. "This don't look like nothin', Tommy. What happened?"

Thomas withdrew his hand, still angry. "I went down to the cafe for supper. Some of the fellas were in there, and I had a misunderstanding with one of 'em."

Noah sighed and shook his head. "Good night of the livin', Tommy. What in the world did he say? Who was it anyway?"

"Some joker named Haynes. I ain't seen him around here 'til lately. He's been hanging around with Archie." Thomas painted his knuckle with antiseptic.

Noah removed his tie as he tried to get to the bottom of the incident. "Archie . . . Archie Duncan from the hardware store?"

"Yeah."

"So what about this Haynes? What did he say that you thought was worthy of a scrap?"

Thomas sat down in a kitchen chair sideways and threw an elbow over the back of it. "I kid you not, Noah. I was settin' there minding my own business and having a bite when Archie and this fella Haynes came into the cafe. Archie saw me when they came in, and he hollered out to me. I waved at him, and the two of 'em

     Jenna Cossey

came over to my table. So they sit down there, and I'm sort of halfway listenin' to what Archie's telling me—"

"Right, right, Tommy. Go on and get to rat killin' here. What'd the guy say?"

Thomas motioned at him to wait. "I'm gettin' there. I'm gettin' there. So I was eatin' and these greens on my plate, you know how they serve 'em at the cafe, they needed salt, but there wasn't any on the table." Thomas saw Noah's patience waning. "This is all part of it. So I get up and walk across to the counter where the salt's at, and when I come back to the table, this guy Haynes looks at me with this fool expression and says, 'You're hitching, boy. You a cripple?' I don't know why, Noah, but that just flew all over me. I mean, here's this dingus I never even met before, and he's callin' me a cripple."

"Tommy, he didn't call you a cripple. He asked if you were a cripple." His sense of decorum enabled him to see a difference.

"You weren't there. You didn't hear how he said it, Noah," Thomas tried to justify his actions.

"Ok, so what'd you do. Punch him from across the table?"

He knew Thomas was impulsive when his temper flared. He had provided countless examples of his hotheadedness over the years. A lifetime of experiences told him that if someone made a remark that did not sit well with Thomas, he would always have a comeback. If someone insulted Thomas, he was apt to slap their face or punch them in the mouth. Since they had moved to Dunnigan, the brothers were still learning all of the people. Noah wondered all along how much time it would take before Thomas got into a fight with one of the townsfolk. He had a chip on his shoulder, especially when it came to his disability. Thomas strongly felt that he was not disabled and constantly tried to prove it.

"Naw, but I wanted to. Archie says to him, 'Tommy's missing a leg. He got it cut off,' and I kinda let it drop, but the guy had to keep on. This Haynes looks at me and says, 'Ah so you got a fake leg, huh?' By that time, I'm really gettin' my fill of this idiot, but I didn't want any trouble so I just told him 'Yeah'. Do you know what that joker set there and said, Noah?" Thomas leaned forward in the chair with his fists on his thighs.

"What?"

"He said, 'That's real cute there, Peg,' and that was it, Noah. That was the last straw," Thomas said with his index finger raised.

"So then you punched him from across the table?"

"Nope. I didn't want to make a scene in the cafe. So I says to him, 'Come on outside here and I'll show you a peg,' and when I stood up, Archie started in trying to smooth it over, carryin' on about how the fella didn't mean it and first one thing, then the next. I just stood there a waitin' on this guy to get up and go out. He knew he had done messed up, but I guess he didn't want to be a coward on top of bein' a jerk, so he got up and went out. Soon as he got out of that door, I took my leg, my bad one, and I reached up and kicked him right square in the tail." Thomas raised his bad leg. "Just about lifted him off the sidewalk, and then when he turned around, I punched that sucker right square in the mouth. I split his lip, and I hope I shoved his tailbone plum up into his gizzard when I kicked him. He deserved every bit of it."

"Tommy, you can't go around havin' fights," Noah said.

"But Noah, this fella—"

"I don't care, Tommy. You can't fly off the handle like that. For one thing, you're liable to run up on the wrong one someday and get hurt bad. For another thing, it won't be good for business. If Mr. Haskins finds out you're fightin' like a wampus cat, he'll fire us."

  Jenna Cossey

Thomas dropped his head. He knew his brother was right. Thomas was about as tough as a boy of sixteen could be, but Noah knew that, if word got around that nobody could whip him, it would not be long before others would try him just for sport.

"So was that all?" Noah was worried.

"Yeah, that was it. I helped the fella up, and he said he was right sorry for insulting me. We shook hands, and I came back here."

"Well, I reckon that's good then. Let that be the end of it."

"We're square, Noah."

The next day as the brothers worked at the station, a car pulled up to the pump. Thomas looked out, saw the driver, and dropped what he was doing. "Reckon what he wants?"

"Who is it?" Noah did not recognize the car.

"It's that fella, Haynes."

Noah tensed. "I thought you said it was square, Tommy."

"It is; it is. I'll see what he wants. Don't worry."

Thomas went out to the car. He pumped gas for Haynes, and they talked for several minutes. He drove away soon after, and Thomas returned to the garage.

"Well, what'd he want? Trouble?" Noah was not convinced things were settled.

"Nope. No trouble. Just came to talk," Thomas said as he continued work unfazed.

"Boy, for somebody you just punched in the mouth, he sure got over it quick. What'd he want?"

"Nothin', just shootin' the bull."

It seemed off to Noah. It was not unusual for two guys to settle a score quickly, but this was a little too easy.

<u>*41*</u>

"Just take the job, Ransom. Work with Robert. He said he could use you there in the law office."

Edward Cahill sat in his office. He had summoned Ransom downtown to tell him the good news he had received from Robert Benson, a local attorney. His law clerk had recently married and moved away, and he needed help. Edward Cahill thought it was a fitting opportunity. He made his inquiry to Robert Benson, hoping that Ransom would take an interest in law under his tutelage and return to college, but he was having none of it.

"I don't want the job."

"Why not, Ransom? This is a great opportunity. You simply cannot continue doing nothing."

"Doing nothing?" He tilted his head back and to the side and haughtily raised an eyebrow.

"Doing whatever it is that you're doing. Frolicking, carousing, acting like you have no upbringing!" Edward's volume increased and his face reddened.

Ransom smiled. "Have I?"

"Yes! You have. You don't have to like me, boy, but you need to get a grip on your station in life. If you take this job, you can go back to school, study law, and—"

"Become the mayor of Dunnigan? How swell. The supreme achievement for which one hopes in life." He nodded his head and tipped his hand as if to a king.

Edward leaned forward in his chair and placed his elbows on the desk. "I'm going to have you in a respectable career if it kills me."

"Respectable? Like your career?"

Edward went on the defensive, "I find the mayoral seat to be quite a respected position, yes."

"I'm not talking about the mayoral seat. I'm talking about *your* career. Respectable? Sure." Ransom may not have desired a career in law, but he was certainly acting as a prosecutor.

Edward slammed his hand down onto the desk. "You don't know what you're talking about!"

Ransom continued to smile with insolence. "Are you sure about that? What kind of a boob do you think I am? You've dragged me to every political event within a hundred-mile radius. Don't you think I've noticed a thing or two about how you conduct your affairs, *Mr. Mayor*? You don't *really* think that I was so blinded by paternal admiration that I haven't watched you prod, bribe, coerce, and beg your way to wealth and prominence, do you?"

"My father was one of the wealthiest men in the state. I'm no beggar!"

"And becoming still wealthier every day, very interesting to say the least, father. Very interesting."

It was true. He had been observant. Edward Cahill may have been respected in some circles, but he was far from respectable in Ransom's opinion. Edward knew that he was telling the truth. The passive-aggressive approach was successful. He sent Ransom away from his office with hardly another word. He was not going to continue the argument, as he knew that Ransom would bring down the wrath of Mrs. Cahill if he pushed too far. He knew exactly how to keep Edward Cahill out of his way.

A respectable career. If Edward Cahill's career was respectable, Ransom had many options, and the one that finally enlivened him was the one Mr. Messina had proposed. He would get to hone his skills of persuasion, something at which he felt he was already quite good. Coupled with a wad of cash, success was inevitable. There had been no indication up to that time as to whom he would be persuading or why, but it made no difference.

He sat in his car later that day at the train station, looking at his wristwatch. *Ten minutes until five.* The August heat stagnated the air inside the car, but he followed Haynes' directive not to get out. He rolled down the two windows, trying to take advantage of any breeze that might have been blowing. The trains were on time more so than not, and he wished the ten minutes away as he perspired in the excessive warmth of his coupe. The minutes ticked away. He reached into his pocket and took out a handkerchief to wipe his brow.

Hurry up, train. Hurry up, Haynes. He heard a whistle in the distance and looked at his watch. *Two minutes until five.*

He sat there waiting when someone appeared at the driver's side window.

"Hiya, Cahill! What are you doing here?"

It was Stancil Stratman. Ransom played a few hands of poker with Stancil and his friends some months before, but had avoided it ever since. He could tolerate Stancil after consuming a few drinks, but otherwise, he found him to be quite an exasperating man. Even worse, he could not keep anything to himself. He told everyone that would listen about the money he won from Ransom during their night of poker. By the time Ransom woke up the next day, Edward Cahill was waiting to chastise him for "fraternizing with ruffians" and "squandering money." Not the least bit happy about his lack of discretion, Ransom politely declined future

                    Jenna Cossey

outings with him. He was the last person Ransom needed standing around when Haynes came by with a bag full of money. He had to think quickly.

"I'm waiting on this train," he told Stancil.

"Is that right? Visitors?" Stancil never ceased mining for information to fuel gossip.

"No. Got a bag on there. Went to Birmingham the other day. They mislaid one of my bags. They sent it somewhere else. It's coming in on this train." *Quick thinking, Rans.*

"I'll say. Lost your bag, huh?" Stancil scratched his head and squinted in the sun.

"Not really lost, just misplaced." Ransom saw Haynes out of the corner of his eye and became desperate to get rid of Stancil. "Hey, I overheard those guys in the freight office talking about a big poker match when I was in the station. You ought to go see if you can get in on it."

"No kidding? I better go see what's cookin' in there!" He took off for the freight office.

Ransom breathed a sigh of relief. No sooner than he did so, Haynes walked up and put the bag through the window into the front seat. He stopped only briefly to say a few words.

"Make sure you get to work on this right away, Cahill. I'll be in touch."

With that, Haynes vanished into the swarm of people disembarking from the afternoon train.

<u>42</u>

He already knew that he loved her. Noah Maclane defied conventional behavior for a young man of eighteen years. One advantage he possessed was an even temperament, and cooler heads among his peers were unlikely to be found. Sara Wheeler sparked an urge for him to break from his standard reactions. He knew that Thomas, shortsighted as a boy of sixteen could be, would not understand his feelings. He did not even bother to share them with him. He wondered how long it would be before he could finally tell Sara what was in his heart. He was surprised at himself for becoming so enthralled by the mere possibility of winning her love.

August progressed with all of the drought and swelter that was typical of an Alabama summer. Noah only let one day lapse before he picked up the phone to call on Sara again.

"Yes, operator, get me zero, six, two, one, please . . . Hello, is this Mrs. Simpson? . . . It's Noah Maclane . . . Just fine, thank you ma'am. I wondered if I might call on Ms. Sara this afternoon . . . Yes'm, I'll wait . . . Yes'm six-thirty. I'll be there."

He took it that Violet intended him to call and request an audience with Sara in advance when she gave him the telephone number. Though he was not sure what she had in mind, he decided it best to err on the side of caution. He certainly wanted to be in her good graces. She had a good reputation of shrewd independence; Noah had caught wind of this during his time in Dunnigan. He always found Violet Simpson to be an overly generous and equitable woman, and he hoped she would be agreeable to him seeing Sara more often. Easton was already an ally. He won him over the first time he serviced his prized toy car, and each time he saw Easton, the boy's partiality increased.

Noah quickly became a regular at the Simpson house. Sara became more at ease around him, but he could feel her hiding or holding something back. He enjoyed the simple talks they shared. It did not take him long to learn that she had a birthday coming at the end of August.

"Next week is Sara's birthday, and we are going to have a big cake! Three layers! With frosting!"

When Noah learned of her birthday, his mind went to work. He rarely allowed himself to spend money on wants. He did invest in a new tie or two after his first visit to see her, but unlike Thomas, he could not commit to spending money on a suit. If Sara's birthday did not warrant spending a little of his hard-earned money, he knew of nothing else that did, but he needed help. One night, after supper and a long porch conversation with Sara, Violet came out to bring the night to a close.

"I believe it's time that we should all be turning in for the night, Noah." She always made the farewell easy to take.

"Yes, ma'am. The time does creep up on us, don't it?" Noah got up from the rocking chair.

Just as always, he wished Sara a good night and promised to see her soon.

The next morning, he had devised a plan. He picked up the phone at the station and placed a call to Violet's house.

Her voice came over the phone, "Hello?"

"Hello, Mrs. Simpson. Noah here. Don't let Sara know it's me."

"Yes?" Violet calmly replied.

"It's Sara's birthday. I want to get her a present, but I don't rightly know what to buy her. I was hoping you could help me."

Violet paused for a moment. "I see."

"See, well, I want to get her something nice, but I don't know what ladies' things cost."

"I understand. I'll be there shortly. Thank you for calling," Violet said as she hung up the phone.

Noah did not know it, but he had already won her favor in addition to Easton's. She thought him a perfect gentleman. He was plain and country, but Violet was, too. She had simply become a little more polished during her years of city life. During his visits, Violet started to see the consistency Noah exhibited. He was confident, but not overly so. She thought he had a good head on his shoulders. She certainly favored the idea of Sara spending time with him over some of the other local boys.

When she hung up the phone, she needed to divert Sara and Easton, who had been sitting at the table when she answered the telephone. "I have to run into town for a moment. I'll be right back. You two finish your breakfast. Easton, help your sister with the dishes when y'all are done."

She changed and headed over to Haskins' garage.

When she arrived, she found the Maclanes already hard at work. Noah came out to meet her.

"Thank you for coming down, Mrs. Simpson. I sure do appreciate it."

"Of course, Noah. Now, what's this you've got on your mind about a birthday present?" Violet came to the point quickly.

"I want to get Sara something, something nice, but I don't even know where to start." He crooked his mouth and placed his hands above his back pockets.

"Well, I don't want to be rude, but how much were you thinking to spend? Maybe we could start there."

"I just want to pick out something nice, Mrs. Simpson. I have the money." Noah had saved his fifty-dollar bill from Ransom Cahill when Thomas spent his.

Violet was surprised. "Oh, well, surely we can decide on a nice gift, then. I tell you what. I'm taking Sara into town this weekend and try to see what catches her eye. Maybe I can get an idea for you too. I will let you know as soon as I can."

"That's mighty good of you, Mrs. Simpson. Mighty good." Noah reached his hand out toward her, but withdrew it when he realized it was covered in dirt and oil. "I never picked out a gift for a girl before, save my little sisters. They're just kids, though. The last time I bought a gift for a girl, it was a dolly!"

"I don't expect Sara would have much use for a dolly!"

They laughed.

"I might as well have you fill the tank while I'm here. I don't want to head back too quickly or Sara might suspect something."

"Surely, happy to oblige!"

When he finished at the pump, Violet paid him and tried to set him at ease, "Don't worry a bit. I will get on the case as soon as I can."

<h1 style="text-align:center"><u>43</u></h1>

"You know, Sara sweet, you've got a birthday coming." Matilda Wheeler tended to a myriad of pots that sat atop a wood-burning stove.

"Yes, Mama."

Her mother always baked her a special cake. Most of the ingredients were on hand, but each year, a few days before Sara's birthday, she would make the ten-mile trip to the nearest town and purchase any ingredients she lacked to make the cake of Sara's choosing.

"I don't suppose I'll be able to bake you a cake this year," said Matilda sadly.

Sara expected no big celebrations, but she had come to count on the cake. "Why, Mama?" Sara was dispirited.

"Well, I have enough money, but," she hesitated, "it's for something else."

"Oh."

"I'm sorry, but if I spend the money on stuff for the cake, there might not be enough for the train fare to go see Violet." Matilda kept at her work, suppressed her excitement, and looked out of the corner of her eye in anticipation.

"The train? Aunt Violet? For my birthday?" Sara leaped to her mother's side and cast her hope-filled blue eyes up at her mother.

Matilda smiled down and gave an affirmative nod. "That's right! I think that seven is a mighty big age, and I think it's about time that my big girl went on an adventure. Don't you?"

Matilda stretched her arms out, and Sara fell against her, hugging her tightly. "Oh, I can't wait to ride the train! And to see Aunt Violet! And to see where she lives!" Each time Sara thought she had finished her sentence, she thought of something else to be excited about.

"This is the best birthday ever, Mama!" Sara spun around in the kitchen as her cotton dress flourished into a banner of floral print.

*　　*　　*

Sara's seventh birthday, and her first trip to Dunnigan, lingered in her mind as her sixteenth birthday approached. Violet convinced her to request a cake, but it was not easy.

"Sara, what kind of a cake would you like me to bake for your birthday?"

"Oh, just any kind. It doesn't make any difference."

Easton blurted out, "Sara likes chocolate cake! I like it, too, with lots of frosting!"

Sara quieted him, "Easton, no. It's ok. Aunt Violet can make any kind of cake that suits her."

"If it's chocolate cake you'd like, I can make the best—my grandmother's recipe!" Violet raised her index finger into the air with confidence.

Sara, reckoning that it was the same recipe her mother used, relented, "Well, alright, as long as it's not any trouble."

"Not in the least, my dear!"

"We'll have a chocolate cake with three layers!" Violet wanted to make it special.

Sara, her mother, and Violet had spent three marvelous days there on her seventh birthday. Each night they would all squeeze into a small bed, and Sara would fall asleep to the sound of the two sisters talking over old times and giggling uncontrollably. Nine years later, she still clung to that happy time. It had given her comfort during the difficult moments, but she felt a bit of sadness that her mother was not there to share the second birthday celebration she would have in Dunnigan. As a child, she never conceived of a time when her mother would not be there to bake her birthday cake. Violet took away part of the sting, and for that, she felt fortunate. There was also someone else that improved her feeling that things would somehow turn out alright.

There was Noah.

<u>44</u>

The Cahill residence was full of dignitaries from all over the greater Birmingham area, a typical guest list for one of Edward Cahill's parties. Some of them overflowed onto the back patio and lawn through the ornate French doors. A few short weeks before, Ransom would have had no interest in being present, but now it was critically important for him. He looked around the room, noting the attendees. There was hardly a strange face in the assemblage. He began to understand why he was the one Mr. Messina had selected to carry out the role.

When he had acquired the bag from Haynes, he found a list inside with additional instructions. As he read the list, he realized that he knew almost everyone on it. He not only knew who they were, but he was also on a first-name basis with many of them because his father was the incumbent mayor of Dunnigan.

"These are the people. You will need to go and see them so that we can get things moving," Haynes had said.

"How do we know these are the right people? What happens if they can't be bought?" Ransom felt it was a reasonable question.

"Mr. Messina has eyes and ears everywhere. These are the right people. He knows who can be bought."

Ransom looked at the list closely. "There's a lot of money in that bag. How do I know what it will take?"

"You see these figures over here?"

"Yeah."

"Those are their monthly salaries. Start with that. You're smart enough to diddle your way through the rest of it."

He stood in the raft of notable citizens, many of his designated subjects among them. He slyly worked the room, making sure to converse with those he planned to see at a later time. He knew how to charm guests. He had endured a lot of forced practice. He had also watched Edward Cahill wedge his way into political circles, garner unlikely supporters, and leverage influential groups into his corner. The governor himself had convinced the Ku Klux Klan to throw their powerful support behind Edward Cahill in his most recent election, mostly because Edward spent a few evenings in Birmingham pandering to him. Ransom found himself at increasing odds with him, but he was not too stubborn to recognize his skillset. Working on Edward's model, he soon found himself in various conversations covering diverse topics. He was not interested in the chats themselves, only the person with whom he happened to be sharing them. He artfully set them at ease until they soon told him all manner of personal details as though he were a lifelong friend. Mentally, he kept notes believing that they would be of use to him soon.

When the night was over, he retired to his room and sat at his writing desk. He extracted his list from the bottom of one of the drawers and placed a small dash next to each person with whom he had spoken. As he did so, he recalled the conversations with each, hoping that he could give a pretense of friendship when he saw them again. Mr. Messina made it clear to him that he was to grease the cogs that would result in a quiet mass of movement. It was secret, yet brazen.

His activities were bound to come to Edward Cahill's knowledge at some point. His defiance was sure to create a complicated situation. Thanks to Cephas, it was not unknown to Ransom where his mother's loyalty lay. She had faithfully supported her husband for the past twenty years, but as he and

 Jenna Cossey

Ransom began to clash, her first and greatest allegiance was to her son. Ransom planned to use it to his advantage. It gave him a type of immunity that no one else in the whole of Dunnigan could enjoy. He had been given the financial means to coerce every entity that posed an obstacle to Mr. Messina's operations. Further, Edward Cahill would be in a strait between avoiding Charlotte's fury and bringing to light the lawlessness of his namesake.

Ransom went about his mission, not knowing he had set the stage for the awakening of a sleeping leviathan.

<h1 style="text-align:center"><u>45</u></h1>

"The watches, Noah. I saw her really looking at them!"

Violet had stopped and asked Noah to fill the gas tank once more. She did not need gasoline, as he had only filled the tank a few days before, but she had taken Sara and Easton to town for some birthday shopping, and she did not forget the request Noah had made. A part of Violet felt that maybe it was too soon for Noah to bring gifts of anything more than flowers and candy, but she was no fool. She could see that he cared a great deal for Sara. On the other hand, she had heard a bit of gossip concerning Thomas Maclane. From her visits to the station, she knew him to be less reserved than Noah, but understood from her own life experiences how differently siblings could be dispositioned. She took little stock in unfounded rumors and was still willing to give both Maclanes the benefit of the doubt, regardless of whether or not the younger was a bit more of a spitfire.

"How will I pick one? Was there one, in particular, she looked at?"

"I'm sorry, Noah. I can't say for sure. Here they come with the cold drinks. Just look at them and pick the one you think most suits her, and please don't spend too much money!"

Sara and Easton emerged from the station none the wiser, each with an Orange Crush in hand. Noah had offered to buy them cold drinks to get them out of the car and away from the pump. He took a folding knife from his pocket, left it closed, and used the end to open the bottles. Easton was astounded.

     Jenna Cossey

"How'd you do that? That's not an opener; that's a jackknife!" He was easily impressed.

"Well, it sorta works the same way if you turn it right, pal. I'll show ya one day when your aunt says you're old enough to have a jackknife." Noah patted him on the head.

Easton took a large swig of the orange soda, popped his lips from the end of the bottle, and asked, "Aunt Violet, when can I have a jackknife?"

She rolled her eyes and tipped her hand to Noah. "Appreciate that, Noah."

They all chuckled except Easton. "What? Why are you laughing? When *can* I have a jackknife?"

"Well, not today, that's for certain! Let's all get in the car now. Noah, we'll be seeing you for supper at six thirty, won't we?"

"Oh yes'm, six thirty. Mighty big cause for celebration today, ain't it?"

"I guess so! I think Easton is mostly happy about the cake. See you later, Noah," Sara said.

They all waved goodbye, and as soon as they were out of sight, Noah walked quickly toward the garage. He went straight to his work, knowing he had to finish in time to get to the jewelry store and make his purchase before they closed. He would have to try and explain his need for an early departure to Thomas.

The day wore on, and the brothers stayed busy with their usual load of repair work scattered with visitors to the gasoline pumps. It was good for business to be on such a well-traveled road, but Noah wished for a brief lull.

"Get Mr. Oakley's car in here. We gotta get some of this cleared out," Noah called to Thomas as he backed a smoothly running Buick sedan out of the service bay.

When he came back in, Thomas climbed out of the car he was bringing in. "What are you in such an all-fire hurry for?"

"Got to get this stuff done in time to get to town before five thirty."

"Five thirty? Oh, and also, don't you think a fella ought to know when he's gonna be left to close up shop?"

"I got something I gotta go do. Place closes at six, and I need to get there before." Noah crouched to the ground, inspecting something beneath the car. "And I've been busy. Just wasn't thinking. You will close up, won't ya?"

"Well, I reckon I can, but you know you ain't the only one that's ever got somewhere to be around here," Thomas said with a hint of agitation.

"Ok, Tommy. I heard ya. Where've you gotta be?"

"Nowheres in particular, but I'll find something to do."

"Don't go looking for trouble, you hear? I don't want to have to hear it from Mr. Haskins again."

"I don't go looking for trouble. Trouble looks for me," Thomas chuckled.

"That ain't funny, Tommy. Now, I mean it."

"Alright, alright. Keep your shirt on."

It was after five o'clock, and Noah was still hard at work. Realizing that he had been busy for quite a while, he checked the clock behind the cash register through the window in the door. *Five forty.*

"Ahh! Tommy, gotta go. You close up good now!" He darted into the back of the station and washed up as quickly as he could. He took a cigar box from beneath his bed that held his savings. He removed from it the fifty-dollar bill that he had earned from Ransom Cahill those weeks ago and put it in his pocket. He dashed out the door and raced into town as quickly as the service truck could take him. He walked up to the door of the jewelry store and pulled on the handle.

Locked.

Noah looked inside and saw the workers covering the glass cases and preparing to leave for the night. He had waited too long. Now everything was closed, and there was no possibility of him showing up with a gift for Sara.

That won't do. He rapped on the door gently at first, catching the attention of one employee who ignored him. He rapped again a little harder, and saw the same employee say something to someone across the store. A smallish man in a well-tailored suit marched to the door. He opened the deadbolt and stuck out his head.

"Sorry, son. We're closed. You'll have to come back tomorrow at eight."

As he began to close the door, Noah slipped his hand through the opening to stop him. "Please, sir, it's a gift, a birthday gift."

"I'm sorry. We close at six," the man asserted.

Noah's hand was still wedged in the door. "I know, sir. I know, but I was working, and the time slipped up on me. Please let me come in and buy a watch."

Knowing the price of most watches, the man loosened his grip on the door and let Noah inside. He estimated that his last-minute customer was so desperate it was a sure sale. "Alright, come in."

"Thank you kindly, sir. Much obliged." Noah returned to his usual reservedness.

"Now, what sort of a watch are you looking for?"

"One for a lady."

"I see, we have a generous selection of ladies' wristwatches. Take a look here." He waved his hand over a counter, "The ones on this end are lower quality, the ones on this end are higher in quality, but all function very reliably. I guarantee it."

Noah quickly scanned the choices. His eyes landed immediately on one in particular. He knew that it was the one. "That one," he said with certainty.

"Ah, yes." The man reached into the case and retrieved the watch. "This is the Miss Liberty by Bulova. Notice, there are fifteen jewels and six sapphires. The case is filled with white gold."

Noah thought it was perfect, but there was an important detail yet to be disclosed. "How much?"

"Thirty-seven fifty, but I can see you are a man with good taste," he pointed to a sale sign behind him, "so I will give you the ten percent off even though the business day has really passed. You buy it on time."

"Oh, that's mighty good of you, sir. I won't be needin' any credit. Thank you kindly," Noah handed over the bill from his pocket.

The man inspected the bill and looked at him. "What line of work are you in?"

"Cars, sir. I work down at Haskins' Mobil. About eight months now."

"I see. Must do a pretty good business over there."

"We do alright. Me and my brother Tommy work together. Mr. Haskins—"

"Lives closer to Birmingham now, doesn't he?" the man interrupted.

"Yessir, he comes into town pretty regular like to check up on us, but he's mostly quit the filling station."

"Yes, yes. I know of Mr. Haskins. He was in here a few months ago, for what I can't recall, but I've done a bit of business with

 Jenna Cossey

him over the years. Good sort of a fellow," the man went on as he placed the watch in a box. "Say, would you like me to have Marla gift wrap this for you? There's no charge."

"That'd be very nice, sir. Yes, please."

The man took the box to the back of the store and returned to make small talk with Noah while he waited, "I don't believe I caught your name."

"Noah, sir, Noah Maclane."

"Good to meet you. I'm Heinzig, Fred Heinzig," Noah immediately recognized the name from the moniker on the building.

"Oh, so *you're* Heinzig?"

"Yes. This is our tenth year here. It's been a very good—" Marla returned with the neatly wrapped package and handed it to Mr. Heinzig, "Thank you, Marla. Yes, it's been a very good place to do business."

"Yessir, it's been good to us too. If your car ever needs anything, bring it by."

Mr. Heinzig handed the small box to Noah. He thanked Mr. Heinzig again and made a hasty exit. He barely had time to get to Violet's house.

_46_

"I've fixed things with Agent Calvert," Ransom told Haynes.

"Yeah? What was the snag?" Haynes did not seem worried.

"I don't know. Guess some just aren't as willing, but once I found out he had a few kids, I was able to convince him." Ransom took his eyes off the road to glance at Haynes from time to time while he talked. "I explained how much more things cost every day, and how his daughters would grow up wanting fancy new dresses for all the events around, you know, sort of shamed him a little about leaving the easy money on the table."

"And that did it?"

"That did it. He hasn't been working the area long. He can always chalk some things up to ignorance, I suppose. Haynes?"

"Yeah?"

"There's something I'd like to know."

"What's that?" Haynes never took his eyes off of the road, even though he was only the passenger.

"What's your name? I don't think I ever knew it."

"Sure you did. It's Haynes."

"Haynes what? Is that your last name or your first?" Ransom pried.

"Look, it's just Haynes. Don't make this personal. Just call me Haynes."

Ransom could not help but wonder why he was so enigmatic about it since Haynes seemed undaunted by the cloak and dagger nature of his work. Ransom was not sure, but his reaction caused him to drop the subject.

They continued down the road until they came to the old cabin where Ransom was to turn. He drove his car down the lane to the clearing and parked it. They got out and surveyed the space.

"Come on, Cahill."

Ransom followed him down the path as before. When they approached the stone corridor, Haynes ran his hand along the wall for only a few feet before finding a switch. The dim light of the singular bulb falling on the once dark hallway of stone surprised Ransom.

"Electricity? Off the main road?"

"Yep, the transmission line was just over on the highway. Mr. Messina has friends at the Alabama Power Company, so we were able to get a line, and after a little work, the place is modernized." Haynes nodded his head in the direction of the switch.

The road that brought them to the cave was a side road off Highway 31 that passed through Dunnigan and on to Birmingham. Ransom gathered that it was not a great distance from it, but he had not thought to notice whether there was a power line in sight as they arrived. When Haynes opened the door at the end of the passageway, he found another switch. He worked his way around the large cavernous room, turning on several lights. The sight was most impressive to Ransom. The empty cavern that had been illuminated by coal oil lamps just weeks before was now filled with modern light fixtures. In the center of the largest space hung a chandelier. Along the walls, there were sleek symmetrically placed art-deco sconces.

"This place looks splendid. I can hardly believe it!" Ransom's eyes followed along the walls soaking in the details.

"Told you it was gonna be something to see." Haynes waved a hand at one of the natural walls in the cavern. "Over here, there will be a large bar. I've got some guys coming in the next two days to get that in. There's a spring nearby, and we've been able to direct the water in just over there behind where the bar will be. Those guys will finish up Wednesday, and by the end of the week, the furniture will be arriving. Simple wooden tables and chairs, nothing too fancy that way. Between the music and the hooch, nobody will notice."

"I'd say you're right about that. Where will we store the alcohol?" Ransom looked around for a nook that could serve the purpose.

"Back around here." Haynes walked behind the stone back bar and into a smaller passageway that concealed a heavy wooden door. "We've moved some of the supply, but it will need to be moved in regularly once we open. What we've got on hand won't last a week."

Ransom, liking the drink himself, was not surprised that such a copious amount would disappear in a short time. He had visited many illegal drinking houses, but this one topped them all on sheer novelty. He was sure that people from the entire greater Birmingham area would flock to the cavernous drinkery.

"I've squared things with Chief Lanham. The shipments can move on Tuesday and Thursday nights," Ransom told him.

"Well done. What did he say about the two joints on the north side of town?"

"They'll be shut down within a week." Ransom swept the lapels of his suit coat aside and hooked his thumbs in armholes of his vest.

"Even better. There's something else. We've got to get a few fellas to move those shipments from downtown. Now you're sure that Agent Calvert understands what he's been told to do when they send those trucks up from Birmingham?"

     Jenna Cossey

"Yes. He knows. There are others that know, too. If he waivers, he'll be out of a job." Ransom lit a cigarette as he talked him through it. "Calvert and Lanham will work together to see that the loads are properly directed. There's only two other men on Lanham's force that are on the take. They will help to smooth things out. As soon as those trucks roll into Dunnigan, everything in them will be as safe as in your mother's arms."

It was a carefully devised network that started several hundred miles south of Dunnigan, but the most important part was what had to be done at the end of the line. Ransom considered who he might interest in moving the shipments to their final locations, but he had yet to decide on anyone he thought was right for the job.

"So who are our local guys?" Haynes queried.

"Well, I've got to admit that I am having trouble coming up with the right ones. I was hoping you might have some suggestions," Ransom took a chance in asking.

"Matter of fact, I think I do. I happened up on a fella downtown, Duncan. Know him?"

"The name sounds familiar. Yeah, I think I know of him," Ransom replied.

"Archie Duncan. Seems to be a pretty regular guy, green as grass, but you know he's not gettin' rich as a hardware clerk, and I cleaned him out in a poker game last week. Probably be happy to make the extra cash."

"Alright, I'll go talk to him. Who else?"

"This Duncan had a pal that we ran into at the diner a few weeks ago, a one-legged fella. I figured him for a dumb kid. Tall and skinny, but I ran my mouth a little too much, and he ended up nearly knocking me out. He split my lip, remember? I had it coming. I've never been hit so hard. I figured a guy with that little fear in him would be useful along the way, so I made friends with him over a game of poker. Pretty sure he wouldn't turn down the money either." Haynes grinned.

He seemed to be describing someone familiar, but it was not clear to Ransom yet. "What was his name?"

"Maclane, Tommy Maclane."

He made the connection. "I know Maclane. He was making a big to-do about a custom job they did for some guy up in Cullman, so I talked him into doing the same on my car. His brother didn't want to do it, but I showed them a couple of fifty-dollar notes, and they did the job in two nights. I'm sure I can interest him in making some extra dough."

Ransom knew that Thomas had been bought once before. The question was whether he would do a job with a much greater risk.

<u>47</u>

It was half past six, and Noah was not there yet. Sara was used to him arriving early, never too much so, but just enough to show his eagerness to be there. His predictability gave her comfort. His manner was unlike that of her father. It was no small wonder that she remained guarded, but she believed that he understood. He never pressed her on the subject of her life before Dunnigan. He just listened, sweetly and patiently nudging the conversation along in his unselfish way. He was always the same, except now it was her birthday, and he was running a little late. Just as she started to let herself worry, he arrived. The 1925 Ford tow truck had a distinctive sound. The tow dolly jingled harmonically with the thrum of the engine, and everyone always heard him coming.

When Sara saw him park the truck, her heart fluttered.

If he hadn't come, I really would have missed him. She watched him attempt to train his hair back into place with his hand. The afternoon sun peeked through the trees and revealed a red cast she had never before noticed. He straightened his tie, and she watched as he retrieved a small box from the seat of the truck. *A gift? He's brought a gift for me?*

She wanted to contain her excitement, so she went away from the window and announced his arrival. It sent Easton galloping across the house and out onto the front porch to meet his big friend. His fondness for Noah only made his attentions more charming to Sara.

"Noah!" Easton called out.

They came inside, and Easton broke the ice in his typical fashion, "Sara! Noah got you a birthday present! Look! It's all wrapped up, and we don't know what's in there!" He put the box up close to his ear and shook it gently. "I don't hear nothing. Is there really something in here, Noah?"

"Easton!" Violet said. "Do you think Noah would bring a box wrapped as fancy as that with nothing in it?"

Easton studied it for a moment. "I guess not."

They all sat down to dinner. Violet had prepared all of Sara's favorite things or at least the things that Easton reported to be her favorites. In reality, they were his favorites. For Sara, it was more important to let him think he snookered Violet than to make any special requests of her own. After the main meal, Violet presented the chocolate cake she made for the special occasion. As she had promised, it was three layers tall and covered in chocolate frosting. It tasted just like Sara remembered and made her think of the moments shared around the kitchen table back at their home in Tennessee.

Violet leaned over and whispered something to Easton, and he darted out of the room. When he reentered, he too carried a small box, but it was not Noah's box. It was a different smaller box.

"Open the present, Sara! Open it!" he shouted.

"For me, Aunt Vi? But you already bought me the things for school," said Sara, having received so much more than she expected.

"There was just one more thing. Go ahead. Open it!"

Sara opened the package. Inside was an olive-colored stone set in a pendant that hung from a silver chain. Sara had never owned a piece of jewelry. "It's so pretty, Aunt Violet. Thank you. Thank you so much," Sara choked back tears.

"I think you should put it on." Violet took the necklace from the box and placed it around Sara's neck. "It's the stone for an August birthday. It's called peridot."

"Do you like it?" Easton asked.

"I love it. Thank you." Sara hugged them both.

"What about the other present, the one Noah brought?" Easton squirmed. The intrigue was too much for him.

"Do you want to give it now?" Violet asked Noah.

"Yes, let me get it. I set it on the mantle in there."

He returned with it, and he was a bit nervous. It was unlike him, but he sat down and placed the small box in front of Sara. "I . . . I hope you'll like it."

Sara opened the gift. Her eyes widened as Noah watched in suspense, waiting for a sign of approval or disapproval.

Easton ran to her side, able to withstand the anticipation no longer. "What is it Sara? Is it—wow! Look, Aunt Violet!"

Sara was still frozen. She knew that he must have spent a great deal of money to buy it. She thought it was beautiful, but she was stunned. "I . . . I don't know what to say, Noah. It's lovely."

"You should put it on, Sara! Oh, look at the sapphires; they are beautiful!" Violet urged her.

She removed the beautiful watch from the box and placed it around her arm. She felt like a princess.

"Mr. Heinzig set it. The time should be right," Noah told her.

"Mine says five minutes to eight," Violet reported.

"This one too!"

Sara looked up at Noah. His face was aglow with happiness, and it was all because he had made her happy. She hardly knew what to say, but did the best she could. "Thank you, Noah. Really, it's . . . it's more than . . . It's perfect."

"Well, Easton, young man, it is time for us to do the dishes!" Violet began clearing the table.

"Let me help you," said Sara.

"No, ma'am! The birthday girl is excused from dishes! Go on, and you two visit," Violet ordered as she motioned them away from the table.

It was a cool night for August, so they opted to take up their conversation from the back porch rocking chairs as they sometimes did. The screen door and the window let the kitchen light shine onto the porch without drawing too many bugs. It made for a pleasant place to sit and talk, and Sara had plenty to say after the birthday endowments.

"How did you know I wanted a watch?"

"I had a tad bit of help," Noah confessed.

"Aunt Vi? But I didn't tell her I wanted one."

"No, but I reckon she saw you looking at 'em, and I hate to admit it, but I schemed with her a little to help me figure out what you'd like to have for your birthday."

"That was a sneaky thing to do," Sara giggled. "But how did you know this was the very one?"

"Well, I didn't. I just picked the one that most reminded me of you."

"Reminded you of me?"

"Yes, the sapphires, they reminded me of your eyes."

"They are so pretty. The sapphires. Sapphires make me think of Mama."

"They do?"

"Uh huh, she used to have a sapphire necklace. I guess it was sapphire anyways. It was blue like these." Sara touched the sapphires on the watch case. "She wore it all of the time when I was small, but something happened to it. I'm not sure, but I think maybe Daddy traded it off somewhere."

"Traded off your mama's necklace?" Noah did not understand.

"Yeah, it didn't make much sense to me then, but I heard them one morning talking about it. They were having some sort of a spat. All I can remember her saying is 'It's the only one I ever had, Walter,' and she was a little sad after that."

"Was she?" He had a way of questioning without being impertinent.

"She was. I think it was special to her, but Daddy didn't care about that. I don't know what he cared about really, Noah, but when I looked into that case at Heinzig's and saw these sapphires," Sara hesitated, and tears welled in her eyes, "I thought of Mama. I thought if I had something like that maybe I could have a little bit of her with me every day. I guess that sounds foolish."

"No, Sara. It don't sound foolish to me at all. Your mama must have been a sweet, good lady. I know you miss her something awful, anybody would." He leaned forward in the chair and placed his elbows on his knees. "It's gonna be alright, Sara."

Realizing that she had nothing with which to wipe her tears, he reached into his pocket and gave her his handkerchief. "Here, don't cry now."

She dabbed it against her cheeks to dry her tears. "Thank you."

There was a long silence. They sat there on the porch in the dim light, rocking gently in the chairs. Noah felt a rush of courage. He looked out of the corner of his eye, reached over, and gently took her hand. It surprised Sara at first, but she quickly felt comforted as his rugged and powerful hand engulfed hers with all the gentleness of a bird lighting on a branch.

"Sara?" Noah broke the silence.

"Yes?"

"I know there's a lot of things that's happened to you, and it's bound to have been mighty hard for you some of the time, but I want you to know something," he said with a quiver in his voice. "Things are gonna turn out. I'm gonna see to it. I'm gonna see to it because, Sara, I love you."

She turned and looked at him. She could see his kindness and honesty. She wondered how she would know if a boy ever loved her or if she loved him back. Violet had told her that actions bespoke love, and she had not been wrong. Noah loved her early on, much longer than she realized, but all she knew was that he had been kind, patient, generous, gentle, and comforting. In the maelstrom of her departure from Tennessee and her arrival in Dunnigan, she had yet to let herself fully believe that life would go on in a new and different way. Sitting there in the serenity of the dim incandescent light and the mellow night air, having celebrated her sixteenth birthday, and holding his hand, she suddenly began to feel more certain that she would find happiness.

What else could it be, if not love?

 Jenna Cossey

<u>*48*</u>

Her happiness was his happiness. Seeing Sara's face light up was all that Noah needed to justify the money he spent. He was not trying to buy her affection, but he aimed to show his love through the gift. It was a big chance on his part. Not only that, after weeks of keeping it in, he was finally able to tell her how he felt about her. She had said nothing in return, but she gave him hope when she returned the grasp of his hand. He knew that she was a bit of a closed book, and he cared little about how long it might take her to open her guarded heart. The frenzy of the evening had left him worn out. When he arrived back at the station, all of the lights were off. He opened the side door that led to their quarters.

"Tommy?" He turned on a light and found Thomas gone.

Noah did not remember him saying that he had anywhere to go, but he knew that he sometimes made his way into town for supper while he was at Sara's. Like most towns of its size, there was not much nightlife. The diner stayed open until nine o'clock when all expectations for a sensibly timed dinner had passed for most people. On the road leading to Birmingham, another outskirt cafe adjoined a motor lodge that stayed open a little later for travelers. A picture show ran most nights, but he thought it unlikely that Thomas would go on a Monday. Though not overly concerned, he did wonder where he might be.

He readied himself for bed, but as he settled in, he could only lie there with his eyes open. Despite his emotional and physical exhaustion, his mind raced. When he closed his eyes, it only grew worse. Hour after hour, he tossed and turned, replaying the day in his mind, and hour after hour, Thomas did not return. Finally, he heard a car pull into the station. He got up to look out a small window just in time to see the tail lamps of a car growing smaller with distance. Thomas came in the back door. He entered, moving under the assumption that Noah was already asleep, so it surprised him when Noah switched on a lamp, flooding the darkened room with light.

"Figured you'd be asleep by now."

"It's after one o'clock, Tommy. Where you been?"

"Been out with some of the fellas." He emptied his pockets on a small bedside table. "Look at this, Noah." Thomas held up a healthy fold of small bills. He laid the money on the table and tapped his finger on it. "Nearly forty dollars right there, brother."

"Where'd you get that?"

"Earned it." Thomas tilted his chin upward. "Won a poker game. I never thought I was much good at it, but I think I'm gettin' the hang of it now!"

"A poker game? Since when did you ever play poker?" Noah had so many questions.

"Since not too long ago. That Haynes fella, you know the one I knocked the stuffin' out of downtown? He came by here that next day and told me again how he was outta line, and said what I done he had comin'. Then he said to show me there weren't no hard feelings he wanted to ask me to play cards with some fellas. So now and then I do."

"Tommy, that's gambling. We don't ga—"

"But just look at this stack of money I earned us!"

"You didn't earn that, Tommy. You won it by chance. There's a big difference. You earn money by working, not by risking it on stupid games."

                    Jenna Cossey

Thomas shook his head. "All I know is that it takes us a lot longer to get it here than it did for me to get this."

"That don't make it right, Tommy."

Noah did not like the idea of Thomas being out late with people he did not know. He liked the idea of him gambling his money on a poker game even less. He had been so busy trying to win Sara's affection that he completely missed the new development in Thomas' social life. He felt responsible for him, but he also knew that he could not hover over him at every turn and force him to do sensible things. Forbidding him to do things would result in a rift, so he had to try another approach.

"Tommy, look. I don't know much about this fella Haynes. I'm just trying to look out for you." He sat back down on the side of his bed and kept his voice calm. "How do you know that one of those guys isn't just a card shark who's reeling you in so he can sit there and take your money night after night? There's guys like that out there, ya know."

Thomas chuckled. "Nah, these guys ain't card sharks. Haynes loses more than he wins. The other guy always bets it all on a sorry hand before we even get started good. It's Archie that wins the most money!"

"Archie Duncan?"

Thomas laughed again. "Yeah! Now you ain't gonna tell me that Archie's some card shark, are ya?"

"I don't know, Tom. It just ain't smart to fritter away money on a card game."

"I didn't! Can't you see?" Thomas tipped his hand toward the stack of cash again. "Besides that, I've got me a side job lined up now, thanks to Haynes."

"What kind of a side job?" Noah continued to feel unsettled.

"Don't worry. It's not gambling. It's work, if you could call it that. Sounds like it's gonna be easy money."

As he did each night, Thomas sat on the side of the bed and began the process of removing his prosthetic leg. It was an unsophisticated thing, but he had made it himself with the only tools available to him at the time: a drawing knife and a pocket knife. When his leg was amputated, Doctor McGee had managed to save about five inches of his lower leg. For a long time afterward, Thomas used a crutch, but when the wound finally healed, he found that to be inconvenient. He fashioned his first leg when he was only twelve. It was rectangular with a long handle that ran up to his waist. If he needed to move quicker, he could use it to propel himself forward, but as he grew into a young man, he wanted something less conspicuous. He finally arrived at a design that not only worked well, but most passers-by failed to notice. His accident generated a determination to do all of the things that people told him were impossible. When his father told him he could not guide a horse-drawn cultivator with his leg, he simply nailed a hook on the back of his prosthesis that allowed him to push and pull with it as needed. When he made up his mind to do something, there was little that could stop him. Noah knew it, but he still felt the need to dissuade him from taking the side job.

"We ain't that strapped for money, Tommy. You don't need another job."

"Don't you get tired of staying here?" Thomas asked.

"Well, it ain't much, but it don't cost us, and we've been saving our money that way."

"Saving for what?"

"I don't know. Maybe buy a little place of our own someday."

"So that you can look after me forever? You don't have to be my keeper. I mean, just look at you tryin' to court Sara. What if you decide to marry her? You gonna take me along, too? Don't make sense."

"What are you saying, Tommy? You don't wanta live here and work here?"

"Naw, I ain't sayin' that, brother. You know we couldn't make it here without each other right now. I'm just tryin' to tell ya that a day is gonna come when you'll have this station and probably a wife and a buncha young'ns, and what'll I have? Still a room in the back here? I just want to work and save up for some dreams of my own, Noah."

Finally, Noah began to understand. It seemed as though Thomas felt constrained by working and living so closely with him. He was so intent on seeing him through life that he missed something. He was unintentionally robbing him of the independence he so desired.

"I can see you're determined to take this extra job, Tommy. If it's what you want to do, I understand," Noah relented. "So who will you be working for?"

"Haynes. He works for someplace out of Birmingham. Some sort of freight operation or something. He needs some extra drivers. It's just Tuesday and Thursday nights for now, but it might get to be more. Pays ten dollars a night."

"Ten dollars a night? To drive a truck? Sounds almost too good to be true."

"Yeah, it does, don't it? But it is. We start Thursday night."

"That's quick. Where's it at?"

"Just have to meet Haynes downtown. Said he'd let me know the rest when I got there. I really ain't supposed to say anything about it to nobody. He said he didn't want the word to get out that he was hiring a driver or two, or all the menfolk around here would get to askin' about a job since it pays so well. So don't let on to nobody about it."

"I won't." Noah had only one more question. "So who dropped you off here? Didn't see the car."

"Oh, Ransom Cahill brung me."

Ransom Cahill? Something seemed off. It was quite an odd combination of people: Haynes, whom he knew so little about, Ransom Cahill, whom he knew but did not care for, and Archie Duncan, who was hardly a model citizen. Noah could see that there was more to it than Thomas knew. He was more than a little naive, but Noah did not want to make him feel any more repressed and drive him away. He decided it was better to wait and see for himself what the whole thing was about.

Jenna Cossey

<u>**49**</u>

"This is a raid! Everybody stay right where you are!"

Fenn Calvert stood in the doorway of an illegal drinking house on the outskirts of Dunnigan with a shotgun trained on the doorman. Police Chief Tipton Lanham and several of his men came through other entry points with guns drawn. It was a medium-sized operation, but they brought enough firepower to contain the bedlam. When Agent Calvert burst through the door, his focus on the doorman provided a brief window of opportunity for some of the patrons to run out, but they trapped their desired targets. When the room emptied some, only a few frightened patrons, unwilling to run from the law, remained.

Agent Calvert motioned the doorman over to a wall where the others were being held. He looked at each one, while the Dunnigan officers began searching and disarming them.

"This is a sorry-looking lot if ever I saw one. Now tell me: which one of you knows where the stash is being kept?" They stood there in silence. He was in no mood for delays. He impulsively selected one of the men from the makeshift lineup and motioned him into an adjoining room. He followed closely, and once they were clear of the doorway, he slammed it behind them. He had a plan.

He seated the barrel of his shotgun tightly against the chest of the man and narrowed his eyes. "I know you can tell us what we need to know." The man started to speak, but Calvert interrupted him, "Shut up and listen. What you're gonna do is tell me which one of those guys in there will lead us to that stockpile of booze.

Do that, and you'll walk free in the morning. If you don't, well, let's just say that you will be . . . rolling the dice."

The young man swallowed hard, and the vibrations of his pounding heart were palpable at the butt end of the gun. "The one in the light blue shirt. He knows where it all is, and he has the keys."

"It's a wise choice you've made." Calvert opened the door and called, "Chief, need you in here."

Lanham made his way across the room and peered into the open door. Calvert kept his voice so low that Lanham could hardly hear, "The fella in the blue shirt knows the whereabouts of the liquor, and he has the keys. I will leave the confiscation and transportation of the goods to you."

"Right." Chief Lanham understood what to do.

Calvert opened the door and motioned the man to rejoin the others.

Chief Lanham began barking orders. "You two, take this one out back and wait for me. The rest of you get these men loaded up and down to the station. Take statements from these people here. They'll come down to the courthouse tomorrow and pay a fine, or else join this lot over here!"

Agent Calvert was glad that his part of the raid was over. After speaking with Ransom Cahill, he had warred within himself. He knew that he was not carrying out his sworn duty. The offer of money caused him to waiver and forget the reason he entered the line of work. Like many other beat cops in small cities, he risked much to work his way up the ranks. When he was offered a job as a prohibition agent, he thought that he had finally made it big in law enforcement. However, he was not getting rich doing it. He had a wife and three daughters, and the oldest two of his children were in school. What Ransom Cahill offered him amounted to

                    Jenna Cossey

one month's pay, and he refused. When Ransom proceeded to triple the amount, Fenn Calvert could think only of the future. After accepting the money and the conditions, he spent the twenty-four hours that followed trying to rationalize his actions. First, he minimized them. Prohibition was not going to last forever. The talks of repeal were strong. The ineffectiveness of the law was glaring. There simply was not enough manpower to continue trying to enforce that for which so many intricate schemes of circumvention existed. If the law were overturned, then the demand for a prohibition agent would be little. He convinced himself of the need to focus on the future, but he still was not at ease. He knew it was wrong and that he had joined hands with the enemy. His pockets were heavier, and so was his conscience, but the die had been cast.

Out back of the building, Chief Lanham and his two officers coerced information out of the man in the blue shirt. With some persuasion from the butt of a shotgun, he finally relented and led them to a large cache of illegal beverage. The entire store of alcohol was loaded into a waiting truck.

At the appointed time, Thomas Maclane and Archie Duncan met Haynes in town. It was nearing one o'clock in the morning by then, but Haynes watched from a window in the basement of the hardware store. Suddenly, a police car went down Main Street. As it passed, it slowed to a near stop just before reaching the alley beside the store. As if mistaken, the car regained speed and continued down the road. Haynes recognized the signal. Under cover of darkness, they emerged from the basement, got into a car, and left. Haynes drove them to a remote location with which Thomas was unfamiliar. There was a structure there resembling a house, but it was empty and unlit. After driving around to the back, the headlights revealed a cargo truck sitting behind it. Haynes gave a few brief admonitions.

"There's the load. Follow the directions I gave you before. Don't stop for any reason, and do not drive fast. Your job is to deliver these goods safely. When you arrive, Cahill will be there to bring you back to wherever it is you need to go. Do you understand?"

They both gave a nod, walked to the truck, and pulled away into the night. There was no one in sight, but back in town, they had been watched.

<u>*50*</u>

"I want you to look your finest for your first day of school."

Matilda Wheeler worked her nimble thin fingers through Sara's hair, braiding it into pigtails. She knew that there was little money for buying new things, but had insisted to Walter that Sara have her new winter shoes for the start of school.

"Mr. Odom will allow us credit until the cotton is in, Walter. Sara will not go to school without shoes. Her old ones are too small," she declared.

The cotton was almost fully harvested from their small field, and with Sara's help, Matilda managed to do her share of the picking. Walter Wheeler's contribution to the harvest fluctuated from day to day. If they failed to bring in the crop, their troubles would multiply. When Sara reached upward to feel her braids, the smooth hair passed between her still-healing fingers. They were raw from the hundreds of boll spurs that had torn at them during the harvest.

Matilda took a step back and inspected Sara's appearance with a proud smile. Sara beamed back at her mother, whose figure was beginning to reveal the forthcoming arrival of Easton. When she finished, Sara's soft medium-brown pigtails lay symmetrically on each collar bone. Her big blue eyes and suntanned skin stood out against the white homemade cotton dress. Sara was a walking burst of color. She blended perfectly into the late summer landscape of Tennessee as she walked to school that morning.

*   *   *

"You're as pretty as a picture, Sara Sweet!"

Dunnigan   *199*

Sara could still hear the words of her mother. She held one of her hands in the other. On her fingers, she felt the scars from picking cotton. She stood in front of a mirror, looking at herself. The scars reminded her that she was still very much herself, but she was not the pigtailed little girl in the homemade dress anymore. Somewhere amidst the chaos of her early life, she had blossomed into a young woman. As she prepared to go to her first day of high school in Dunnigan, she could not help but feel nostalgic. She stood there in a lovely room, of a lovely home, in a store-bought dress, wearing one of the many new pairs of shoes that she possessed. Hanging from her neck was the silver peridot necklace Violet had given her on her birthday and on her small wrist was the stylish fifteen-jeweled watch that Noah gave her. She felt like a butterfly making ready to exit the silky swath for its maiden flight. The heaviness of her life in Tennessee, which she had carried for so long, was, at last, beginning to dwindle. She finally began to feel a sense of calm and safety. Sara tried not to feel guilty. She knew that, if her mother were there, she would be happy for her and step back just as she had years before to say to her again, "You're as pretty as a picture, Sara sweet!"

Sara paused for a moment longer in front of the mirror, imagining her mother saying the words. On that morning, she especially had her mother in her heart. She gazed into the reflection of her own eyes and took a deep breath.

Just before she turned to leave, she spoke faintly to her reflection, "Alright, Mama. Here I go."

51

The unremitting August heat gave way to a milder September, and the nights became crisp and pleasant. Leaves began to abandon their lush green tones for scarlet and burnt orange. The diverse Alabama countryside revealed the spectrum of color with harmonious perfection. The summer solstice had come and gone, and the daylight hours became truncated as time marched toward the autumnal equinox.

The increasing hours of darkness presented no hindrance to Haynes and Ransom. They moved with efficiency in the night. The attraction they had worked to nestle into the Appalachian mountainside was beginning to gather people from border states. Ransom knew the right people, and he helped to draw a clientele that revealed the usefulness his superiors saw in him. The people who came to "The Thirty-One Grotto," as it was aptly named, had money to spend, and they did it with little hesitation. The club was in operation for little more than a week before a few choice acquaintances of Ransom's from Birmingham visited. They departed as satisfied customers, happy to spread the word about the rustic yet elegant nightspot. The Grotto boasted of the best alcohol, the finest entertainment, and the friendliest service anywhere. To further monopolize the market, every small-time illegal establishment within reasonable driving distance was shut down by Chief Lanham and Agent Calvert. They did it while government officials all over the greater Birmingham area heaped praises upon them. Profits were made quickly, and the investment that Mr. Messina made in the venture proved worthy of the risks.

"Our man on the inside says that Carollo's trucks leave New Orleans on Sunday afternoons. They make a stop in Mobile, but they plan to come right down Highway 31 on Monday nights. They have three trucks, and they leave out about an hour apart from each other. They do other business in Birmingham, but these shipments are not part of that," Haynes filled Ransom in on the plans for keeping a steady supply of beverages rolling into the establishment.

"So why are they trucking these shipments? Surely a fella like Carollo could smuggle a shipment onto a train," said Ransom.

He was right. Sylvestro Carollo neared complete control over the illegal liquor trade in New Orleans. It poured into the harbors about as smoothly as it did into the glasses of recalcitrant citizens who were unwilling to give up the vice. Carollo's goods found their way as far as Chicago, and when the goods needed to be delivered, he found a way to get them there.

"Oh, believe me, there's liquor on the trains, but the Feds have started to tighten up. It's getting harder and harder by the minute to move booze on rails. Carollo's outfit is using every form of transportation available." Haynes twisted his hand to mimic flowing water. "There's more liquor floating on the Mississippi River than you could possibly imagine. Mr. Messina thinks that, if we can send some by truck through Birmingham, we can keep our customers swimming and have plenty to spare."

Ransom took everything in as they talked in the office at the Grotto. Outside, the noise of high-spirited customers and jazz music swirled together. It was the same room he had sat in not long ago when first meeting Mr. Messina. He did not know then what a detailed operation was being planned, nor did he understand the magnitude of the inherent danger.

 Jenna Cossey

"So we take the merchandise off the highway after it leaves Birmingham, sell it here, and warehouse the rest for resale to small-time gin joint owners outside of our area," Haynes explained, "so as not to interfere with our customer base, but still make dough off the shipments."

"How long can we expect Carollo to keep moving liquor through here if all of it is getting confiscated, though?" It was a logical question.

"That's just it. The law is confiscating it," Haynes said. "That's the point. To everyone else, it looks like we have some top-notch lawmen around here keeping the area free of booze, but we know better!"

Ransom finally understood the entire procedure. He realized in retrospect that, as he went from Birmingham to Decatur meeting with government and law enforcement officials, he paved the way for them to control a large swath of the main thoroughfare in the state. It was a monumental undertaking and required him to exercise his persuasive talents to the uppermost limit. So far, it had been successful, and they had already acquired enough liquor to keep the Grotto open for months while managing to store another large quantity not far from Dunnigan.

"How long do you think we can keep the drivers in the dark?" Ransom asked, assuming that most of them had no idea that they were participating in illegal activities.

"What makes you think they don't already have an idea?" Haynes had a sly look on his face.

"I don't know. Maclane is just a stupid kid after an easy dollar. I knew it the first time I sat across the poker table from him. Duncan—same. The others? They're old enough to know better," said Ransom.

"But still too young to care, right? They may not be as ignorant as you think. We'll just have to feel them out. If we end up paying them a little more, it's no big deal." Haynes leaned back in his chair. "But if they end up getting in the way, we'll have to take a different approach."

Ransom paid the boys who moved the shipments more generously with each trip, and up to that point, it kept them from being too curious. Haynes was right—Thomas Maclane was eager to make the cash—but Ransom hardly even believed his own declaration that he was just a "stupid kid." He wondered how long it would be before he and the others would have to make the same conscious all-or-nothing choice he had made there in the cave those months ago. He wondered, *How would they choose?*

<u>**52**</u>

The season was not the only thing changing in Dunnigan. In spite of the way Noah tried to keep Thomas under his wing, it was not working. His relationship with Sara began to blossom, but the lifetime of closeness he shared with his brother faded at a gradual yet perceptible pace. The balancing act weighed Noah down. He loved Sara and wanted to be in her life, but he also wanted to keep Thomas in his life. He started to wonder if the divergence was inevitable.

A few weeks passed, and Thomas's overt sense of independence began to manifest itself in different ways. He was a young man with an income that afforded him new luxuries.

"Whatcha think?" He stood there in a brown three-piece suit with windowpane striping, and his weight shifted toward his good leg.

"Looks nice. Must've set you back a pretty penny," said Noah.

"Most I've ever spent on a suit of clothes, but it sure does make me feel good when I'm wearin' it!" He looked in the mirror and straightened his bright red tie.

"Don't you think you might be a little overdressed for the county fair?" Noah wore his typical ensemble of slacks, a dress shirt, and a tie.

"Where else better to wear a new suit? I won't be the only one. You could afford one, too, Noah. Don't you think that little gal of yours would like to see you in a suit?"

Noah chuckled at his suggestion. "If she would, she ain't ever said so."

There was a growing tension between them. Both were changing and seeing the future through new lenses. Noah's constant dissonance over the troubling changes he perceived in Thomas produced a sense of worry that became more difficult to ignore with each passing day.

"Why don't you ride out to the fair with us?" Noah asked Thomas.

"Nah, Archie's comin' by to get me."

"Can't you just meet Archie there?"

"Well, I could, but . . . y'all just go ahead."

Riding to town with Sara and her family did not promote Thomas' new sense of style. Noah did not mind that he wanted to go with his friends. He only had misgivings about what they might be doing that they did not want him to know. When Violet Simpson's car pulled up to the gas station, there was no more time for him to worry about it. He tried to include Thomas in his plans, but he was not interested. More and more often, it left Noah in the unpleasant position of going on without him and trying to enjoy himself anyway.

"Well, there they are. You sure 'bout goin' with Duncan?"

"Yeah."

Over the preceding weeks, it became a regular occurrence for Sara and Noah to go places with Violet and Easton in tow. He favored having them along, and they started to feel like family to him. He understood Violet's need to watch over Sara, and he recognized in Sara a greater level of ease when they were with her. He hoped that she would learn to trust him as her new family learned to accept him. Although they took Violet's car into town, her sense of propriety led her to give the driving responsibilities over to Noah.

The county fair teemed with people from miles around. It was the time of year when people frequented every nearby festival as part of their ritual to ring in the upcoming season. Some thought the carnivals brought unsavory characters into town, but for most, it was an important social event. The Dunnigan fair included a circus in addition to the rides and games. They all found enjoyment at the fair, but Noah made it his priority to see that Sara enjoyed it to the fullest.

After a thorough visitation of the attractions, the four of them sat down to enjoy some of the food. There was little doubt that it would be Easton's favorite part, and none of them were surprised when he managed to make himself first in line.

"Can I go?" He stood between Violet and the food counter.

She grinned at him. "Yes, go on." She looked back at Sara and Noah. "That boy must be hollow on the inside. He can eat more than anybody I ever saw!"

As he and Sara stood in the line behind them, Noah spotted Thomas across the midway. Archie Duncan, Ransom Cahill, Haynes, and one or two others Noah did not know stood with him. They were all sharply dressed, and each had a swagger that set them apart from the crowd. Noah watched, sure that Thomas had not seen him, and availed himself of the opportunity to observe his behavior in the presence of his new friends.

Haynes stood with his hands in his pants pockets. His fedora rested squarely on his head, and he casually leaned against the corner of a booth. Archie stood there talking incessantly, waving and greeting passersby. Ransom had his thumbs tucked into the armholes of his vest, and a cigarette hung loosely from his lips. He also wore a fedora, but it was cocked slightly to the side, giving an added appearance of smugness. Thomas wore no hat, and his dark thick red hair was parted to the side in perfect wave atop his head. Noah watched as Ransom casually slipped a flask from the inside pocket of his coat, took a sip, and handed it over to Thomas, who did the same before returning it. The six of them walked together down the midway. Noah kept an eye trained on them.

"What will you have, Noah?" Sara broke his concentration.

"Whatever you're havin'. I ain't picky." He took out his wallet and retrained his eyes on the six.

He watched as Ransom and Thomas overtly directed their eyes at various ladies who walked down the midway. It was hard to tell from that distance, but it appeared that they were whistling and catcalling to them. Noah was infuriated.

"Hey," Sara again caught his attention.

"Oh." He quickly moved to help gather their food from the counter.

After they ate, they wrapped up the night by granting Easton's request for cotton candy.

He waited for Thomas to come home that Saturday night. He was glad that it took a while because he needed the time to calm down. All along, he feared that Thomas was going to find trouble, and what he saw at the carnival did not ease his mind. He decided it was time for the two of them to have a serious talk.

Thomas returned to the station before midnight. When he came in, Noah observed his behavior, wondering just how drunk he might have become. He was surprised to see that Thomas had his wits about him, but he also detected an unusual slackness.

"You still up?" Thomas rhetorically asked.

"Yep."

"What for?"

"Waitin' on you."

"Why?"

                    Jenna Cossey

"Thomas, it's time we had a talk."

"What kinda talk?"

"A talk about these new friends of yours."

"What about 'em?"

"I'm not sure I like you hanging around with them, spending all that time with them. They seem like ruffians to me, and—"

"Ha! You've got to be kiddin' me. Ransom Cahill's daddy is the mayor, and they've got money running out their ears. What kind of ruffian can a guy really be with all those important people in his family?"

"I don't care who his daddy is. I saw you at the carnival tonight, Tommy. You, Archie, Ransom, that Haynes, and whoever them other two was, I don't even know, but I saw you'ns. Y'all moved around like a pack of wolves." He became more forceful in his speech, being careful not to raise his voice.

"Good grief, Noah! Can't a guy have a little fun? You sound like Maw nagging me." Thomas removed his tie and emptied his pockets.

"Fun? That's your idea of fun? Passing around a hip flask and ogling girls?" Noah crossed his arms.

"We didn't—"

"Don't deny it, Tommy. I saw you with my own two eyes. First staying out late, then gambling, now drinking. What's come over you? This ain't how we was raised to act."

"We ain't little boys no more, Noah. I'm a man. I can do what I please."

"I won't stand for it."

"What do you mean you won't stand for it? You can't tell me what to do!"

Noah sat there without a word, contemplating what he could say or do to change his mind, but he could think of nothing that would not further inflame the situation. In a matter of hours, he had come to an impasse with Thomas. He continued sitting there while Thomas changed his clothes and hung up his suit. Finally, Noah made another attempt to reason with him.

"I just don't wanta see you in trouble, Tommy. I don't like where these fellas are leadin' you." Noah momentarily paused. "You ain't the same as you used to be."

"I don't know what to tell ya, Noah. They're my friends."

"I'm not so sure."

They both went to bed that night without another word, but neither slept. When the morning came, Thomas broke the silence.

"Noah, I think it's time I moved out of here."

Noah said nothing.

"I think . . . I think we've just spent too much time together. This place is cramped, and I've saved enough money to take a room in town. I think we'd both be better off."

"I need your help here, Tommy. Who am I gonna get to help me?"

"I'll still help you. I don't see any reason why we can't keep working together just because I don't live here no more. I reckon it's up to you, though," Thomas explained.

"If you think living in town will make you happier, I ain't gonna stand in your way, Tommy, but it doesn't change how I feel about the people you're runnin' around with."

"That just ain't something you get to decide, brother. I ain't never picked your friends for you, and you ain't pickin' mine. If you want my help here, I'll keep working with you, but I'm done being cramped up here in this dump. There's better things in life, Noah."

Noah was in a strait. He could not keep the station running without his help, and he knew of no one else he could count on to do the work. If he pushed too far, he would lose Thomas completely. He decided he would have to accept his terms if there was any hope of them retaining their relationship. "Alright. I guess you have to do what you think's best."

That Sunday evening, Thomas gathered up his belongings and took them into town. Noah knew that things would never be the same between them. Torn, he could only ask himself one question. *Did I do the right thing?*

<u>*53*</u>

Ransom jogged lightly down the grand staircase. It was early in the day, but there had been a noticeable change in his habits. Those in the house saw that, although he still found a late card game and a bit of liquor from time to time, he was miles away from the careless college castaway who lacked purpose in the months prior. Charlotte Cahill was not sure what he was up to, but for the moment she was pleased to see him busy at something. He wore a perfectly fitted suit, and when he reached the bottom of the stairs, he entered the main room with an added air of confidence about him. His mother deemed it the appropriate time to make a few subtle inquiries.

"Ah, son, you look as handsome as ever. The day is still young. What are your plans?"

He leaned down and kissed her on the forehead as he straightened the cuffs of his shirt between his gold cufflinks. "Not a terribly busy day, mother. There's a man coming to the house directly on business." Ransom looked at the clock. "In about an hour, he'll be here. I was hoping I could trouble Zennia to make me a bit of breakfast."

Just as he mentioned her name, she appeared out of nowhere, a skill Zennia often exercised with proficiency. "Mr. Ransom, I don't know why you don't get you'self up when the rest of the folks eats breakfast. How am I s'posed to get a lunch and an afternoon tea fixed when I'm settin' in there still fixin' you fatback and hen fruits?"

Ransom shifted his weight to his left side and, as was his habit, hooked his thumbs into the armholes of his vest. "Don't trouble yourself, Zennia." He poured out charm. "Really, the last thing I would want to do is put you to any extra trouble!"

Her irritated expression melted, and her jutted chin receded into a simper. "Oh, you rascal, you know I can't have you walking in, out, or 'round this here house sayin' you hungry. I'll get you a dab a breakfast out just shortly." She looked at Charlotte Cahill and shook her head back and forth. "I don't know how he do it, Mrs. Charlotte, but he do. Every time I say I ain't gonna do it, he go and talk me into it."

"He does seem to have that ability," Charlotte Cahill giggled and smiled at her son.

"So what kind of business is it that you have to conduct, Rans?"

"Oh, you know, just business. I wouldn't want to bore you with the details, mother," He deflected.

Without warning, Cephas entered the room. "Mr. Ransom, they's somebody here to see you out back."

"Out back?" Ransom had asked Haynes to do the very opposite when he arrived, and it was early.

"Yessir, out back," Cephas repeated.

He could not understand why Haynes would deviate from his instructions, but he made his way to the back entrance. When he passed through the kitchen, Zennia warned him that his breakfast was nearly ready. He stepped outside the back door, but it was not Haynes as he expected.

"Mornin', Mr. Cahill."

"Maclane? What brings you here?"

"It's about my brother, Tommy."

"He's alright, isn't he?" Ransom was baffled by this unexpected visit.

"I suppose, but you dropped him off last night."

"Last night?" he played dumb.

"Yes, last night. At least it was your car. I couldn't mistake it. I know what it looks like, I know how she runs, and there ain't another one like it around here," said Noah.

"Alright. So I dropped him off."

"It was nearly midnight when you dropped him off. That's late, but it's still a sight earlier than some of the nights."

"He's not a baby, you know," Ransom underplayed the situation.

"No, sir, you're right. He ain't a baby, but he is my baby brother, and I don't like it much him being out so late and me not knowing what he's up to."

"Seems to me that you should take up the matter with him, not me." Ransom crossed his arms.

"I did take it up with him. Now I'm takin' it up with you too," Noah coolly continued. "He's not a little boy, but he's a boy, and I know him. I don't want him in any kind of trouble. Me tellin' him to stay out of trouble, why, it's like talking to that wall right there."

"I see."

Ransom was unsure what to say. Noah Maclane seemed to be under the impression that Thomas was up to no good, but to probe him about what he knew could give away too much. Thomas was the kind of young naive guy they needed, but Noah was more calculated. He was more likely to ask questions, figure out what was going on, and hamper the entire operation.

"I'm gonna get right down to it, Mr. Cahill." Noah put his hands in his pockets. "Tommy told me that he was working a second job for that fella Haynes as a truck driver for some place

                    Jenna Cossey

out of Birmingham. I didn't like the idea to start with, but he seemed set on making a little extra money, and I didn't want to stand in his way. I've gotta know. What's this job?"

"It's just as he told you. He drives a truck for us," Ransom answered.

"Where does he drive to, and what for? He couldn't be going far, because he doesn't leave until after eleven."

"All I know to tell you is that Tommy made a deal with us to do a job, and that's what he's doing. He has to keep his end of the deal. We're keeping ours. He's getting paid well."

"Alright, fair enough." Noah could see that he was getting nowhere, and he was even more sure than before that Thomas had gotten himself involved in something nefarious, whether wittingly or not.

"Good day to you," Ransom said as he reentered the house.

Noah stood there, rigid with disgust at the outcome of the conversation until the back door slammed and ordered him back to attention.

"Your breakfast gonna be cold now, Mr. Ransom! After I've done fixed it up fresh and hot for ya!" Zennia was agitated all over again.

"Thank you, Zennia. I'm sure it's as good as ever."

Ransom quickly ate his breakfast, knowing that the time for Haynes to come was near. When he finished the last bite, a knock came at the front door. This time it was Haynes. Cephas let him in, and Ransom met him at the landing to shake hands with him.

"Let's go into the study, shall we?" He led him into the large study that belonged to his father. He shut the large door, and they proceeded over to a pair of armchairs to take up their business.

"Are you sure we are safe to talk here?" Haynes looked all around the large study.

"Of course we are. The mayor is downtown in his office. Mother is preparing for guests. There's nothing to fear," Ransom reassured him.

"Okay, let's get down to it. I'm told that Carolla's sending a special shipment of goods through here soon, just as I discussed with you before."

Ransom jostled a cigarette from a package and took it in his mouth to light it. "Alright, so where do we need to have it go? We are fully supplied at the Grotto."

"Two of the trucks will need to be taken to the warehouse. One needs to go to the Gray Fox Club in Garden City," Haynes said.

"Which of the fellas should we send to Garden City?" Ransom asked.

"What about Maclane? I'm sure he can handle himself," Haynes opined.

"Eh, I'm not sure. It might be better to send one of the others and have Duncan and Maclane go to the warehouse. It's an easy drop-off. I don't think we should chance the young fellas knowing too much of what's going on just yet, and if we send one of them to the Fox, it will be as plain as day."

"There you've got something."

"I had an unexpected visitor just this morning." Ransom crossed his legs and sunk a little further into the chair. "Tommy Maclane's brother, Noah."

"Oh yeah? Did Tommy say something to him?"

"No, I don't think Tommy knows anything to tell. It seems like his brother has become concerned with him finding trouble. He knows I drop Tommy off a lot of nights because he knows my coupe. Tommy does seem to have told him he's working for you driving a truck. I suppose he couldn't find you, so he came here," said Ransom.

"What did he want?"

"He was questioning me about the work Tommy was doing for us. I don't know for certain, but I think he may become a problem for us." Ransom looked at Haynes seriously.

"He's not going to be a problem. One way or the other, we will keep him out of the way."

"What would you have me do about him?" Ransom sat up in his chair.

"Nothing for now. Let's just wait and see."

"Alright, if you say so."

"Besides, Cahill, we don't want to have any trouble where we can avoid it."

"That's true." Ransom considered the entirety of the situation and felt more confident.

"So we wait," said Haynes. "We wait."

<u>54</u>

Since Noah could remember, he had performed the duty of being Thomas's keeper. At first, it was easier, but eventually, the time came in their lives when he no longer appreciated the instructive discipline of his elder brother.

"You better see to it that Tommy don't cause any more trouble. It's your responsibility to look out for him, Noah. He's your little brother," Gertrude Maclane had said.

Noah's attempts to corral him were less successful over time, but he understood his need for autonomy.

One fall, William Maclane learned that workers were needed in a nearby heading mill after the planting season. He suggested that his two oldest sons go there, sure that Mr. Blackwood, the owner, would be glad to hire them. Though they were both capable of doing a man's work, at fourteen and twelve years of age, the law only required that they receive half wages. Noah hesitated at the suggestion, but the idea of earning a bit of money excited Thomas. Noah decided it might just keep him busy enough to stay out of any other trouble. He was mischievous, but he was a hard worker. Having a job when the crops were in greatly appealed to him, but their work in the Blackwood heading mill proved catastrophic.

The heading mill was part of the booming Alabama cooperage industry. It produced heads for the many wooden kegs that would contain the substantial tonnage of nails manufactured at the steel mill in Birmingham. A steam engine and a network of belts powered the mill. The leather belts would often creep their way off of the wheels they were meant to turn, and sometimes the boys spent more time trying to keep the saws running than actually using them. One day, as they worked, a belt had once again loosened. Thomas quickly attempted to jump the belt back onto the wheel, but he miscalculated the timing of his release. The belt flung him through an opening in the wall where, on the other side, a large circular saw meant for blocks of wood made quick work of his leg. The steam whistle usually signified working hours, only singing out of time in emergencies. Noah never forgot the way the whistle cried that day.

In the months following the accident, Noah was afflicted with intense guilt, feeling that he had failed in his duty to watch over Thomas. He vowed within that he would watch over him more carefully for the rest of their lives. Yet, there in Dunnigan, Noah realized that, in his eagerness to give his love to Sara, he fell short in steering Thomas away from the likes of Haynes and Ransom.

He motored down the road back to the gas station, wondering what he could say or do that might cause Thomas to forget the driving business. He knew that the likelihood of him listening to what he had to say was almost nil. He thought that there had to be some way for him to appeal to Thomas effectively, but he was not sure what it was. He only hoped that the entire thing would turn out better than their stint at the Blackwood mill.

The Monday after Thomas moved out, he reported to the station for work just as he agreed. They worked as diligently as ever. Their conversations mostly revolved around the work. Before Thomas left, he mentioned in passing that he would have to work late that night.

"I guess I better shove off. I plan to get me a little cat nap in before I go out tonight."

"Alright. Want a lift?" Noah offered, knowing he would not accept.

"Nah, it's only a good stretch of the legs—well, leg, you know."

Thomas gave a slight grin. Noah understood his self-deprecating joke. He knew he was trying to keep the conversation light. They were never good at being mad at one another.

"Yeah, I know. See ya tomorrow, Tommy?"

"Yeah."

Needing to figure out a way to stay in the loop, Noah conversed with him the next morning. He did so mindful that, if he said too much, it would seem atypical to Thomas.

"Late night last night I 'spect. You tired?"

"Nah, I got a few hours of sleep. I'm good as new."

"How'd it go, the driving?"

"Simple, easy money," said Thomas.

"Ah. You driving again tonight?"

"Nah, not sure what else I've got this week."

"So what will you be doing tonight then?"

"No plans. You?"

"Well, Mrs. Simpson thought that the little fella might enjoy going to see this picture show that's on at the Lyric. We all got to talking about it the other night and reckoned that we'd just all of us go together. One of those Rin Tin Tin dog pictures, you know, like we seen a time or two?"

"Yeah, I know the ones. That dog is really somethin' else, ain't it?"

Noah saw an opening. "Say, why don't you just go with us?"

"Nah, don't wanta horn in on y'all."

"It wouldn't be hornin' in. Come on, go with us." Noah tried not to seem overeager.

Jenna Cossey

"Well, I don't know. I figured on going to bed a reasonable time tonight."

"Ah, we'll be back pretty early. We was planning on going to that early show, then going for a cone or somethin' after. The boy has school. Mrs. Simpson makes him take an early bedtime." There was a pause, and Noah grazed his arm in a punching motion. "Come on, Tom."

Thomas thought about it for a few seconds. "Alright, ya talked me into it. I'll go, but I don't want you buying my ticket. I'd be mighty embarrassed if you was to do that in front of the ladies!" Thomas always wanted to keep his pride intact.

Noah continued working and talking at his usual frequency after they made their plans. He was happy that, for at least one night, Thomas would not spend time with his new cohorts.

"Mrs. Simpson was planning to come by here and have us go in her car. There will be plenty of room for us all, and no grease on our pants from the truck seat!"

Noah set his unsettled feeling aside for a while.

_55_

The light rocking of the passenger car lulled Alfio Colucci into deep thought. He had developed a sense of hyperawareness of his surroundings that disallowed him from napping on trains. He often passed into the Southland by the "Dixie Line" for his work, but he could never forget his first trip.

*   *   *

"I do not like this thing you do, Alfio."

Alfio packed his bags. "Mamma, it's a decent thing."

"Sì, but I still do not like it. Your old friends, Mattie and Leo, they used to be good little boys, no?"

"I never knew them to look for trouble, but we were kids then, Ma."

"Esattamente! And look, now the two of them have been turned into rotten eggs! You should have seen their mother's faces after the papers came out last week. They walked to market with shame in their eyes." Emilia Colucci paced about the room.

"I'm not like Matteo or Leonardo, Mamma. If I don't do my job, then it will only be ones like them left for everyone to talk about."

"I know, but your work—it is dangerous. It was bad enough when you stayed here. Now they send you to New Orleans. What about the notte terribile? Surely you have not forgotten the words of your Uncle Renzo."

"You shouldn't dwell on it, Ma."

"It is not an easy thing to forget."

Alfio knew the story. In 1891, a few years before he was born, his uncle Lorenzo lived in New Orleans. The rest of his family members were in Saint Louis. He left them to move to the Crescent City and was working there as a stevedore. A group of Italians was arrested and incarcerated over an alleged connection to the murder of New Orleans' chief of police. When Renzo learned that most of them were subsequently tortured and lynched by an angry mob, he fled the city in fear, calling in a favor from a friend on a riverboat crew to make a hasty exit. He rejoined his family in Saint Louis, but the event made a lasting impact on Renzo Colucci. Alfio never heard his uncle tell the story in English. It was far too intense for him to try and keep command of his second language as he recounted it. Alfio and his brothers never dared not to listen to the story in its entirety if they happened to be present when "Zio Rennie" started to tell it.

"They will mark you. With a name like yours, it will be easy."

"Mamma, you forget—I changed it," he reminded her.

"So what? You have the look about you. They always know." She squinted and waggled her finger at him.

"This is what I want to do, Mamma. It's what I need to do. I've worked for it. It's my dream. Did you and Papa not follow your dreams?"

His mother shook her head and sighed. "Sì, figlio mio, sì." She patted him on the cheek and restrained her tears, knowing that they would not keep him from his commitments.

His mother had become accustomed to his excursions over the years, though it never really grew easier for her to watch him go off into the fray. He did not take thought of the danger as she did, except in the ways in which it was wise to do so.

*   *   *

He never stopped being "Alfio Ettore Colucci" inside, but being "Alfred Lucas" on the outside had spared him a bit of trouble along the way. The negative cliches did not concern him. At first, his approach was to defy them every step of the way. He wondered if he had been changed by his line of work. The pursuit of his dream carried him back and forth across the country, and now it took him to Dunnigan, Alabama.

56

Sara felt an indescribable change within herself. Her circumstances had conscripted her into a battle for her life and the freedom to write her own happy endings. The conflict raged for years, and her mother's death delivered a blow so catastrophic that she barely had the will to fight. With time and care from Violet, she was forging ahead through the chasm of her guilt and sadness. The affection Noah showed only bolstered her confidence. She had a knack for taking the threadbare pieces of her life and using them to moor herself. She was a fighter, even if she did not recognize it.

The five of them took in the picture show together that Tuesday afternoon. Having Thomas along added a different dimension. He was gregarious and talkative. It was impossible not to notice the contrast between him and Noah, but they all enjoyed his company. Where Noah tended toward the reserved side, Thomas always had something to say, and most of the time, it turned out to the amusement of the entire group, especially Easton.

The group sat around a small table in the ice cream parlor that afternoon. They talked about the first few weeks of school for Sara and Easton, the stifling late summer heat, the theatrical heroics of Rin Tin Tin, and the satisfying taste of the ice cream. Unlike the drugstore fountain, the ice cream parlor was near the cinema. The owners discovered the advantage of staying open past the first few evening shows; people often came looking for something sweet to eat once they were over. Suddenly Thomas raised his hand in a wave. Noah and Sara had their backs to the large window in the front of the parlor. Noah turned to see who Thomas waved to: Ransom Cahill and Haynes.

Sara detected a tension in Noah's reaction that Violet also noticed. As Thomas waved, the two men stopped and smiled. Haynes said something to Ransom, and they turned and entered the ice cream parlor.

"Howdy, fellas!" Thomas greeted them.

Ransom smiled slyly. It was obvious that he considered himself mightily superior to everyone else, but Thomas was too gulled to recognize it. "Hello there, Maclane," he said as he approached the table.

"Hey, Peg." Haynes outstretched his hand toward Thomas.

"Peg? That's Tommy," Easton interjected.

"Easton." Violet motioned for him not to talk over the men.

Haynes grinned at Easton. "Easy there, partner. Who are your friends here, Peg?"

Thomas started around the table. "Well, this is my brother, Noah, and his girl, Sara. Her aunt, Mrs. Simpson. And this here's my friend Easton."

"I'm her brother," Easton pointed to Sara.

Haynes looked around the table. He did not extend any verbal greetings, but offered a collective nod. "Looks like he's kinda busy tonight, doesn't it, Mr. Cahill?"

"Yes, it does." Ransom scanned the faces at the table. Unlike Haynes, his upbringing prompted him to make an introduction. He looked at Noah. "I believe we've met before. Pleased to meet the rest of you all as well, Sara, Mrs. Simpson, Easton."

Sara was impressed at his immediate recall of the names, knowing how terrible she was at remembering new ones.

"Well, we won't hold you up any longer. Saw you in the window there and thought we'd drop in on you. We'll see ya around, Peg," Haynes said.

"Yeah, see y'all 'round," Thomas replied.

They made their way to the door, and Thomas finished eating his ice cream. Noah's apprehension was apparent. Sara did not know what was going on, but the sense of conflict made her uneasy.

"Ransom Cahill. That's Mayor Cahill's son," Violet remarked.

"Yes'm, it is," said Thomas.

"How do you know him?"

"Well, me and Noah did some work on his coupe, and I just started working for him a few nights a week a while back."

"Is that right? What is it that you do for him?" Violet pressed further.

"Well, I just do a little driving for him. Delivery trucks."

"Deliveries? What kind?" asked Violet.

He realized that the line of questioning was outrunning his knowledge. "I don't rightly know. I don't ask many questions. I just do the work and get paid."

"I see," Violet said.

Noah had been sitting silent. "I thought it was Haynes you were working for anyway."

"Well, it is."

Noah looked straight at him. "But you just said you worked for Ransom Cahill. Which one is it?"

Thomas became flustered by the barrage of questions. "It's both of 'em. I work for the both of 'em. I don't see what's so hard to understand about that."

An awkward silence hung over the table. Sara had never seen this side of Noah.

Easton cut through the stagnation, "Tommy?"

"Yeah, pal?"

"Ain't your name Tommy?"

His brow relaxed. "Yes sir, young man. Well, it's Thomas, but folks always called me Tommy, sometimes Tom."

"Why did that man call you Peg?"

"Oh, that's just something he calls me. It's because of my leg." He reached down and rapped on his wooden leg.

"Your leg?" Easton was even more puzzled by the sound he heard.

"Yeah, see?" Thomas raised his pant leg, revealing a small part of his smoothly crafted leg.

"Your leg is wood?"

"Yep."

"Why do you have a wood leg?"

"Easton." Once again, Violet tried to quiet him.

"Oh, it's alright, Mrs. Simpson." Thomas could not help but be amused by his wording. "Well, when I was younger, only a few years more than you, something happened to the bone in my leg. So now, instead of my leg, I have a—"

"A wood leg?"

"Right, I've got a wood leg. Sometimes people call these things a peg." He pointed to his prosthesis. "So Haynes there, he sometimes calls me Peg."

Easton's wonderment over the "wood leg" grew as he stared down at it. "I don't think I like Peg. I think you should just be Tommy."

"Tommy never liked Peg either," Noah interjected.

Noah and Thomas looked across the table at one another. They were not staring each other down, but their recent rift was still fresh. Sara grew more anxious over the dynamic, and Violet could see it.

"Well, I suppose we should be heading back. Someone here will have to be in bed soon!" Violet tousled Easton's hair.

The car ride back to the station was much quieter than the ride into town. Noah drove them. He and Thomas sat in the front seat in silence. Sara was thankful that it was only a short distance to the place where he stayed because the astriction in the car was even worse than it had been at the ice cream parlor.

Noah slowed as they approached the boarding house and let Thomas out on the sidewalk.

"Pleasure joining y'all, Mrs. Simpson. See y'all around."

Easton rode quietly up until then, but he could contain himself no longer. He stood up, leaned over the front seat, and stuck his head out of the rolled down front passenger window. "Tommy!"

"What is it, pal?"

"What happened to your bone leg?" He had to know before Thomas left.

"A bear bit it off!"

Easton giggled as Violet urged him to sit down. Sara and Noah remained expressionless.

They arrived at the gas station, and Noah got out of the car.

"It's a fine car you've got here, Mrs. Simpson. Always enjoy the drive," he said as Violet prepared to take the wheel over from him. "It was a nice evening. I'll see you soon, Sara. Bye, y'all."

When Sara said goodbye, she did not look at him.

<u>*57*</u>

"I sorta got the sense that Maclane's brother wasn't thrilled to see us."

Haynes leaned against Ransom's Chevrolet coupe just down the street from the Lyric Theater and the adjacent ice cream parlor where they had spotted them.

"In the times I've talked to him, he tends to be a man of few words. After that visit the other day, I couldn't tell if he was sore or not, but he could be," Ransom said.

"What about those other people? You know them?" Haynes latched his arms across his chest.

"I've seen Mrs. Simpson around. She's lived here for a while, school teacher. She was married to a man named Joseph Simpson. He worked for one of the big banks in Birmingham."

"A lot to know about somebody you don't know," Haynes quipped.

"Well, the fella died in an accident." Ransom paused to light a cigarette. "Nobody really knows what happened, but he managed some big accounts, and his family was well known there. It was all over the papers earlier this year."

"So the Simpson lady is pretty well fixed then, I bet."

"I'd say so. I remember Cephas telling me that the Simpsons in Birmingham were pretty well to do in the first place," Ransom said as he got into his car.

"What about the girl? You know her?"

"No, don't know her." Ransom recollected the department store meeting. "I did meet her once when I went into Stillman's, but I don't exactly know her."

"I figured you knew all the pretty girls in Dunnigan!" He playfully punched Ransom's arm.

"Most, but not all," Ransom jested. "Besides, she isn't from around here."

"No?"

"No, she moved here, but I can't recall where from."

"Oh well, it's a good thing we ran into Maclane, though."

"Why do you say that?"

"Well, his brother Noah . . . You say you're afraid he'll make trouble for us."

"He might try, but he can't stop us." Ransom was confident.

"But if he interferes, it may make things more difficult," Haynes continued. "And now we know who his brother's girl and her family are."

"I'm not following, Haynes. What are you getting at?"

"If Noah Maclane gets in the way, we'll hit him where it hurts the most."

His fear was confirmed. He was fairly certain about what Haynes was implying, but he was unsure how to feel about it. *Is he saying we might hurt these people?*

Ransom fell silent, pondering Haynes' meaning when he suddenly connected the dots. He remembered what Mr. Messina had told him in the beginning. *"By any means necessary . . ."*

His heart began to beat faster. He knew that he could not preclude the possibility of Noah Maclane or others trying to obstruct their newly established operation in Dunnigan. He also knew that he could not, therefore, preclude the possibility of violence. He did not see himself as a man of violence, but he had joined Messina's ranks in acceptance of the conditions. At that moment, he knew he might soon face unpleasant duties. A small part of him said to get out, but it was too late. He was committed. If he defected, the violence would come *his* way.

By the time they reached the Thirty-One Grotto, Ransom had made up his mind. He would have to stay the course, no matter what it required. Too many bridges had been burned with Edward Cahill, and though his mother had faithfully stood by him in his stubborn, prideful, and often self-destructive behaviors, he knew that even she had her limits.

The wheels were in motion. There was no turning back.

Jenna Cossey

<h1 style="text-align:center"><u>58</u></h1>

The rest of the week passed. On Sunday, Noah went to Sharp's Creek. It was the only place he could clear his head enough to develop a plan. As usual, he took his cane pole with him. The whirlwind of life events consumed his thoughts. It had started so long ago, before they moved there, before Thomas lost his leg, before they left school. The position he found himself in was the culmination of a lifetime spent trying to protect someone who did not want protection. He harkened back to the final skirmish that had brought them to Dunnigan.

*   *   *

"You're a cripple. Ain't nobody gonna hire on any cripple to work for 'em."

It was a cold declaration. The words made Noah wince when his father said them to Thomas. He knew that it would deepen his anger and resentment. He did not blame Thomas for his reactions to William Maclane's patronization. After all, he could not help having lost his leg. Like most sons, he longed for encouragement from his father, not ridicule.

"It ain't kept you from working me like a borrowed mule around here, has it, Paw? Has it?" His face flushed red.

"You gotta earn your keep somewhere, boy. Only way you're gonna help us is workin' here, 'cause ain't nobody else gonna take you on with that bad leg," William repeated.

It was not true.

Thomas did not have the brute physical strength of his older brother. He was a spindly fifteen-year-old kid who happened to have one leg, but he could work steadily alongside any hired hand in the county, and his father knew it. Noah never fully comprehended why their father criticized Thomas for being lame until he realized that they were viewed as debtors to him. From the time they were old enough to help farm and bring income to the family, William made sure that they understood their stations by treating them like tenants. It started simply enough: if they did not help in the fields and with the livestock, they did not eat. He was a hard man, and soon his requirement that they work for their food morphed into a different one: if they did not work to his complete satisfaction, they did not eat. When the boys grew older still, William worked them in the fields during planting and harvesting, and then demanded they take other jobs during the off season. When he found work for them, it was not a mere suggestion. Their other employers were much easier to please than their father. Like most of the boys they knew, they received no compensation for helping on the family farm, despite working hard enough to cover the duties of four men. When they took work away from the farm, William demanded that they pay rent for living at home. Time after time, Thomas tried to find work off the farm to escape the unreasonable conditions, while Noah felt obligated to the family.

"Nobody'll take me on? You won't let anybody take me on. Every time I get a job lined up, you either do me out of it before I start, or you come behind me sayin' that I'm slow movin' and crippled 'til they decide maybe I can't do the jobs after all." Thomas clenched his fists. "You're the cause of me not bein' able to keep work around here anywhere. It's you! You're so afraid that you're gonna lose your free help! Well, you ain't gotta worry about it no more because I'm leavin'. I ain't your slave no more."

           Jenna Cossey

"Leavin'? You ain't leavin'! You ain't got nowhere to go!" William Maclane raised his hands and looked all around.

"I'll just have to find somewhere then, won't I?" Thomas walked toward the house with his fists still clenched.

Noah stood there aghast, seeing clearly how cruel his father could be. "Paw, I can't let Tommy go."

"He ain't goin' nowhere! Where could he——"

"No, Paw. He's leavin'. Sure as I'm standin' here, he's leavin'. You've done pushed too far."

"He won't make it a week by himself."

"I know it, Paw." Noah started to walk away. "That's why I'm goin' with him."

*   *   *

The scene flooded anew into his thoughts as he sat on the bank of Sharp's Creek. Noah had always stayed with Thomas when he veered from the expected course. Now he feared that Thomas was going where he could not follow. He needed to think about how he could confirm or deny his suspicions.

"Hey there, you."

He was deep in thought, and the voice, though sweet sounding, startled him.

It was Violet Simpson.

He jumped to his feet. "Mrs. Simpson. Didn't expect to see you here."

"I can't say as I expected to see you here, either. You don't have to get up," Violet replied.

He reclaimed his seat on the soft grass. "Sara told me that y'all come here now and then. Guess we just never were here at the same time."

"I do come here from time to time, mostly when my mind is unsettled about something."

"Know what ya mean," Noah said as he looked out over the creek.

"You know, I'm glad to see you here. Since there isn't anyone around, perhaps it's a good time for us to talk." Violet took a seat in the grass next to him.

"Yes'm. What'd you have in mind?"

"I'm not very good at these kinds of things, so I'll save us both the trouble and get right down to the heart of the matter. It's been nearly two months now that you've been coming to visit Sara regularly."

"Yes'm."

"I have certainly enjoyed having you come to visit with us. Easton adores you, talks about you all of the time, and Sara," Violet hesitated, "Sara cares for you, Noah."

"Oh, well I care for her too, Mrs. Violet," Noah blushed.

"If you care for her, then surely you understand that I'm her guardian and that I'm responsible for her well-being."

"Yes, ma'am, I understand that." He was unsure of what she was driving at.

"So then, I must ask. Are you involved in the same work as your brother?"

His throat constricted. She was not referring to the work at the garage. "You mean, with Ransom Cahill?"

"Yes."

"No, ma'am."

"I see. It just concerns me that Sara is so fond of a young man whose brother is involved in such," Violet spoke in a calm tone. "I would have forbidden you coming back when I learned of it, but I happen to like you very much. I've even grown to trust you somewhat, and I don't know how Sara would handle the disappointment if I were not to let her see you anymore."

     Jenna Cossey

He could not believe what he heard. "Not let her see me anymore? Mrs. Simpson, I don't understand."

She saw the gap in his understanding. In good faith, she decided to explain it, hoping he would see her concern. "Noah, you're fairly new in Dunnigan, but I've lived here for almost a decade now. As a school teacher, I've gotten to know many of the community members, and I feel that I have a pretty good grasp of what goes on here."

"Yes, ma'am?" he listened intently.

"I think you should know that the word about town is Ransom Cahill, along with this Haynes fellow, whoever he is, is running an illegal drinking house on the south end of the county. The last time I stopped by Stillman's, Jacob told me he'd gotten wind of some suspicious activity next-door. As it happens, Ransom frequents their store, so Jacob made a few subtle inquiries and came away with the impression that the rumors were true. Now, I don't know what Thomas is involved in. I don't know what he knows. After questioning him in town the other night, I couldn't decide whether he didn't know or if he was just trying to dodge the questions, but to say it concerns me would be an understatement."

In an instant, Violet had confirmed his fears. Noah had no reason to doubt that she knew what she was talking about. She was known and respected by a great many people in Dunnigan. The question was one of what to do about the whole thing. He sat there and rested his elbows on his knees.

There was a period of silence before he spoke. His voice cracked just enough to reveal his uneasiness. "I was feared of this. I . . . I don't know what to do. I should have known Tommy was in trouble. It's all my fault."

"It's not your fault, Noah. Do you think he would be working for Ransom if he knew what was going on?" Violet asked.

"I can't say for sure, but I'd hope not."

"Then it seems to me that the only thing to do is to try and convince him," Violet said.

"How can I do that?"

Violet looked out over the creek. She heard his question, but she was still thinking. "When does Tommy work again?"

"It's different sometimes, but Monday nights here lately," Noah said.

"Alright. I think it's better if Sara doesn't know about this for now. I'll see you later this evening. I need to think on this," she said.

Violet left Noah at the bank and walked home.

He made his way back to the station, wondering what to do and whether she could actually help him devise a plan. All he knew for sure was that he would do anything within his power to help Thomas.

<u>*59*</u>

Living in the house with Walter Wheeler meant living in a state of constant uncertainty. He had been so erratic.

Matilda Wheeler began to refer to the old life more often, the life before her husband turned into the unstable version of himself. "It wasn't always this way."

Sara wanted to believe that her father possessed some redeeming qualities, but as she grew up, she found it increasingly difficult. Sometimes she concentrated with intensity, trying to remember as far into her past as she could. She clamored for good memories. No matter how hard she tried, her earliest and only memories of her father were of his untrustworthiness. After a time, she decided it was best to block it from her mind. Her survival was far too important for her to expend too much emotional energy searching for the good in him. She needed every ounce of it to keep going. She learned to ignore and pretend at all of the right times, but sometimes she had to help Easton too.

Easton had adjusted wonderfully in Dunnigan. Sara envied his youthful spirit, the part of him that still saw the world through the lens of childlike innocence. It seemed as though he hardly even thought of their old home anymore. It saddened her, in a way, that he would never know their mother the way she had, but she was also happy that he would never have to miss her as much. She understood that her mother had been a very good woman in a terrible set of circumstances who tried with every fiber of her being to give them the love they deserved despite the challenges.

Violet and Noah gave Sara the gift of dependability, but after the incident at the ice cream parlor, the variation she sensed in his steadiness alarmed her. Her experiences had conditioned her to protect herself, to flee at any sign of danger, but how could she run from Noah? She *loved* him.

Her mind told her to shut down and prevent any possibility of being hurt, but her heart told her that it was worth the risk. Once again, she was in a situation she did not know how to handle. Violet was an ever-flowing fountain of support, love, and helpful advice. She was the only person in the world Sara could go to about such things. Having given the matter much thought in the days following the occurrence in town, she awakened Sunday morning, intending to discuss the entire complicated issue with her confidant.

Not fully awake yet, she held on to the banister railing and went downstairs. She heard no movement in the house and smelled no coffee brewing, a rarity as Violet enjoyed a few cups each morning. She looked out the window and noticed that the sedan was still there. *She can't have gone far.*

She went back upstairs, changed out of her nightgown, and pulled her hair away from her face. She walked lightly across the hallway, peeked into Easton's room, and found him sleeping soundly as he always did, with his arms thrown above his head and the covers kicked away.

She heard Violet come through the kitchen entrance and went down to meet her.

"Good morning," Violet said.

"Morning, Aunt Vi."

"I'm ready for my coffee! Let's fix something for breakfast. What'll we have this morning?" Violet asked.

"I don't know. I'm not very hungry."

"Not hungry? Is it too early?"

"No, it's not that. I just don't feel hungry much this morning," Sara said.

"Are you feeling alright?" Violet placed a hand on Sara's forehead.

"I suppose so."

"Is something bothering you, Sara?" Violet sat down in the chair next to her. "Are you ok?"

"I'm worried about Noah," Sara confessed. "He's been acting different ever since Tommy went with us the other night. Something happened. I don't know what it was, but he's not been the same, and I don't know what to do about it."

Violet was in a precarious situation. She knew exactly what was going on with Noah, but felt that she did not need to reveal her conversation with him. Instead, she took a different approach.

"What do you mean he hasn't been the same?"

"I don't know. I can't quite put my finger on it. When those two came in at the ice cream parlor—I can't think of their names— something wasn't right. Since then, he's been much quieter. I'm afraid to ask him what's going on, Aunt Vi."

"Why?"

"I'm afraid I won't want to know. I'm afraid he won't *want* me to know."

"Why does that make you afraid?"

"I'm afraid that it will be something I don't like, but I don't want him to hide things from me. I don't want to hide things from him. I . . ." Sara hesitated, "I think that I love him, Aunt Violet. Well, I *know* that I love him, and I thought that he loved me, too, but if he won't tell me what's going on, then maybe he doesn't love me enough to trust me."

Violet considered what Sara said, weighing it against what Noah had told her. "You might not be thinking exactly right about it, sweetheart. Maybe he just needs time to tell you in his own way. I happen to believe that he cares for you very much, and he's told you as much, because you and I have talked about it."

"So, what do I do?" Sara asked.

It was a big question. Violet understood her concerns, and she saw what Sara could not see both about herself and Noah. She did not know whether it was the right thing to do or not, but she gave her the only advice she believed.

"Don't be afraid. Fear . . . it's a powerful thing. It causes us not to see what's right in front of us. If you're afraid, you can't run from it. You may find out that what you fear isn't worth being afraid of at all," Violet said as she patted her hand.

"What does that mean?"

"Do you love Noah?"

"Yes."

"Then just talk to him, Sara. Talk to him."

_60_

"They said some cold-blooded things. They did."

Zennia and Cephas talked with hushed voices in the backyard while he held the laundry basket from which she plucked damp clothing. They each had their own kind of worried expression.

"Like what?" He believed her, but he wanted more details.

"I couldn't hear everything they said, but I hear most of it. First, Mr. Cahill say something 'bout Mr. Ransom gone too far. Then Mrs. Charlotte say he a grown man and have to look out for hisself."

"I knew it was just a matter of time before Mr. Cahill found out," Cephas said.

"You shoulda told Mr. Cahill what was goin' on. You saw them friends of his waitin' downtown that night. You shoulda told him then and maybe he coulda stopped Mr. Ransom," she chided him.

"You crazy, Zennia. Somebody in our shoes don't tell things like that. Liable to end me up dead somewhere!" Cephas became riled, and his voice rose before he hushed himself again.

"Then why'd you go lookin' if you wasn't gonna do nothin' 'bout it?"

It was not an unreasonable question. Cephas and Zennia had known for several weeks that Ransom was up to no good. The change in his activity was noticeable to those who watched, and they watched. They also listened. Zennia found it hard to understand Cephas's reaction to the new revelations, but she did not know all that he knew.

"'Cause since the day Mr. Ransom was born, I been looking out for him. I promise Mrs. Charlotte's daddy before he died that I look out for the boy," Cephas said.

"Mr. Palmer musta been mighty good to you for you to stay on this fool's errand tryin' to wrangle that boy. It don't look like there's any doin' it. What's the use?"

"Mr. Palmer—rest his soul—he was a mighty fine gentleman, and he always done right by me. Fool's errand or not, I gotta keep my word."

"Now he's in a peck of trouble, and Mrs. Charlotte know about it too 'cause that was partly what I heard 'em talkin' about," said Zennia.

"Mrs. Charlotte been knowin' about it all along, Zennia." He looked around before continuing, "She knew Mr. Cahill were gonna find out about it soon enough. She had plenty time to decide what to do 'bout it."

"You mean you told her?" Zennia was surprised.

"Had to, part of my promise even if I don't like it none."

"Well, she sure was loaded for bear when Mr. Cahill lit into her about Ransom. They went back and forth for good long while." She took another piece of laundry from the basket and hung it on the line. "But there was one thing about it all that left me scratchin' my head, Cephas."

"What's that?"

"When they finally came to a real standoff, and all the spittin' and snappin' was over, Mr. Cahill told her that, if Mr. Ransom brought any embarrassment onto the Cahill name, it would be the last straw. Then Mrs. Charlotte asked him what he was meanin' by the last straw." She took the last piece from the basket. "He told her he would disown Ransom forever if he shamed the family, but she turned right around and told him that there was plenty of

 Jenna Cossey

shame to go around. She told him that she hadn't pandered to all these gov'ment crooks all these years without learning a thing or two. She said if he do Ransom wrong that she'd tell the whole world how crooked him and his boon companions really were."

Cephas fixed his expression. "Yeah?"

"Yessir, and then he say she had some secrets, too."

"Did he?"

"Yeah, and he say she know what he mean, and he would tell everyone her wretched little secret and that it'd be the ruination of her *and* Ransom."

"Mercy." He exhaled a short breath.

"What you think he talkin' 'bout, Cephas?"

"We best be gettin' on with the rest of the chores, Zennia."

"I can tell by lookin' at your face you know what they talkin' 'bout, Cephas. My mama didn't raise a fool."

There was only silence, and he made his way toward the back of the house. Zennia followed after him.

"Cephas! Cephas!" she tried to stop him with her voice still stifled. "Now I told you everything I heard 'em say 'cause you asked me. It ain't fair of you not to tell me what's goin' on!"

He stopped and turned around. "Shh! Now hush up, woman! Look here. They's just some things you don't know about—wish I didn't know 'em myself. Only reason I know's 'cause I'm older than Methuselah, and I been with Mrs. Charlotte family since she were just knee-high to a duck herself."

"I can't see why that keeps you from tellin' me what's goin' on," she snapped.

"Zennia, *The Good Book* say everybody sins gonna find 'em out . . . mine, yours, the mister and the missus, Ransom, everybody. All I can tell you is that time may come soon for some."

Zennia looked into his eyes and saw in them a gravity she had never before seen. With that, Cephas turned and disappeared into the house.

Jenna Cossey

61

Noah went to dinner after his chance meeting with Violet. She confirmed that Thomas was in trouble, and it was a tremendous distraction for him. Once again, Sara found his demeanor and attention changed as they sat in their usual places on the porch. She talked, but he did not seem to be listening.

"Noah?"

He stared out into the clear shimmering night sky that sprawled over the treetops. He thought about how to intervene in a way that would force Thomas to see the folly of participating in the schemes of Ransom Cahill.

"Noah?"

Swaying Thomas was not easy. A lifetime of experience told Noah that convincing him to drop his newfound source of income would only be possible if he confronted him with unavoidable reasons to do so. He had to figure out a way to present the facts before it was too late.

"Noah!"

He heard the desperation in Sara's voice. "Yes? I'm sorry. What is it?"

"Noah, please tell me what's the matter."

He saw fear in Sara's eyes. It jarred him, but he did not want to burden her. "Ah, don't worry about me." Noah smiled disingenuously, hoping to quell her concern.

"It's too late, Noah. I'm already worried. You haven't been yourself for the past several days since the night at the ice cream parlor. I haven't stopped thinking about it all week. I know something is going on between you and Tommy. I'm not dumb, you know," she said.

"Sure you're not. I never said you was. Don't know why you'd even think a thing like that." He turned toward her and put his elbows on his knees.

"Because you're acting like I don't see it, but I do. Whatever it is, you can tell me, Noah. You don't have to keep everything all bottled up like—"

They looked at each other, and neither said a word for several seconds. It had been true since their first meeting that he knew very little about her life before Dunnigan. He knew that she was delicate in certain ways, so he did not pry into her emotions. He tried to be patient and wait for her to share what she would in her own good time, but she never did. The moment Sara stopped herself, he knew that she understood the irony of her proposal. She was asking him to do what she had not done.

"Like you?"

Sara looked down at her lap. "Yes, like me."

Several seconds passed before she spoke again. "I haven't kept things from you because I don't trust you. I've tried so hard not to think about the past . . . about the way things were before I came here. I never thought I'd be happy again, but here . . . here, I'm happy. I just don't want to spoil it. Things were bad before I came here, Noah, really bad."

He took hold of her hand in his gentle way. "It's alright, Sara. I understand it."

"I'm not so sure you do."

"But I want to; I want to understand."

"I just didn't want your pity. I don't want anyone to feel sorry for me. It just seems like everything always goes bad somehow. It seems like everything that means something to me goes away. I was afraid—I'm still afraid, that if I loved you too much, you'd go away, too."

He leaned a little closer still. "I ain't goin' anywhere, Sara. If you love me too much, it'll be the best thing that ever happened to me."

For a moment, when she smiled at him, he forgot everything that weighed so heavily on his mind.

"I do love you, Noah. I just haven't been able to let myself tell you because I'm scared of losing you. I'm scared of losing everyone. I never imagined I'd be here without Mama." She choked back tears. "I miss her so much. I wish she were here. Every time something good happens here, I still want to tell her about it. Then I catch myself and remember that I can't."

Noah's heart was soft, and a part of him did feel sorry for her, but he did not want to do the one thing that caused her to delay telling him in the first place. "I know. It's got to be hard, but you're gonna be alright. I'm gonna see to it. I've told you before, I love you, and I'm gonna do everything I can to make you happy."

He realized that by keeping the situation with Thomas to himself, he left her believing that he did not trust her. *I have to tell her.*

He started to tell her, but he wanted to honor Violet's request that he not do so. So he forged a compromise. "Sara, I can't tell you everything that's going on with Tommy. Mostly because I'm not sure myself what it is. Things have been touchy with us for a while. Partly it's just how Tom is, but the other part I ain't too sure about. I've got some figuring to do on it." It was the best he could do to let her in and still do as Violet had asked. "I reckon I better be headin' back so you can get to bed. I don't want you bein' tired for school tomorrow." He rose from his chair still holding her hand.

When they stood, she was inadvertently close to him. Wondering if the time was right, he made a swift decision. He took her other hand. His blocky figure overshadowed her slender frame, but he leaned toward her and lowered his voice to a whisper. "Good night, Sara." He gently pressed his lips to her cheek.

"Good night, Noah."

Noah made his way home that night with his mind racing. He could yield himself to love or focus on rescuing Thomas. The balancing act was ripping his heart into pieces.

Jenna Cossey

<u>62</u>

"I have bad news."

Ransom and Haynes were in the office at The Thirty-One Grotto. It was just past noon, and the place was empty.

"Burt rang the house earlier. I told him never to ring the house, but under the circumstances, I suppose he had no choice," Ransom said.

"Yeah? What's the trouble?"

"Well, you know he works in the shop at the rail yard. It seems that he burned his hand very badly this morning. Something about one of the locomotives he was working on."

"Now what?" Haynes was unconcerned about the injury.

"I'm not sure. I never wanted him working for us in the first place. That job in the yard is dangerous. Coupling it with sleep deprivation was a recipe for disaster, but he's a friend of Chief Lanham's." Ransom snuffed out his cigarette in a bronze ashtray on the desk. "He insisted we cut the guy in somehow. He's too uncouth to be working inside here nights. Putting him on the road for us seemed like the best way to keep Lanham happy."

"Those trucks are coming through tonight. How are we going to get Burt's load up to the Fox in Garden City?"

Ransom threw his right leg over the other, hooked his left thumb in his vest, and pressed his right finger down onto the desk. "The two of us need to be here, but two of those trucks are going to the warehouse, and that doesn't take much time. If one of us does a warehouse run, we can send one of the others up to Garden City."

"That might work. I'll take the run. You stay here, but," Haynes gave a side-eye look, "who will we send to Garden City?"

"Whoever we send has to be the one least likely to go around making a lot of talk about it. You know the options. There's Duncan, and there's Maclane."

"You know those guys at the Fox can be a little mouthy. I don't want Maclane blowing his top if one of them gets a little wise with him," Haynes said.

"No, but we have to think about which one of those guys is the most likely to be able to handle things if he has any trouble."

They sat there for a few minutes. Ransom, indecisive and uneasy owing to the importance of the matter, lit another cigarette as he waited to hear what his associate had to say.

"It's got to be Maclane. That's just all there is to it. For one, this job pays double. It takes longer, and it's more dangerous. Archie's liable to tell every cat in town if he gets too much money in his pocket. Plus, he's just not as tough as Maclane. Period. Trust me on this." Haynes rubbed his chin, remembering the time Thomas had biffed him.

"If that's what you think is best, I'm in agreement. We've got to send one of them. Bringing somebody else on would be too hard on such short notice. I'll go meet with Burt tomorrow and see how long he expects the hand to keep him from driving. If it's too long, then we can think about bringing somebody else on, but I'd like to avoid it."

"From what I understand, Carollo's gonna keep Mr. Messina sending those trucks through here as long as things keep going like they are. We're gonna need someone if Burt can't stay on. Anyways, I guess you better track Maclane down and see if he's gonna be on board to do this thing."

     Jenna Cossey

"Oh, he'll be on board. I can make it worth it to him. It's not often a yokel like him makes money like this. He'll go for it." Ransom patted the breast of his coat where his wallet was.

A little later, he cruised through Dunnigan in his coupe. He rarely had reason to visit Thomas at the gas station during working hours. The one on the south side of town was much closer, but this was a special case. Hoping to circumvent the need to fabricate a reason to talk to him, he pulled up to the gasoline pumps in the front of the station.

Thomas recognized the car. He knew that Ransom must have been there on business and made his way across the parking lot, maneuvering with his distinctive gait. When he reached the vehicle, he asked the usual question. "Fill 'er up?"

"Yeah, go ahead."

He filled the tank on the car and leaned his arms on the ledge of the open passenger side window.

"Sixty cents was all it held. What else can I do you for?" He expected something more than just payment for the fuel.

"Change of plans tonight."

"No deliveries?"

"Yeah, just need you to do a new one."

"Not goin' to the warehouse?"

"No."

"Alright, so where to?"

"Garden City."

"Garden City? That'll take a while."

"I know, but it pays double."

"It'll take me more than double time to get there and back."

"You're right about that. I'll throw in a little extra, make it worth your time."

"Ok, I can do it."

"Haynes will tell you everything you need to know when you get downtown tonight."

"Alright."

"Here. Keep the change." Ransom handed him a dollar bill for the gasoline and drove away.

That night Thomas walked down to the alley by the hardware store. It was not far from the boarding house. He stepped into the alley and tapped on the red door. Haynes was there to let him in as usual, but Archie was not yet there.

"I'm glad you got here early, Maclane."

"Yeah?"

"Yeah, I wanted to talk to you about this trip," Haynes said.

"Shoot," Thomas replied.

"I don't want Archie to know the particulars. He'll know you've made a different trip before the night's over, but that's about all he needs to know. You'll just tell him you've gone to another warehouse."

"But I'm not going to another warehouse?"

"No. You're gonna find out when you get there either way, so I'm gonna go ahead and let you in on the secret. You're going to a place called the Gray Fox."

"The Gray Fox?" Thomas raised an eyebrow and shifted his weight to his good leg as he stood there waiting for more information.

"Yeah, the Gray Fox."

"What's the Gray Fox?"

"It's a speakeasy." The word dropped like a hammer.

"A speakeasy?"

"Yeah, a speakeasy."

"So I'm taking this truck to a gin joint?" Thomas tried to connect the dots.

"That's right." Haynes waited on his reaction.

"So you're telling me that in that truck is—"

"Yep."

Thomas stood there and made no immediate response. He clenched and relaxed his jaw rapidly, causing his jaw muscles to twitch.

"What's it gonna be, Maclane?"

_63_

Noah wasted little time waiting for Violet to help him decide what to do about the situation with Thomas. He had made up his mind when he saw Ransom Cahill pull up to the pump that morning. He needed a little more information, but he had to take care not to be too forceful in getting it, or he risked being shut out.

Thomas came walking back to the garage and resumed his work. After a few moments passed, Noah posed a question. "That was Cahill's coupe, weren't it?"

"Yeah."

"I'd know the sound of it anywhere. We did a good job on that one," he tried to neutralize the conversation.

"Yeah, I reckon we did. He goes on about the car all over town."

"How come him to be all the way over on this side of town?" It was a mildly invasive question to which Noah did not expect an answer.

"Little change up in my driving schedule tonight. It was gonna be a longer trip, so he was just lettin' me know."

"Ah, ok." Noah let it drop, not wanting to seem overly curious.

By the end of the workday, Noah had a plan in mind. He was not sure if it would work, but he needed to act. He was not due to go over and see Sara that night, but needed to talk to Violet. They passed by the station on their way home each day, and it was their habit to stop, if only to say hello. He opted to wait and see if they stopped. It paid off. Every few days, Violet needed her gas tank filled, and if the weather was warm, she would treat them to a

                    Jenna Cossey

cold soda. Easton especially enjoyed the thrill of getting to pick out his own. He tried every flavor they stocked in Haskins' station. When he got through them all, he tried them again, never settling on a favorite or having the same one twice in a row.

Violet pulled in alongside the pumps and climbed out of the car. "Looks like I could use a bit of gasoline this time, Noah."

"Sure thing, Mrs. Simpson. How we all doin' today?" He smiled at Sara.

"We're all just fine, thank you! Look at that little rascal running across there! He's already decided on a grape soda. He said it as soon as we got in the car this afternoon!"

Sara watched him barreling toward the door and took a precautionary measure, "I told him I wanted a Coca Cola. I guess I better go see that he remembers."

Noah could not have planned it any better. It was just the moment he needed to talk to Violet about his plan.

"Mrs. Simpson," he looked toward the garage and kept his voice low, "I believe I know what I need to do. You know, about that situation I was discussin' with you."

"Yes?" Violet was listening.

"I've got to see if I can see for myself what he's up to. I've got to know where they're goin' with those trucks they're drivin'."

"How do you propose to do that?"

"Well, I thought about volunteerin' to get in there and go with him, but I think it'd be a suspicious thing to them boys if I did that."

"I'd say you're right."

"So the only other thing I can do is try to follow him when he goes tonight."

"Are you sure you can do that without them knowing?"

"No, I'm not, but I know about what time he meets, and I know they meet downtown. If I can watch from afar, then I'll be able to see which truck Tommy is driving and follow him. I can spot him from a mile away, but I need your help."

"I can try. How?"

"I need to use your car. I can't go in that service truck. It makes too much racket, and it don't run fast enough to follow anything."

"I see," Violet pondered the situation in its entirety. "Alright. You can take the car, but you must be careful, Noah. Should I leave it here now?"

"No, let's don't do that. I'd have to give y'all a ride home and then try to explain to Tommy why you left it here."

"That's true." Easton and Sara emerged from the station.

"I'll call the house a little later," Noah said.

"Alright."

It was about seven when he called the house, and Violet answered. "Hello? . . . Yes, I can do that . . . If that's what you think is best . . . Alright, bye now."

He simply asked that she leave the key inside the car. It was a clear night, and he planned to walk from the gas station. He thought it would give him a chance to expend some of his nervous energy. There were other options, but he did not want the neighbors to see the Haskins truck sitting at the Simpson house all night. There was too much potential for idle talk in that. He thought it out and decided his plan was best. He told her he would have the car back the next morning.

About ten o'clock that night, Noah arrived at the house. Almost every light in the neighborhood was off, save one or two folks who had mistakenly left their porch lights burning when they went to bed. There was not an unnatural sound anywhere, and it suddenly occurred to him that starting a car that late at night

 Jenna Cossey

would surely wake the entire street. It was parked nose-first in the driveway, which had a slight grade to it.

I could coast it out of the driveway, at least. It was the best he could do. Once the car was out in the middle of the street, he counted on the Ford's V8 engine firing up as faithfully as always. He took the car out of gear, released the brake, and waited until the last possible moment to turn the engine over. He eased off as quickly as he could without being too aggressive. Banking on the slow-moving nature of most delivery trucks, he parked up the street nearly a block to prevent the car from being seen by anyone in the vicinity of the hardware store. He waited in an adjacent alley and watched for some time. It seemed like hours, but it was only twenty or thirty minutes before he saw Thomas walk down the street and dip into the alley. He knew it was him because of his peculiar gait. A little later, he saw Archie Duncan go in. Soon, three trucks parked in the alley, and the drivers were picked up by a car that Noah did not recognize. Three men emerged from the basement door of the hardware store, but none of them were Thomas. Noah waited.

He waited an hour, but Thomas never emerged. He did not know what to do. If he crossed the street, he risked being seen, but he could not understand why Thomas had not left the building with the others. He started replaying the scene in his mind. *Tommy went in. Archie went in. Three came out, but not Tommy.*

He knew that there had to have been two men inside before Thomas ever arrived. Upon that realization, he made his way across the street. He had no idea what he was walking into, but Thomas was in there, and something was off. When he reached the solid red door, he found it padlocked from the outside as if no one else was expected to exit. He did not spare the silence in the alley. He banged loudly upon the door.

Dunnigan

"Tommy! Tommy!"

He heard nothing. His adrenaline rushed. He hurled himself into the door twice before the padlocked hasp, and the inner locks gave way under his immense power. The door dangled open into the dark basement. He called for Thomas again, but heard nothing. He tried to still himself and listen over the sound of his heart pounding in his ears. He instinctively moved toward the first noise he heard.

"Tommy?"

Finally, a faint choked voice replied, "Noah? Is . . . is that you?"

Unaccustomed to his surroundings and having no idea where the lights were, he closely listened for the weak sound of his brother's voice. He could not see in the pitch darkness. His eyes began to adjust, and he tried to get his bearings. He called out again. "Tommy? Where are you?"

"I'm just over . . . here," Thomas struggled.

He moved a few paces closer to the weak voice. He could make out a heap on the floor near him. He knelt. "Your matches, Tom, your matches!"

"In . . . my . . . pocket," Thomas barely got the words out.

Noah fished the matches from his pocket and struck one of them, hoping to see something, anything.

When the dim light of the match encircled Thomas's body, Noah broke out in a sweat. He was badly beaten. Cuts covered his face. His scalp was encrusted with blood from a sizeable split just below the part in his thick red hair. Noah did the only thing he knew to do. He gathered up the weak, frail body of Thomas and carried him back to the car. He did not know where to go. Banking on the good-heartedness of Violet Simpson once again, he drove to the gas station, placed Thomas in his old bed with a cool rag on his head, and picked up the telephone.

It was past midnight, and the ringing phone pierced through the house like the scream of a bobcat. Violet leaped from the bed and darted to the phone. "Hello? . . . Oh no, is it bad? . . . Call Doc Weathers. I've got it right here. It's 4362 . . . Don't worry about the car . . . Please, it will be alright. Call me if there's any change." She hung up the phone and sat down in a nearby kitchen chair just as Sara came down the stairs.

"Sara . . ."

"What's wrong, Aunt Violet?"

"I guess there's no point keeping it from you."

"Was that Noah on the telephone? I saw the two of you talking earlier today. I heard the car go down the street."

"It was Noah, yes. He went downtown to see what Thomas was up to. He found him, but he's injured. It sounds pretty bad." Violet looked up at Sara.

"How bad?"

"I don't know, but he's going to call a doctor. We'll just have to wait here and see if he calls back. You should get some rest."

"I haven't been asleep since I heard the car leave, Aunt Vi. It's no use now. Noah told me something was wrong. He wouldn't tell me much, but I knew it was bad."

"I was hoping to keep you from the strain of it all, but I suppose I only delayed the inevitable," Violet confessed.

"Those men that came in to talk to Tommy the other week after we'd gone to the movies, they're no good."

"How do you know?"

"I've seen them out and about a time or two. I just have a feeling about them. Especially the one with the dark hair," Sara said.

"Ransom Cahill, the mayor's son—I'm afraid you're right. He doesn't seem to be a very good apple." Violet got up from her chair. "It troubled me greatly to see that Tommy was palling around with them. It troubled Noah too. That's why he told me about it."

"I know. You always seem to have the answers, Aunt Vi. So what now?" Sara fell into her open arms.

"I don't know, Sara. I just don't know. I guess we'll have to wait and see what tomorrow brings."

Back at the station, Noah tried his best to clean Thomas's face. He removed his bloodied shirt and dabbed the defensive wounds on his hands to clean them.

"It took two of them scoundrels, but they got me down, Noah. I got in some good licks before one of 'em hit me upside the head with somethin'." Thomas still spoke weakly and winced with every word. "I don't know what it was, but that's the last I remember. They musta walloped on me some more after I went down. I think my ribs are busted."

"Just be quiet, Tom. Doctor's on his way," Noah tried to calm him.

"It's missin'."

"What?"

"My leg, it's missin'. Them no 'counts took my peg," Thomas said as he grimaced.

While evacuating Thomas from the basement of the hardware store, getting him to the station, calling Violet and the doctor, and trying to clean him up, he did not even notice that the very important item had gone missing in the fray.

"Don't worry, Tommy. We'll figure it out."

His only hope was that Thomas would make it through the night.

     Jenna Cossey

<u>*64*</u>

"The boy's brother made a report this morning. The kid's hurt bad. He may not make it."

Chief Lanham sat behind his desk with his hands interlocked and his chin resting in his thumbs. He was expecting an explanation from Ransom Cahill, but he had none.

"I was at the Grotto. I had nothing to do with it."

"Oh, that's just swell. I'll be sure and tell the fellas in the department that," Chief Lanham's words dripped with sarcasm. "In case you didn't know, that doesn't help my situation here."

"Chief, you've been paid to overlook these 'situations,' and handsomely paid, I might add." Ransom reared back in the chair and glared at him.

Lanham pounded his fist down on the desk. "I did not—" he lowered his voice, "I did not agree to this, Cahill. I did not agree to attempts at murder."

Ransom took time to think before giving a response. "No. I suppose you're right about that. What you did do, however, was take an enormous bribe. You've done it more than once now. All I have to do is drop a little anonymous word to Carollo's gang down in New Orleans and give them the inclination that you've turned over on me. You'll be dead by the end of the week."

"Maybe you forget that I could do the same thing," Lanham threatened.

Ransom's green cat-like eyes had an evil glow, and his face fell into cold placidity. "You must have lost control of your senses, Mr. Tipton Lanham. I'm the son of a wealthy bureaucrat, the son of one of the oldest families in Birmingham, the son of the oldest money in New Orleans. Who would believe a charge like that from a fool like you, the son of a filthy coal miner? You haven't the social or political clout to impugn the Cahill name."

He was so indignant. He was not in favor of the actions Haynes and his cohort took in the beating of Thomas Maclane, but Chief Lanham forced him to take sides. He chose the unscrupulous side, as he had become comfortable doing. He was too heavily involved to renege. With each passing day, he moved his piece on the board, confident that he would be able to play himself out of the mess with the next move.

"Alright. I can see that I'm in a corner here, but what would you have me do? This Noah Maclane is going to expect some action on our part. He's going to want something to be done about this!" He turned his palms upward in a pleading gesture.

"Figure it out. That's part of what you're paid to do. Send him on a wild goose chase," Ransom advised.

"He was up here Tuesday morning and again today. He's not going to let it go. I've seen his type many a time. If it hits the papers, there'll be a whole other slew of questions, and heaven forbid the boy should die, then we'll have a murder on our hands!"

"Well, maybe the elder Maclane needs a little persuasion to help him let this go," said Ransom.

"I want no more violence, Cahill! It's going to be hard enough to explain this Monday night fiasco away!"

"Don't worry. I think I know exactly how to quiet him. That is if he is what I expect." Ransom casually lit a cigarette as though discussing a triviality.

"My hands are tied, but I'm begging you, please, no more violence," Lanham said.

         Jenna Cossey

"You knew it could come to this. Surely, you knew."

Tipton Lanham sat there helpless. He had bet on a thread of decency in the son of a well-known politician raised by two high society families, but he wagered in folly. Now, the magnitude of that folly rose before him in all of its ugliness and depravity. He did not like what he saw, but he was helpless to stop the very beast into which he had helped breathe life. He could not deny the words of Ransom: like him, he was too involved to go backward. Ransom left the office feeling that it was time for a different kind of move in the sordid game he was playing.

If I handle this myself, I can keep Haynes out of it. I know what to do.

The wheels continued to turn.

65

The afternoon bell rang at Dunnigan High School, and Sara gathered her belongings. She left the school building with no reservations about walking the two blocks to Main Street from school. She and Violet had already discussed it.

"Sara, dear, I have a short meeting after school this evening. It shouldn't take very long, a half hour I'd say."

"Alright. Can I walk to Main Street after school while I wait? I'd like to get a thing or two from the five-and-dime."

"Sure." Violet took a bill from her clutch and gave it to Sara. "Here's a dollar. Is that enough?"

"Yes. Thanks, Aunt Vi."

"I'll pick you up there. Be on the lookout for me."

The crisp September air made the walk pleasant, and the sights along the street helped her clear her mind. She was worried about Thomas, and Noah had not been to see her. He watched Thomas as closely as he could and tried to keep up with his workload. She understood, but she missed him. All she could think about was how to help him, how she could repay the kindness he showed her. She did not yet know how best to do it, but she was determined to figure out something. She mulled it over on her foot journey. Not too many minutes passed before she turned onto Main street. On the corner, there was a cafe, and the smell of fried chicken wafted from the open door. The calls of the cooks came over the service bell that rang each time they completed an order. She reached the dime store and entered. When the door closed, it muffled the sounds of the street behind her.

"Afternoon, miss! What can I do ya for?"

"Well, I was thinking on a pad of stationery. Nothing fancy, just something for letters," Sara explained.

"This is what most use. It's a five-by-eight pad. The pages are lined on both sides, and they tear away at the top." He fanned open the pad and fluttered the pages with his thumb. The paper looked like the kind she had seen her mother use for writing letters. It seemed like an appropriate choice.

"Alright, I'll take one of these. Also, perhaps an extra pencil or two."

"Sure thing, miss. Anything else?"

"No, I think that's all."

"That'll be thirty-three cents." She handed him the dollar bill. "Sixty-seven cents is your change, miss. Have a nice evenin'."

Sara thanked the man and walked out of the store. She looked down at her watch. The sun glinted off of the jewels around the face, and she repositioned herself so that she could see the time: three fifteen.

Sara expected that she had enough time to go to the drugstore fountain. She never grew tired of the aroma of sweet confections. She took a seat at the counter, and a friendly young man with rose-colored cheeks approached. His white soda jerk hat was tilted to the side over his neatly combed, pomade-coated blonde hair.

"Afternoon, Ms. Sara!"

"Hi, Milton."

"Good to see ya. Where's the others?"

"Aunt Violet had a meeting. They'll be picking me up here shortly."

"Oh, I see. Well, what can I get for ya? Cone? Soda?"

"Chocolate soda. It's getting to be my favorite!"

"Chocolate soda? Coming right up."

Sara watched as he grabbed a tall downturned glass from the ornate back bar. He delivered a shot of chocolate syrup into the glass, opened the refrigerated case in the fountain, and added heavy cream. After returning the bag of cream, he fetched a long metal spoon and vigorously stirred the concoction. With the jerk of a handle, a small quantity of carbonated water jettisoned into the glass. He added ice cream, stirred gently, and added a bit more soda. With the final bob of the spoon, the flavor was distributed. He was very efficient. *I bet he could do this blindfolded.*

Suddenly, she developed an unsettling sensation. It broke her concentration on Milton, and she began to fiddle with the small paper bag that held her purchases from the dime store.

"Whipped cream and a cherry?" Milton distracted her from the sense.

"Oh—yes, yes. Sorry." She continued to sit there with the unusual feeling. She could not identify it, so she tried to ignore it. She started to drink the soda. She stopped. She could not continue to ignore it. Then she realized what it was. *I'm being watched.*

She shifted around in the stool, trying not to appear uneasy. She faced forward, but cut her eyes left and then right. Several people moved about in the room. *Maybe I'm mistaken.*

She took another sip of the soda and raised her eyes from the glass. Someone was sitting next to her. She had not heard him approach. *Where did he come from?*

"Creme de menthe, Milt."

It was him. Her heart raced. She knew Ransom Cahill was involved in the beating of Thomas, even though she did not know how. She wanted to run, but she was frozen. She sat there passively swirling her straw in the soda, trying to figure out what to do.

 Jenna Cossey

"Sara, isn't it?"

It startled her. She did not expect him to speak to her. It created more tension. *How does he remember my name? How long has he been watching me?*

"I believe we've met before. Once or twice, perhaps. Not too long ago at the ice cream parlor, I believe it was." He oozed a fake charm that turned her stomach. The barrage of questions all but forced her to give some response.

"Yes, I remember," she said as she tried to remain calm on the outside.

Ransom rested one foot on the brass railing along the floor beneath the marble counter. He spun to face her and moved his drink a little closer to her. She felt trapped.

"Noah Maclane. He's your beau?"

She said nothing.

"Terrible thing, what happened to his brother."

She cut her eyes at him. *No! Why did I do that? Control yourself.* He had struck a nerve. *I've got to get out of here, or I'm going to scream.*

Sara placed a few coins on the counter and calmly rose. Ransom was between her and the door. She nodded at him, "Afternoon, Mr. Cahill." She sidestepped his left foot that was kicked out behind her stool and moved toward the door at a steady pace. Her heart raced, and sweat covered her hands. She opened the door. She had been holding her breath, and the fresh air made her gasp. She turned toward the dime store.

Aunt Vi, where are you?

Someone caught her by the arm.

"You forgot this." It was Ransom Cahill with her bag from the dime store.

She took the bag and turned back around, but he did not let go of her arm. She looked into his green dagger-like eyes. He tightened his grip.

"Let go," Sara weakly said.

Ransom tightened his grip. "Listen, doll," he stepped even closer, "you tell your beau he better let this thing drop with the law."

Sara could not say anything else. Her jaw clenched shut as his fingers began to touch around her small arm.

He spoke in a low gruff whisper. His breath smelled of scotch and creme de menthe. "If he makes any more trouble, that brother of his will be the least of his worries." He gave her a quick, violent shake.

Still in his clutches and unable to speak, Sara stood there. *Someone help me, anyone.*

"Take your hands off of her!" Violet's voice cut through the air like a knife.

His head snapped around toward her voice. He shoved the paper bag at Sara and stormed away. It lasted forever in her head, but it happened so quickly that no onlookers even noticed.

Violet retrieved the bag from the ground. "Come on, get in the car."

In the car, Sara sat numbed by fear and unable to speak. She could not even cry. She cradled her throbbing right arm and looked through the windshield of the car. Her eyes were glazed over with terror.

Easton was in the back seat. "Sara? What's wrong? Aunt Vi, what's the matter with Sara?"

"Sit down and don't say another word, Easton. Not another word," Violet demanded. "This has gone far enough," Violet said quietly, almost as if to herself. "It's gone *too* far."

 Jenna Cossey

<u>*66*</u>

Noah watched Dr. Weathers examine Thomas back at the station. The aroma in the room caused his mind to drift backward.

*   *   *

His weak, clammy body lay outstretched on the bed. Thomas was pale and his lips were encircled by a crust of dryness that remained despite the copious amount of water Noah had offered him. The room wreaked of a hot ferrous odor. It was poignant, but not foul—the smell of blood. The open doors of the farmhouse beckoned a fall breeze through it. Damp cloth in hand, Noah dabbed Thomas' arms and face to cool his skin. He opened his eyes and looked at him.

"Am I gonna die, Noah?"

"No, Tommy. You ain't gonna die. I ain't gonna let ya. You just lay still there."

He was too weak to lift his head, but he cast his eyes downward to look beyond his waistline. "My leg, it's 'bout plum gone ain't it?"

"Well, yeah. I reckon it is." Noah reluctantly affirmed.

"If I don't die, I won't be no good for nothin' anyways. What am I gonna do with my leg gone?"

"Don't talk like that, Tommy. Doc McGee said once this heals up, you'll be fine. Yours ain't the first leg he's seen took off. When did you ever let anything stop you before?"

"Never, but I used to have two legs."

"So what? Now you got one and part of one. We're gonna get you goin' again, little brother. You bet on it. You and me's gonna be doin' all the stuff we always done here before too long."

"I hope you're right."

"Say, don't you remember old man Looper? He ain't got but one leg," Noah said.

"Well, at least I ain't the only one."

"'Course you ain't!" Noah half smiled.

"That don't make me feel no better about it."

"Maybe not, but don't you remember all them time's he chased us out of his orchard for pickin' fruit? Don't slow him down none!" He did his best to give Thomas some encouragement, but he began to feel he was doing more harm than good.

"No, reckon it don't." Thomas stared at the ceiling in the room and a tear fell from his eye and ran behind his ear. "It hurts real bad, Noah. I feel awful sick."

"It's gonna be alright, Tommy. I'm gonna look out for ya. Don't you worry none. Get some rest."

*　　*　　*

"He needs to be hospitalized immediately. His condition is worsening. Without more rigorous care, his decline will continue," Dr. Weathers said.

"So let's get him there." It seemed plain to Noah.

"The facility in Dunnigan would be of some benefit, but if we could have him transported to Birmingham, I suspect it would significantly increase the likelihood of his recovery."

"Birmingham?"

"Yes, they have some of the best physicians, and the most modern equipment available in the three states. If you so desire, I can contact them. We'll put him on the evening train, and they'll receive him at the depot."

"They can do that?" Noah was surprised.

"Yes, in fact, we did just that after the mining accident a few weeks ago."

It was no question in Noah's mind. He had to get Thomas to Birmingham. He was buried in work at the station, and the backlog continued to grow. He needed to call Mr. Haskins to make some arrangements, but he did not know where to begin. Everything that he needed to do created a vortex of panic that he had never before experienced. *Keep it together, Noah. Keep it together.*

He glanced at Thomas who lay there with limp body and shallow breath. "Alright, Birmingham it is."

"Very well. When I return to my office, I will phone them. You'll want to make the appropriate arrangements with the rail office." Dr. Weathers gathered his belongings and began his departure.

"Yessir. How much do I owe you?"

"We'll settle it later, Mr. Maclane. Goodbye."

He forced himself into a razor-sharp focus as he made a series of phone calls. The first was to the rail station to arrange for him and Thomas to travel on the evening express to Birmingham, and the second to Mr. Haskins. He mercifully spared him any chastisement and agreed to keep the gas station open without his help for a day or two. "I'll need you back here in a few days, or I'll be forced to find someone else to come in and do the work as bad as I'd hate to do it."

"Yes sir, I understand. If I can have just a few days to get Tommy situated, I'll get back to work. I'll do it as quick as I can. You have my word."

Mr. Haskins knew that his word was good, and he was empathetic to the degree that his business sense allowed.

Noah prepared a small satchel of items for the trip. It was not long before the train would leave the station. All of the money he possessed, he put in a sock and placed it in the satchel. He felt like he was forgetting something.

Sara. I've got to call Sara.

He returned to the office and picked up the phone. He gave Violet an update on Thomas, informed her of Dr. Weathers' directives and the travel plans, and then asked to speak with Sara.

"I'm afraid she's unwell this evening, Noah."

It hit him like a bullet. "What's the matter? She's sick?"

"Yes, you could say that. She—"

"I'll be right over."

"I don't know if that's the best thing right n—"

He hung up the phone, checked on Thomas, and darted out the door to make his way to see Sara before he left. He jumped into the service truck, and sent it jangling down the road with the motor wound out. When he pulled up to the house, Violet met him halfway.

"Noah, you've got to listen to me. I don't think it's the best time to try and talk to Sara."

He was still confused, running on high octane, and wasted no time. "What's going on here? I'm missin' something."

"Trust me, just trust me. She is in no position to talk right now, going away or not. I'll give her your regards," she said.

"Why? Tell me *why!*" His frustration grew.

"It's for the best." Violet stood there with arms folded and chewed her lower lip.

"Listen, Violet—Mrs. Simpson—I've never wanted to be a nuisance to anybody, but that's exactly what I'm about to be. Now Tommy is laying back at the shop, and he's liable to wake up any minute. They're comin' to get him and take him to the station at four thirty, and last time I checked, it was after three. Now if you don't want me to see Sara, then I reckon I'll just have to accept that, but I'm tellin' you right now that I ain't leavin' from here until you tell me *why*!"

His words came through strong. He was serious, and Violet knew that she had no choice but to tell him the truth.

There was a brief silence and she would not look at him. "Now I mean it. I can't abide with this hem-hawing around. Tell me what's goin' on here!"

"Alright. Alright. Frankly, I was hoping to spare you this, but you've left me with no choice."

"Yes, come to it," he urged her on.

"This afternoon, Sara was downtown at the drugstore. She was to wait for me to pick her up on Main Street. When I arrived . . ." Violet hesitated.

"Yeah, go on."

"Ransom Cahill had Sara up by the arm out on the sidewalk. He was threatening her. She closed up on me, and I practically had to pry it out of her. It seems as though he threatened her with violence. I don't know if he hurt her otherwise—I can't tell yet— but she's in quite a shape."

Noah was addled. It made no sense to him. *Why is Ransom Cahill threatening Sara?*

"She wasn't very clear, but in not so many words. He told her that if you pressed this thing with Tommy, there'd be more trouble. She was shaken by the whole thing, Noah. Her father . . . She lived in fear for years before coming here. This has given her quite the setback."

On the front lawn of Violet Simpson's house, Noah's armor cracked. He felt completely helpless. For so long, his life had centered around the shelter and protection of Thomas. He found, in Sara, someone he wished to protect even more, and he had failed on both counts. His fists were balled in anger. He looked off into the distance because he could not bear to look Violet in the eyes.

"I see. I . . . I don't know what to say, Mrs. Simpson. You'll please give Sara my regards, and . . . and tell her I love her. It's a terrible mess I'm in, and I can see where nobody, least of all her, would want any part in it." His fists relaxed, and his head dropped. "Goodbye now."

The strong, square-framed young man wilted. He was furious and devastated. As he opened the door of the truck, he felt like overturning the vehicle with his rage.

He was trapped.

Ransom Cahill and his associates deserved a fight, but he could not give it to them. Too many lives hung in the balance. He slammed the door of the truck and reached for the gearshift. He pressed the starter to the floor, and the engine chugged to a start.

"Wait! Noah! Wait!" Violet jogged to the side of the truck and hung on to the window. "Maybe I can help."

"No, Mrs. Simpson. Stay out of it. I've caused enough trouble for everybody already," Noah said as he looked out the windshield.

"Truly, Noah. Listen. At least I could try," Violet tried to show compassion. "Maybe it won't do any good, but we won't know unless we try. You go on to Birmingham with Thomas. See him well."

"If you say so," Noah was doubtful, "Bye now."

The men that Dr. Weathers had summoned to transport Thomas to the rail station arrived on time. They carefully loaded him into the back of a combination car and saw him onto the

     Jenna Cossey

train headed for Birmingham. The whistle blew, and the forward jerk of the cars awakened Thomas.

"Noah?"

"Yeah, little brother?"

"Where we goin'?"

"Goin' to Birmingham, Tom, to get you better."

"Am I gonna die Noah?"

"Just try to rest, Tommy. Just try to rest."

<u>**67**</u>

"Mrs. Charlotte, you know it don't give me no pleasure to have to tell you such."

Cephas stood before her, wringing his hands. The oversized room engulfed the high-backed chair in which she sat. The house was quiet, and it seemed that even the noise of Zennia's culinary efforts ceased to carry forward from the rear of the house. Charlotte glared out one of the large front windows.

"Who else knows of this?"

"Don't rightly know, ma'am. I only happened up on it myself. Mr. Ransom don't even know ol' Cephas seen him."

"No crowd was gathered I hope." Her chin rested in her right hand.

"No'm, it was over'n done with jus' like that," Cephas snapped his fingers.

"Who was the girl?"

He did not understand what difference it made, but answered anyway, "I don't rightly know, but I'm fairly certain the little filly is Violet Simpson's kinfolk what's come to town to live with her. That's the lady that broke it up."

Charlotte Cahill dropped her forehead into her palm. "Oh dear. Violet Simpson."

"She a spark," he said.

"Yes. She's been very vocal in the public meetings. She's so nouveau riche."

In truth, Violet was beyond reproach among most in Dunnigan. She was the kind of woman that others admired. She was tenacious, brave, and independent. When Joseph Simpson had died earlier in the year, she wasted no time wallowing in self-pity. She found other ways to give of her time, like volunteering to teach in the local "opportunity schools" for adult education. She was vocal concerning the budget for the area schools and the need for more transparency from people like Mayor Cahill. It endeared the locals to her, but she made all of the blue-blooded sons and daughters of the South cringe. What loathed Charlotte Cahill and her afternoon tea party patrons even further was her indifference to their opinions.

"Cephas, do you believe Chief Lanham is involved in this?"

"Yes'm, 'less I been misinformed, he bought and paid for."

"So then I'll write a letter. You will deliver it."

"What kinda letter, Mrs. Charlotte?"

"The kind that warns him of the distinct possibility that Violet Simpson will bring this to the police, and the kind that also warns of his being dealt with if he doesn't dispense with the matter as I direct." Her eyes intensified.

"Oh."

Cephas disliked the idea, but his loyalty to Charlotte Palmer Cahill was paramount to his misgivings. She prepared the letter, including with it an undisclosed sum of money. It lacked the etiquette of her typical correspondence and read:

Chief Lanham,

Should one Violet Simpson present herself at your precinct with a complaint concerning Ransom Cahill, it would be in your best interest to see that it is dismissed out of hand as a fallacious attack intended in retaliation against Mayor Cahill for his recent decisions from the mayoral chair. It is widely known that Mrs. Simpson has been a vocal critic of the mayor. Should you give her false accusations credence, it will be to your detriment.

C.P.C.

As directed, but much to his chagrin, Cephas delivered the letter to Tipton Lanham the next day. It was not the first time that Chief Lanham had received directives from Mrs. Cahill. The letter achieved its purpose, and the days following proved her correct in her assumption about Violet Simpson's immediate course of action.

As was so often the case for her and her ilk, she underestimated the wit, influence, and sheer determination of a woman like Violet. Her sense of self-importance prevented her from conceiving that Violet might be a step ahead of her.

68

Sara went to school the morning after the encounter with Ransom, but she did so with no sleep. She could not focus on anything. As each class came to an end, the bell signaled a space of time completely lost to her. *What was the teacher talking about? My paper is blank. What's the assignment?*

Overwrought, she quickly mined information from her classmates to figure out what she needed to do to keep up. When she arrived home that afternoon, the accumulation of work was greater than she expected. She sat down at the writing table in her room. Her arm still ached from where Ransom had snatched it. She stared at the books spread across the table. For the first time since the beginning of the school year, she was behind, if only a little.

Alright, be big about this. You've got to get this work done. She tried to coax herself to begin the work. She reached for a pencil, but when she started to write, the soreness in her arm made her wince. She withdrew it into her lap and lowered her head to the table.

For months, she had been waiting on the other foot to fall. She constantly beat back the nagging feeling that happiness and normalcy could not last. The game that Ransom Cahill played had turned her fear into reality. He successfully flung her backward into the hopelessness she thought she had left behind for good.

The sleeplessness from the previous night caught up with her, and she dozed off with her head on the writing table. Half asleep, her mind began to swim in the roiling current of memories that Ransom Cahill had summoned with his rotten behavior.

*   *   *

"Daddy, please don't disturb her. She was awfully sick today, and she's only just now gone off to sleep. I'm making supper. She doesn't need to be on her feet," Sara tried to reason with Walter Wheeler.

The air in the room felt stagnated, and the smell of the wood burning in the cookstove mingled with the scent of moonshine that effused from Walter Wheeler's dirty sweat-covered body.

"I never thought I'd live to see the day when my sass-mouthed daughter would order me 'round under my own roof."

Sara kept her voice very low, hoping that he would take the hint, "Daddy, please."

He squinted at her and turned his head as if he strained to hear. "What? Girl, if you've got somethin' you want to say, speak up!"

"Shhh! You're going to wake mother. Now please, Daddy, please stop hollering."

He bit his lip and paced around the kitchen, while Sara finished cooking the remaining parts of the meal.

"Where's that boy?"

"He's down at the creek, playing. He'll be along in a minute." She had purposefully not summoned him when their father arrived home in his condition.

"Where's my razor strap? I'll get him up—"

Sara intervened by placing a large pot of green beans on the table. It was littered with halved potatoes and flavored with fatback. "Here, sit down and eat, Daddy."

The distraction was successful. He subsided into one of the thin creaky chairs that surrounded the table. She placed a few more items in front of him, the last of which caught his attention: fried cornbread patties.

"Ah, slide me that butter." His mood quickly swung to extremes, as it was apt to do when he was drunk. "These are good, taste almost like Tildy's. Tildy! Get in here!" he shouted.

"No! Stop, Daddy! Don't wake her!" Sara begged once again.

Like a cannon, he exploded into a fit of rage. "Stop tellin' me I can't call your mother in here to this kitchen table! Tildy! Tildy! I want the whole family settin' right here at this table!" He slammed his hand into the corner of the table.

The bedroom door creaked, and Matilda Wheeler appeared in the doorway. She was pale and dark circles hung beneath her eyes. Her soft brown hair was disarranged over her thin shoulders. Barely having been able to leave the bed, she leaned against the door facing and weakly cradled the bump she carried at her midsection.

Sick, feeble, and heavy with child, she mustered the strength to speak. "Walt, what is going on in here?"

He was unfazed by her condition. "Well, I'll tell ya what's goin' on, Tildy. I want to sit around this table and break bread with my family. Now's that too much to ask?" He snapped his head toward Sara. "I don't think it's too much to ask. So I want you to sit down here, Tildy, and I want this sass over here to go out and call that boy a mine up here, and we're all gonna set down and eat together!"

Matilda gave Sara a look that let her know she intended to humor him in hopes of alleviating the trouble. The smell of the food drifted into her nostrils, and her lip curled. She took a deep breath as her stomach turned. Sara watched as her mother expended reserves of energy she could not spare to make it across the kitchen and lower herself into a chair. She was bewildered by her attempt to appease the drunken irrationality of her father. She turned toward the back door. She knew her father wanted her to call Easton, but she saw the potential for him to bear the brunt of their father's tirades.

"I won't do it," she said it before she could stop herself.

"What'd you say?"

Better me than Easton. "I said I won't do it."

Walter Wheeler charged across the room. He slapped Sara hard across the face, and she fell against the wall.

Matilda leveraged herself up from her chair. "Walt! Stop it!"

"Shut up, woman! She's sassed me for the last time! She'll think twice next time."

He barreled through the house. They knew he was going after the razor strap.

"Sara, go!" Matilda cried as she moved in front of one of the openings that led from the kitchen. The blow left Sara addled. Her ears rang. She heard the instruction, but it did not register with her until he barged through the opening.

She saw it in slow motion.

He collided with Matilda and sent her crashing to the floor. Sara shoved the screen door open with both hands and tried to run. When her foot touched the top step, she felt the hand of her father around her arm. He yanked her backward as she tried to propel herself forward. He struck her with the strap. Her legs pumped forward, and he struck her again. Then she slipped.

She was falling. He was falling. Both were falling down the porch steps, and he still had her by the arm as they tumbled.

Sara hit the ground head first. Everything went black.

She awoke to a small voice, "Sara! Sara!"

It was Easton. "Sara, wake up! What's the matter with everybody? Wake up!"

                    Jenna Cossey

Her ears still rang. Her arm ached. Her head throbbed in time with her heartbeat. She gathered herself off of the ground with a helpful tug from Easton. Nearby, Walter Wheeler lay unconscious from the combined effect of his intoxication and the fall.

Mama. She remembered seeing her mother knocked to the floor. She forced her heavy feet to carry her back up the porch steps and into the kitchen. Matilda lay on the floor in a pool of her own blood with shallow breath.

"Mama!" Sara dropped to the floor and cradled her head in her lap. "Mama? Come on, Mama! Easton, get that dishcloth! Go dip it in the bucket. Bring a dipper full of water! Hurry!"

He skittered out to the porch and returned with the items. Sara laid the damp cloth across her mother's forehead and lightly tapped her jaw to try and rouse her.

"Mama?" Her eyes cracked open. "Mama, come on. Come on around here now. You've got to wake up." She let out a faint groan.

Sara thought as quickly as she could, trying to figure out what to do. "Easton. Listen to me. Are you listening? Stop crying now. Mama needs your help. Are you listening?" He nodded. "You've got to run to the Banks' place. You have to run as fast as you can. You have to tell Mr. and Mrs. Banks that Mama is hurt and have them come and bring their truck. You run. Don't stop. You hear? Run! Go!"

Over half a mile separated the Wheeler and Banks houses. Easton ran as fast as his legs could carry him down the rough dirt road.

Sara stayed with her mother and continued to keep her awake, "Mama? Mama, can you hear me?"

She lost track of time, but some minutes later, Matilda opened her eyes. All of the color was gone from her face, and she labored to breathe. She looked at her daughter, and her eyes filled with tears, "Sara sweet."

"Mama, it's gonna be alright. Easton's gone to get help. It's gonna be alright." Sara began to cry too.

"I love you, my sweet," Matilda forced out the words, and her eyes closed.

"Mama?" she tried to wake her again. "Mama?"

*   *   *

Sara jerked upright in the chair with her heart racing. She clutched her aching arm, the memories were more vivid than ever.

<u>*69*</u>

"There were no other witnesses to this occurrence?"

"I cannot answer that, sir."

Violet wore a resolute expression that had oft prompted people to take her seriously. She was not a "temperamental woman" as some of the men in the law-making and keeping organizations in Dunnigan tried to characterize her. She was, in actuality, quite the opposite. When tempers flared and untruths permeated the general populace, her cool head prevailed in the public meetings. Much of the community held the young widowed teacher's opinions in surprisingly high regard, which helped to convince them on a great many matters when it came to the education system in Dunnigan. It was that same unwavering resolve that ushered her into the office of Chief Tipton Lanham after Ransom laid hold on Sara.

He twirled a fountain pen between his thumbs and fingers. He listened to her complaint with an aggravated expression. He knew full well that she was not one to make false statements, but he had received a separate directive that was too big to ignore. "Mrs. Simpson, of course, you understand that it's very difficult to make a report with so little information."

"Just exactly how much information do you need, Officer Lanham?" She remained unperturbed.

He dropped his pen. "Without anyone to corroborate your claims, it is no more than that—a claim. I can't be expected to waste my time on every spat that happens in the street."

"This was not a spat. Ransom Cahill assaulted and threatened my niece. Who knows how far it would have gone if I hadn't shown up when I did?"

"Alright, alright. I'll look into it." Lanham was dismissive.

"I see. I think I understand exactly what you mean to do." She got up from her seat.

"I'm sure I don't know what you mean, Mrs. Simpson."

"Don't play daft with me, Officer Lanham. I wasn't born last night. I know the hold that the Cahills and their cronies have in this town. How many people are going to have to be hurt before you stop this boy and his pathetic little mob from terrorizing innocent people?"

"Mrs. Simpson, please. That's enough. Now I've told you I'll look into the matter and—"

"Yes, you'll look into it. Tell me, will you look into it as thoroughly as you are looking into Thomas Maclane's beating?" She gave him a cool stare as she stood by the door of his office.

He began to understand that his allegiance to the Cahills was conspicuous. He wanted to be ashamed for shirking his sworn duty, but he was chained to those who purchased the power of his office. Deep down, he knew that he was very wrong. A part of him even cared about the corruption. His throat tightened, and he uttered a final perfunctory assurance.

"I'll . . . ahem . . . I'll look into it, Mrs. Simpson."

She remained calm during her attempt to spur him to action, but the trauma Ransom Cahill had inflicted on Sara stoked a fire within her that was difficult to contain. After all, Sara had suffered enough at the hands of her father. The loss of her mother by tragic circumstances was enough to break the spirit of any person, young or old. Violet had tediously worked to integrate her into a new comfortable life where she could regain hope and free herself from the weight of her old life. Who was Ransom Cahill to interrupt that quest for tranquility? Who did the Cahills think they were that justice and fairness should not be brought to their doorstep?

When Noah had visited before his departure to Birmingham, she stupidly let herself believe that she could prompt some action on the part of Chief Lanham and his force. Her mission at the precinct was a boondoggle. As she left town, her mind churned with anger and frustration. She turned down Ketcherside Drive. Easton was with the Carson children, and she saw them playing together in the yard. She stopped in front of the Carson house. "You ready to come on home, little man?"

"Aww! Can't me and them play a little longer?"

She looked at her watch. "Alright. Just a little longer. I'll call for you in a little while. You be listening for me!"

"Yes, Aunt Vi! I'll be listenin'!"

His childish innocence once again left him oblivious to the events of the day before. At least, Violet thought, she could be thankful for that. *There has to be something I can do about all of this.*

She walked into the house and listened. "Sara?" Hearing nothing, she felt a slight panic. *Where is she?*

She made her way up the stairs. When she reached Sara's bedroom, she found her sound asleep at her writing desk. It only fueled her ire. Neither had slept the night before. Both were taken aback by the incident downtown. Sara had very little to say, and Violet found that she did not have any words that seemed adequate to soothe her. One of the few things Sara managed to tell her was, "I couldn't get away. When he grabbed my arm, it was . . . it was like someone else was there. It took away all of my strength, Aunt Violet."

Indeed, it had temporarily taken all of her strength. Violet knew that she was hurting. She knew that Ransom Cahill's actions had reopened some of her deepest wounds. Now Violet was in a terrible position. She knew something needed doing, but she could not depend on anyone influenced by the Cahills to do it. One thought prevailed in her troubled mind. *Joseph would've known what to do.*

She returned downstairs, went into her room, and sat at her bedside. A picture of Joseph still rested on the bureau, and she looked at his likeness as if she expected it to direct her what to do. Underneath the photo, she kept some of his personal effects in a drawer. They were mostly things taken from his desk at the bank in Birmingham. She knew the significance of some, but others she did not. She had often combed through the items, but she did so again, looking for answers or at least a distraction. There were several letters in the drawer. They had all been opened by the engraved silver letter opener that lay alongside them. She picked up the small bundle of envelopes and thumbed through them. One return address caught her eye: "U.S. Department of the Treasury." She vaguely remembered looking at it before, but she slid the paper out of the envelope and read it. It was a letter thanking Joseph for his assistance in a money laundering case.

Suddenly, murky conversational details Joseph shared just weeks before his death became clear again. She remembered it all now. In confidence, he had told her that he was assisting a federal officer in poring over several financial documents. They were linked to an operation based in Chicago that was doing illegal business in Birmingham. When the agents traced funds to his bank, they asked him to aid their investigation from within. He later learned that they investigated him for some time before asking his help. In the end, his knowledge of the bank, its funds, and transactions provided tremendous assistance to the Treasury Department. Violet was never able to dismiss the possibility that his cooperation had cost him his life. She could only take solace in the fact that he had showed great bravery. Joseph Simpson was called upon to aid law and order at great personal risk, and he did so without hesitation.

Violet knew that bringing Sara and Easton to live with her would come with challenges. She was not their mother—she was not even *a* mother—so she was forced to rely on her personal and professional experience as she tried to help Sara traverse the deep waters of her life. She was more unsure of herself than she ever could have imagined. She constantly worried whether or not she was truly giving her niece the advice she needed. Self-worth, intelligence, love, and the ability to be loved were all things that she wanted Sara to have, but she could not give those things to her. All she could do was nurture and protect her, but as it concerned Ransom Cahill, she had failed in that effort. When she attempted to resolve it in her mind, there was a moment when she blamed Noah, but as she sat there trying to figure out what to do, she too felt a little bit helpless. She had a thought. *I guess this is how Noah feels . . . helpless.*

She knew he loved Sara. She had never seen a young man with such a good heart. She was nothing if not a keen judge of character. She saw his goodness, and she knew that he would never have intentionally brought harm or danger to Sara. She really wanted to deliver them all from the plight, but she did not know how. Inspired by Joseph anew, she decided on a course of action. She was not satisfied that it was the right thing to do, but she knew that tackling the mess Ransom Cahill continued to create would require an unconventional approach. All she could do to keep her word to Noah was try.

___70___

Hospitals seemed odd to Noah. The smell of ether filled his nostrils and permeated the fibers of his clothing. The days felt long, and they were punctuated by Thomas's elusive periods of alertness. Every hour that passed without him becoming able to sit up and converse caused Noah to grow more concerned. Most of the time, he did not know what the nurses and doctors were doing as they scurried in and out of the room, but it appeared that they were doing everything possible for his brother.

The weekend approached, and he knew that he could not stay in Birmingham if he wanted to keep his job. Mr. Haskins was understanding at the outset, but if Noah stayed gone too long, it would force him to make a difficult business decision and hire someone else to do the work or risk losing customers. Friday afternoon came, and there was little improvement for Thomas. When a group of men in long white coats came to visit, Noah listened intently as they bantered.

"As indicated, our radiographs show that the patient is suffering from a pneumothorax."

They all nodded.

"The pneumothorax appears to be the result of trauma to the ribcage. Notice the contusions along here." The doctor removed the covers, revealing the still bruised side of Thomas. "Complicating the matter is that all signs seem to be pointing to a cerebral hemorrhage. With the patient's lack of consciousness, it is difficult to fully understand all of the symptoms."

There was more head nodding and chatter.

 Jenna Cossey

"I move that we pursue an attempt to deal with the pneumothorax. Improving the oxygen supply could give the internal systems what they need to promote consciousness."

The group of men agreed once again, and began to shuffle out of the room.

Noah had listened intently, but was unable to glean anything from it. *Pneumothorax? What's that? What's cerebral hemorrhage? I don't know what cerebral or hemorrhage means.*

As the team of doctors disappeared into the hallway, he darted out of the room behind them. "Excuse me, sir, sirs, doctors."

They stopped and faced him before they directed their eyes toward the eldest-looking of the crew.

"Um, ah, excuse me, sir. I hate to trouble y'all, but, um . . . that's my brother in there y'all was talkin' over, and I was listening to what y'all was sayin'."

"Yes?" said the doctor.

"Well, I'll tell ya, none of it made a lick of sense to me. Could I trouble you to tell it to me so I can understand what's going on? Can you tell me why he's not waking up?"

The seriousness on the doctor's face melted into an understanding expression as he waved the rest of the team away. "Of course, son. You say this is your brother?"

"Yes, sir. I'm his brother. Name's Noah Maclane."

The doctor extended a hand to him. "I'm pleased to meet you, Noah. I'm Dr. Brand. I'm very sorry that your brother is experiencing this. We are doing all that we can to bring him around, but he has suffered severe trauma."

"Yessir."

"In short, he has a lung that most surely was punctured by a broken rib. I believe his inability to breathe normally is affecting his recovery just as much as the head injury. It appears that the blow he took to the head, while severe, did not fracture his skull. However, there is some pressure on his brain from the bleeding. You see, the brain rests inside the skull with a bit of room to spare." He raised a closed fist and shielded it with his other open hand. "When someone takes a blow to the head, it causes the brain to rattle around inside." The doctor let his closed fist bump against his open hand, giving Noah a visual.

"Oh." Noah immediately wished he had not asked for the discouraging information.

"He can make a recovery, but we need to operate so that the lung will be able to heal and allow him to breathe more efficiently. Perhaps the head trauma will resolve with more time."

"Doc, I'm not a kid, so I don't want you to beat around the bush about this. Is he gonna make it?" He looked into the doctor's eyes with a somber stare.

"Son, I'd like to give you some guarantee, but he is just in a very delicate condition presently. We are doing all that we can, and I assure you that we will continue to do so." He put his hand on Noah's broad, thick shoulder and gave him a few pats of reassurance.

"Alright. Thank you."

The doctor walked away, and Noah leaned against the wall, trying to process all of the news. He had rarely done so since moving away from home, but he felt a need to contact his mother and father. *Mother would want to know that Tommy is hurt.*

He went to the hospital entrance where a small army of receptionists busily coordinated the movements of the patients and visitors.

"Excuse me, miss. Where can I send a telegram?"

"If you go down the street one block, there's an office on the opposite side of the street."

 Jenna Cossey

He made his way down the street, pondering what to include in his message. When he arrived, he greeted the cable messenger who advised him to include only the necessary information on the form.

Ma and Pa,

At Hillman Hospital Birmingham. Tom badly injured, might not make it.

Please come.

Noah

The gravity of Thomas's condition did not settle in until Noah wrote the words.

He might not make it.

There was only one other person he wished he could talk to that afternoon: Sara. He wanted to call her, but he could not bring himself to do it. He felt that he had failed her just as much as Thomas. Not knowing what he would say, he did not place the long-distance call to Dunnigan. Instead, he resigned himself back to the bedside of Thomas and hoped for a breakthrough.

71

The death of Thomas Maclane was like a bolt out of the blue for Sara. Everything happened so quickly that she missed the real urgency of his condition. When she received the news, emotions flooded her. She could not help but feel sadness for Noah. When Violet finally revealed the circumstances surrounding the injury and death, it angered Sara. Ransom Cahill and Haynes had fast managed to create serious havoc in their lives. She was surprised to think that she could have doubted one man's ability to destroy multiple lives when she had seen it before. In the back of her mind, she developed a persistent fear of what else might come from the hands of Ransom and his crew. She loved Noah. She wanted to offer him the comfort and patience he had so freely given to her when she was new to Dunnigan and struggling with her own portion of grief. The deep admiration and trust she had for him began to overpower the emotions Ransom had rekindled in her. All she could think of was how to help Noah through it.

Her love for Noah was lifting her from the despair into which she had regressed. As quickly as she had plunged, her tremendous desire to give him her steadfast support picked her up. She felt beholden to him, because he had helped her gain a sense of self-worth that she never knew she was lacking. He made her believe that she deserved a life of love, happiness, and fulfillment. He had showed her that there was much more to life than what she had come to expect. She made a pact with herself. She would strengthen herself in order to strengthen Noah, but she also

     Jenna Cossey

pledged that she would never again let the dark times in her life cast a shadow on the happiness that she learned was possible.

She tried to turn the page. Violet told her she would always miss her mother, but she knew her mother would have wanted her to have a good life. Despite the unexpected turn, Sara was determined not to be a victim of her past. She tried to have peace about the things she could not change. After all, the terrible situation she encountered before leaving Tennessee did bring her to Dunnigan, and there she had received the care and guidance of Violet as well as the unconditional love of Noah. If she was to embrace her new life, she had to do some letting go.

<u>72</u>

"This is nothing but a little bump in the road, Cahill. You've done enough to keep Lanham and Calvert quiet. There's no way those two are going to get in our way. They are making more money than they ever could have dreamed! They'd never risk the scandal we could bring down on 'em if they jumped ship now."

It was midday. The Thirty-One Grotto was not yet open for business, and Haynes and Ransom both sat at the bar with a glass of whiskey. Ransom nursed a cigarette between gulps of his beverage. He reached upward and pulled on his tie, leaving it hanging loose and cocked slightly to one side. The whiskey failed to improve his mood, and he was restless.

"I know, but there's a limit to what they can reasonably sweep under the rug. I never figured Tommy for the strait-laced type. I guess he's more like his brother than I expected. I still wish you and Rackley hadn't roughed him up so bad," Ransom confessed.

"Back off, Cahill. It was all fine until Duncan got there. The kid shot his mouth off to Duncan as soon as he came in. I just knew he'd take sides with Maclane, and that would have blown the whole thing, but when he saw how we shut Maclane up, he changed his tune."

"I know, I know. Don't get heated." Ransom added more whiskey to their glasses. "We've both done what we had to do here, but now Tommy Maclane is dead. I think I've done enough to keep his brother from trying to press the issue with the law, but he may still come looking for trouble."

 Jenna Cossey

Haynes peered into his glass. "You're right. And Archie Duncan—we've got to keep him quiet some way."

"Guess so. I'll just have to pay him more." Ransom shook his head, thinking about the absurd amount Archie Duncan was already making to do a menial task.

"There's only one other guy can place me and Rackley there that night, and that's Duncan. I'm not willing to bet all the chips on him keeping it to himself either, more pay or not." Haynes' tone was low and forbidding.

Ransom sensed that his comrade had other plans for keeping Archie Duncan quiet. He asked no further questions and figured that ignorance of the stratagem was the best option for his sanity. He regretted that the beating of Thomas Maclane resulted in his death. He regretting having threatened Sara Wheeler. However, he was no paragon of sympathy. His regret and displeasure stemmed from the convolution of otherwise simple matters. He ultimately did not care what happened to Archie Duncan, but the play of the game was complicated when people got hurt. Haynes often opted for excessive force, and he directed Frank Rackley to do the same at the Thirty-One Grotto. Extending diplomacy in the aftermath of violent encounters was an ongoing annoyance to Ransom. He was none too surprised that the men acted so fiercely when Thomas objected. Haynes put tremendous confidence in Ransom's ability to sway people, and he never expressed any doubt that he would do so in every needed situation. It gave rise to a carelessness that placed a greater burden on Ransom at the negotiating table.

He realized too late that he was the face of the operation. If things went too far askew, all of the government officials, law enforcement officers, and employees he had paid off would identify him foremost. He concluded that Haynes had wanted it that way to keep his own skin out of the game. What served as a constraint for him provided freedom to Haynes—the freedom to be too brutal and then send him to clean up the mess with crisp banknotes.

Ransom decided to take the same preventive approach with Archie Duncan that he had with Sara Wheeler. He would personally deliver a stern warning to him about keeping quiet at the earliest opportunity. He hoped it would save any further distribution of unnecessary barbarism from Haynes and Rackley. Though he thought himself much more important than the likes of Thomas Maclane, he still understood that many in Dunnigan liked the Maclane boys. Archie Duncan was a widely known hometown boy. They needed to avoid added mishaps that could result in the loss of such lives. It was the wrong kind of attention.

He tried to downplay the importance of Archie Duncan's silence to keep Haynes at bay, "I can persuade him to stay quiet, Haynes."

"Well, you have it your way, but if he gets to be a liability, I'll take care of it my way." Haynes poked himself in the chest with his thumb.

Ransom extinguished his cigarette in the tray and emptied the glass of its contents. The reasons he had adjoined himself to the operation seemed less than adequate with the passage of time. He mostly intended to needle Edward Cahill, but what he managed to do instead was to create an even more uncomfortable situation for himself. He was determined to answer to no one. Instead, he shifted his dependence from one controlling interest to another— from Edward to a New Orleans mobster who was in a power struggle amongst the ranks of Sylvestro Carollo. His youthfulness had urged him to pursue the lifestyle characterized by frivolity, vice, and calculated danger. He had jumped headlong into a

 Jenna Cossey

serious game of life and death with no guarantee of safety. The empty glass before him was a perfect representation of his achievements. He had missed the mark on all counts. As his options dwindled, he felt that all he could do was charge forward on the swiftly narrowing pathway.

73

The train lurched into the Dunnigan depot. Alfio Colucci watched through the window as it came to a stop. He stepped onto the platform with a Gladstone bag in one hand and a briefcase in the other. He scanned the swarm of people for a porter.

"Pardon me, could you tell me which way to the hotel?"

"Yessir. You'll go down the street about a block, and it's on the other side there. Can't miss it. They's big letters painted 'cross the top of it: 'Dunnigan Hotel.'" He used two hands as he described the moniker.

"Thank you."

Alfio set out on the short walk to the hotel. Dunnigan was not the size of Birmingham, but it seemed to benefit from the overflow of activity in the nearby metropolis. He noticed a variety of storefronts as well as a movie theatre in the distance. He spotted a small bank and caught a whiff of sourdough bread baking in a nearby bakery. The place seemed benign enough to him, but experience told him that looks often deceived. He was conditioned to wonder what deprivation lurked in the dark corners.

Having checked into his hotel room, he took the opportunity to freshen up. He took off his hat and revealed the smooth jet-black hair tucked beneath it. He removed the suit coat under which he wore a shoulder holster with a .45 caliber Colt pistol. He straightened his tie and smoothed it down beneath his vest, and then gently tugged the front of the vest into the desired position.

He rinsed his face and used a fine-tooth comb to fix his hair neatly back into place. He was not only particular about his appearance, he was particular about details in general. It was exactly what made him good at his work. He looked at his watch and decided he ought to proceed toward his destination if he intended to be there on time. He peeked out of the curtained window, trying to surmise where to go. He put on his coat and hat again and went down to the lobby of the hotel. He approached the desk clerk.

"Hello there again, Mr. Lucas. Settled in already? What can I do for ya?"

The overt friendliness was refreshing to him. "Could you tell me how to get to the courthouse?"

"Oh, sure. It's on our side of the street, but it's on down further. If you leave out through those doors and go right, you can't miss it."

Alfio tipped his hat and left the hotel carrying only his small briefcase. The directions proved true. He was not far from the hotel when a large and seemingly important building came into view. Its red brick facade rose two stories into the air. Freshly painted, decorative white woodwork trimmed it. He made his way inside and surveyed the tags that hung over each door. Not seeing the one that interested him, he made his way up the central staircase. When he reached the top, he spotted the sign: "Mayor."

He knocked on the large wooden door, and a deep, clear voice came from within. "Come in."

The room was large for an office. The ceilings were high, and the decorative style of the interior matched the exterior woodwork.

"Good evening, sir. I believe you're expecting me. I'm Agent Lucas."

A tall, portly man with mixed gray hair stood up behind his desk. "Ah, yes. I have indeed been expecting you. Please sit down, Mr. Lucas. Could I interest you in a cigar?" Edward Cahill raised the lid on an ornate cigar box.

"No, thank you."

The mayor took one for himself and proceeded to trim the cap from the end. "I want to thank you for coming in, Mr. Lucas. I reached out to Governor Graves in confidentiality. Bibb is a personal friend of mine, and as luck would have it, he was able to arrange to have you come."

"I'm not personally familiar with the governor, but when I get orders, I generally take them," Alfio quipped.

"I'm sure I don't need to explain, but this matter is highly sensitive. It involves members of my family. It's put me in quite the quandary." He rolled the unlit cigar back and forth in his fingers.

"Breaking the law often puts one in a quandary, Mr. Cahill, especially when it's a federal law."

"Yes, yes. Notwithstanding, I have promised the governor that I will fully cooperate to bring this issue in my city to a halt. There's already one young man dead, and if something isn't done, I believe there will be more bloodshed."

"I'm afraid I've witnessed more than my fair share of it, mayor, but with the information we have gathered already, I believe that we can shut this down quickly. Now what we discuss here must be kept confidential. If you were to reveal any of it, the terms of your immunity would be invalid, and not even the governor would be able to justify helping you then," Alfio told him.

"I understand."

"According to the information I have, the liquor that has been passing through here is originating with one of the biggest

 Jenna Cossey

bootleggers in New Orleans. The outfit we're talking about here has managed, in the past, to ship liquor from the Gulf all the way up to Canada. There's been an inside man on this operation for months. It seems that what's going on here, in Dunnigan, is just one leg of that much bigger operation," Alfio explained.

"I can't believe it." Edward Cahill was dumbstruck.

"It's a tricky situation, to say the least. Sylvestro Carollo, known to many as Silver Dollar Sam, is shipping liquor through here on trucks. He is keeping those trucks coming right through here, and the men here are intercepting it as if they are doing their job, but it's ending up right back in the hands of Carollo's people. The police force is involved, although we can't be sure yet which officers, or to what degree, but in order for the agent who now works in this area to have been unaware of all this is a near impossibility."

"So you're telling me they've compromised my entire police force, *and* a federal officer?"

"Possibly so, as well as officers in several other localities along Highway 31 from Mobile to Athens." Alfio leaned forward in his chair. "Mayor Cahill, all of our reports indicate that your son is behind the bribery of dozens of officials between Birmingham and Garden City. He's doled out thousands in just a few months in order to keep this operation going."

It was that which Edward Cahill had feared the most when he had caught wind of the enterprise. It was much worse than he had anticipated. "I . . . I'm not sure what to say. I'm afraid my culpability in this situation is, well, it's very great." He took a deep breath and spoke with nervousness in his voice, "I should have taken action sooner. I knew the boy was up to no good. This town is growing, but it's still small enough that hardly a secret can be kept. I knew about this nightclub of theirs the first week it opened," he admitted.

"What kept you from going to the authorities about this? Why did you wait so long?" Alfio had to inquire.

"It's a complicated matter." Edward's face reddened with embarrassment. "I did approach Chief Lanham about it, and he assured me he was trying to get to the bottom of it. I took him at his word. However, since we are speaking in confidentiality here, it was also because of my wife."

"She wanted you to ignore your son's involvement?"

"Well, yes, but . . ." Edward hesitated. "Let's just say that I have done some things as mayor that may not have been fitting of the dignity of the office. It's not easy getting these big companies to do business with our city when Birmingham is so nearby. I may have offered unauthorized incentives at times. I know it wasn't right."

"And your wife—she threatened to damage your political career if you went to the authorities over this whole thing?"

"Yes, and not just my political career, but the family name. The Cahills have been a respected name in this state for a great many years. She and her son are jeopardizing all of that."

"Her son?"

"Yes, her son."

"You mean your son," Alfio clarified.

"No, I mean *her* son."

Alfio was shocked by the divulgence. His experience in criminal investigations enabled him to hide his reaction, but he could see now how Edward Cahill had weighed his options and come to the decision about Ransom.

"You're telling me that you are not this young man's father?" Alfio wanted to make double sure.

"That's it. I knew he was not my child, but to save my wife the shame I took him as my own, and this is how I'm being repaid. She has never allowed me to correct him. He's been a thorn in my side from his youth. His entire life he's been spoiled beyond imagination. I sent him off to the best college I could get him into, thinking it would tear him away from her clutches and give him room to straighten out, but he found trouble there too. Thankfully, I avoided that scandal by persuading all of the right people, but when he returned home, he became more reckless than ever. I cut him off financially months ago. I suppose this is how he made up the difference. He's gone too far this time. This rabble he's aligned himself with, they are terrorizing people everywhere. With this boy dead, I can't stand idly by and let it go on regardless of what he and his mother might try to do or say about me."

"So his illegitimacy is not common knowledge?" Alfio asked.

"Absolutely not."

"Not even to him?"

"Not even to him."

"Mayor Cahill, I thank you for your complete disclosure. Agent Calvert will be reassigned for the time being, and I'll be working this area in his stead. It's of the utmost importance that you act none the wiser as it concerns my activities with the department here. If I can blend in and get the right information, we can end this."

"Good. That's what I want. I want it brought to a halt."

"Well, thank you for your time, mayor." Alfio walked toward the door.

"Agent Lucas?"

"Yes?"

"I hope you understand that I'd like you to avoid any unnecessary violence. I'd rather the boy be tried in a court of law than dead, you understand."

"I can't make any guarantees, sir. We never know how these things will turn out."

"I know. Just do what you can," Edward pleaded.

"I will."

Just as Alfio Colucci had suspected upon his arrival, the city of Dunnigan was one of illusions. On the surface, it spoke of happiness and growing affluence, but underneath churned a destructive force that threatened to ruin it forever.

<u>**74**</u>

Noah rode the train back to Dunnigan. He vacillated between a sense of dread that Thomas would not be there and anticipation over returning to Sara. He could have stayed in Oneonta, but there were scores to be settled. Not only did he owe money to Dr. Weathers, he needed to talk to Mr. Haskins and decide what future, if any, he had at the service station. He was not opposed to being a farmer, but he was more confident in his mechanical ability and wanted to continue in the trade if he could. There was a far greater need for his services in Dunnigan than his hometown. He also intended to avenge Thomas's death somehow. For the most part, he knew who the responsible parties were, and if the police department did not mean to do anything about it, he did. It was immaterial to him whether the perpetrators were prominent and wealthy. They would not go unpunished if he had anything to do with it.

He had seen to it that Thomas was buried in his favorite suit. He remembered Thomas showing it off to him, and doing what he thought he would have wanted gave him a bit of peace. It was such a strange feeling for him to be thinking about what he *would* have wanted. The real tragedy of his death was in his youthfulness and the fact that he had so much more life yet to live. It created a new sense of urgency in Noah. He was always the easy-going one, while Thomas was high-strung, but he now developed a sudden need to embody some of the vivacity of his little brother. He thought if he could do that, Thomas would always be with him.

When he stepped off of the train in Dunnigan, he walked toward Haskins' garage. Autumn was now fully encamped in the Alabama landscape. The sun beamed down on him, but the brisk air kept him from breaking a sweat. He carried only the small broken-down travel case he had packed before leaving town. It was not long before someone pulled alongside him, someone he knew from the station.

"Hey Maclane, want a lift? Headed to the station anyway."

"Sure."

Arriving at the station without Thomas was a difficult moment. Memories the two had shared there engulfed him. The months they had spent in Dunnigan seemed like both a lifetime and the blink of an eye. He went out into the garage to speak with his employer.

"Glad to see you back, Maclane. It's been a sight without you around here. If there's one that pulls in here and asks for you, there's ten every day. That's the truth!" Haskins shook his finger at Noah, but smiled. "I sure was sorry to hear about Tom. He was a good'n."

"Yeah, he was." Noah looked around at the undone work.

"It's a mess, ain't it? This place falls to pieces if you ain't in it, I reckon," Haskins tried to cheer him.

"Ah, I've kinda learned that things go on whether we are here to tend to 'em or not, Mr. Haskins. The world don't wait on nobody."

"Ha, I guess you're right about that, son, but I hope you're back for good just the same."

"Well, I'm the last person that could tell ya what tomorrow will bring, but I reckon I'm here for at least a little while. However, if you don't care, I've got something I need to tend to this evenin'. I'll be here in the mornin'."

 Jenna Cossey

"That's alright, Noah. This stuff ain't goin' nowhere. I get it done by and by. I'm just a heap slower at it than you boys—" his face reddened when he referred to the two of them, "than you are."

"I'll get in here tomorrow. I give you my word," Noah promised.

"Alright, Noah. Use that old truck if you need it now, ya hear?"

"Yessir, think I will. Thank ya."

The first thing he wanted to do was go and see Sara. He knew it would comfort him to see her again under better circumstances. When she, Violet, and Easton had showed up in Oneonta for the funeral, it filled him with gratitude. When he fell in love with Sara, Easton and Violet also became dear to him. They were like family, albeit an unconventional one. More than ever, he knew that she could understand his sense of loss. As he came to a stop in front of her house, she came out and met him halfway.

"I heard the truck coming. I knew it was you," she said through a smile.

"Hard to mistake that ol' thing, ain't it?" he kidded, but the joy was missing from his voice.

"I'm so happy you're back."

"You wanta go for a walk?" he asked.

"Yeah, let's." Sara ran back up to the house and called in to tell Violet they were going down to the meadow.

Though they did not have much time before dark, the two of them sauntered down the road side by side. Noah had both hands in his pockets, and Sara clasped hers behind her. They were going toward the meadow, but neither cared if they made it that far as long as they got to be together. They walked several minutes without talking.

"I sure am glad the heat's finally left us," Noah said.

"Oh, me too."

There was another long silence, and then Sara spoke, "I think the fall is my favorite time."

"I like spring better. Everything's new then. In the fall everything's dyin'."

Sara reached up and hooked her hand around his arm. She walked a little closer to him as they went down the road, he with his hands in his pockets, and she with a hold on his arm.

Finally, they reached the edge of the woods and found the footpath. It was not wide enough for them to walk side by side, so he took her hand, and she followed him down the path. When they came to Sharp's Creek, the water flowed in the peaceful way they had come to expect. They stood there listening, looking, and saying very little, just as they had the first time they met there.

"You know, Sara, I wasn't sure I wanted to come back here. It just didn't seem like it would be right without Tommy here."

"I know. I'm so sorry, Noah."

"But I got to thinkin' about it all, and I knew I had to come back. I just can't let them fellas get away with this. I don't know what I'm gonna do, but somehow they have to pay for what they did to him, and to you. I let both of you down."

"You could never let me down. I don't want you to be hurt, Noah. They are cruel. They don't care who they hurt."

"I really wish those guys woulda left y'all out of this whole mess," Noah said as he threw his arms across his chest.

"But they didn't, and now it's serious. I wasn't hurt but—" she stopped herself.

"I know. But you coulda been. I could just tear that guy limb from limb!" The veins in Noah's neck bulged.

　　　　Jenna Cossey

Sara tried to calm him, "But it wouldn't do any good. His daddy is the mayor, and you know they'd put you under the jail if you laid a hand on him. He knows that, too."

"I know he does. That's how this whole thing's happened. He can do whatever he wants, and them fellas up there at the police station, they ain't gonna do a thing about it. They all but laughed at me when I went in there, Sara."

"Maybe there's something else that can be done. Aunt Violet, she always knows what to do. Maybe she'll think of something. There's nothing to lose, Noah."

"Yes, there is, Sara." His gentle gray eyes intensified as they stared into hers. "I didn't come back here just to straighten them out. I mean, that was part of it, but there was only one thing that really coulda brought me back here. It was you."

Sara's eyes welled up. "Noah, I . . ."

"I don't know what I'd do without you. There's nothing for me back there. Being at home without Tommy is too hard. He's a part of everything I see there, but here—you're here, and I don't want to be anywhere or do anything where there's no you."

"We can make it through this together," she said.

"Sara, if you love me, I can make it through anything. If you love me, I can take on anybody."

He took her gently into his arms.

"I do love you, Noah. I love you."

Sara dissolved into his powerful embrace. His heart pounded as he leaned into her to seize the long-awaited moment. He pressed his lips to hers, and all of the grief, fear, and uncertainty faded away for a few seconds. She loved him, and he felt unstoppable. As their lips parted, he gazed into her eyes. They understood one another. Amid the upheaval, their blended perfection conquered the ugliness of their trials.

<u>75</u>

Cephas sipped on the coffee Zennia made. He held the cup with two hands and tapped his fingers against it between sips. Only a few days earlier, he had taken a great risk in warning Violet Simpson of Ransom's growing impetuosity.

"You did what you thought was best. You can't set there worryin' 'bout it. That boy . . . Well he ain't no boy anymore for one thing, but he done gone off the deep end. Maybe you saved him from worse trouble," she tried to reason with him.

"Mighta, but ever since I did it, I been frettin' about whether I done right or went too far. Mrs. Charlotte or Mr. Ransom either one find out about it, and I'll be the next one dead." He shook his head and tapped his fingers against the cup some more.

"But if you hadn't told her, she mighta got herself dead. I sure 'nough wouldn't put it past that bunch a heathens Mr. Ransom been tearin' around with, and you saw for yourself how he snatched that little gal up right there in the street in front of everybody. Who knows who saw it, and who knows what he'd do if there wasn't nobody around! You think he had a hand in that Maclane boy's death?"

"That Haynes—he the one helped kill that boy," Cephas said.

"How you know Ransom ain't helped?"

"'Cause I overhear 'em talkin' about it. It was Haynes and that other, but it don't make no difference."

"Naw, he just as guilty 'cause he knew 'bout it, and what'd he go do?"

"He's got brave, ain't no doubt about that. I know Mr. Cahill's privy to it, but he ain't gonna get in the way either or—"

He stopped himself. They had worked together for fifteen years, and neither of them had any family of their own. There was no romantic relationship between them, but each was all the other had in the way of companionship. He trusted her so much that even those secrets he dared tell no one came close to slipping from his tongue.

"What Cephas, or what?" She focused on him, awaiting another revelation.

"Nothin'. All I know's that if Mr. Cahill try to line that boy of her's up, it'll be Katy, bar the door." He pointed his bony finger at her.

"I can't understand that. This his house, and he the mayor. It don't make no sense to me."

"You just have to take my word for it."

"I s'pose I will."

Ransom Cahill was headed toward self-destruction like a fast-moving train, and Cephas could see it. It was bad enough that Haynes and Frank Rackley had injured Thomas Maclane so severely, but when he died, the situation intensified so rapidly that Cephas saw no way for Ransom to escape what was surely coming his way.

"It's just a matter a time before he goes too far with all this foolishness," Zennia said.

Cephas emptied his coffee cup and exhaled a breath. "Maybe he already has, Zennia. Maybe he already has."

76

"What do you mean you've been reassigned?"

"Just what I said. They're having me go somewhere else," Agent Calvert gave a clipped response.

"That's ridiculous. You've only been covering the area for a few months!" The news agitated Ransom.

"Tell me about it, and I bought a place in Birmingham. They assured me I'd be around for a while."

Fenn Calvert and Ransom Cahill sat in the office at the Thirty-One Grotto. He took a phone call that morning suggesting that he "meet F.C. at the office." They had devised ways to transmit information over the phone so that operators and other interlopers to the conversations would have no indication of their meaning. Naturally, he went into a mental tailspin as he considered possible reasons for the federal agency to remove Agent Calvert. It was too well timed with the commotion surrounding Thomas Maclane's death.

Maybe someone knows something.

"Are you sure that the Simpson woman isn't the cause of this? I thought I had her pretty well convinced not to press this any further," Ransom said.

"No, I really don't think so. I never saw her. Lanham said she came in and kicked up a bunch of dust, but we never pursued the matter. You don't think she knows anyone at the bureau, do you?"

"Doubtful. She's just a yokel that came into a little money when her husband died. She doesn't have any influence around here."

"I hope you're right."

"So who's the new fella? Do you know?" Ransom was already planning his next move.

"I don't know too much. I hear he's been up North helping to disrupt some of the bigger operations, but I can't tell you anything about him," Calvert said.

"You can't, or you won't?"

Calvert put up both of hands in defense. "I tell you I can't. I just don't know. Look, I've got as much to lose as anybody here. I've got no reason to lie about it."

"Ok, ok," Ransom calmed him down. "Here's a little parting gift. Something for your troubles." He tossed an envelope of money across the desk.

Calvert took it and stuffed it inside his coat. "Thanks." His eyes were downcast, as if he still felt a sliver of shame over being bought out.

"Hope it helps, wherever you're going. This place is taking in money like you wouldn't believe. I'm just sharing the bounty, Calvert. When should I expect to see this new fella?"

"Oh, he's already in town. When they reassigned me, they already had him here. It's a done deal."

"What's his name?" Ransom asked.

"Lucas, Agent Lucas."

"I see. Well, best of luck to you, Fenn." They shook hands and Calvert left.

Ransom had to figure out what to do next. While the timing of Agent Calvert's reassignment was unfortunate, there was no real reason for him to believe that there was a breach in their chain of corruption. He remained confident that Edward Cahill would not get in the way, believing that his mother would make sure of it just as she had always done. Chief Lanham was powerless, because if he turned on him, he too would be implicated, which was true of practically everyone else on the payroll. Further, he was one of the few who could tie the death of Thomas Maclane to Haynes. His perceived control only emboldened him more. In his mind, he had the least to lose. *How could someone in my position be considered a criminal?*

Later, he made his way to Agent Calvert's old office. His belongings were gone, and just as expected, a new man was behind the desk.

Ransom knocked on the facing of the open door. "Afternoon. I hear you're taking Agent Calvert's place."

"Yep, looks like both of us have been reassigned."

He extended a hand. "I'm Ransom Cahill. My father is Edward Cahill." Ransom despised him, but he did not mind dropping the name when it was convenient.

"Ah, yes. Alfred Lucas." He shook Ransom's hand.

"May I?" Ransom motioned that he wanted to close the door.

"Please."

He sat down in the chair and took out his package of cigarettes. "You mind?"

"Not at all," Lucas said.

"Agent Lucas, I'm going to get right down to business. I have certain arrangements here in Dunnigan."

"Yes?"

He exhaled a large cloud of smoke as he lit the cigarette. "Yes. These arrangements are convenient for everyone involved, you understand. I'm a businessman. I simply like to keep the business operating smoothly."

"And what exactly is your business, Mr. Cahill?" Agent Lucas queried.

"Same as your business."

"Is that so?"

"Yes."

"You've got quite a lot of nerve coming in here like this," Lucas asserted.

"I can't argue with you there, but in my business—pardon me, *our* business—you just don't get very far without it."

"So what is it that you're proposing?"

Ransom removed from his coat an envelope that bulged with cash and tossed it on the desk. "I'm proposing that we make a deal. That we work together instead of against each other."

Agent Lucas glanced out both of his office windows to see if anyone was watching. He picked it up, looked inside, and estimated the sum to be no less than a thousand dollars. "You understand that I could have you arrested right now, don't you?"

"Yes, but you're not going to." Ransom grinned.

"How do you know that? Perhaps you underestimate me, Mr. Cahill."

"Of course not. Everyone has a price, Agent Lucas. Perhaps this will help." He removed a second envelope of equal size from his coat.

Agent Lucas shifted in his seat and chewed the inside of his jaw as silence engulfed the room.

"Alright."

"We have an agreement?"

"Yes."

"Good. I felt sure you were a reasonable man. Now there are some things I need to make you aware of, but I'd rather not do it here. I'll be in touch with you soon. Where are you staying?"

"The hotel here in town for now."

"Very well. It was nice meeting you, Agent Lucas."

Ransom walked out of the office certain that business would continue as usual.

77

The day was long for Noah. He was distracted and worked feverishly in the garage to keep his nerves at bay. He wanted to believe he had made the right choice, but anxiety and doubt crept in. Because of Ransom, Thomas had ended up dead, and the way he saw it, there were only two options: he could confront him and make a reprise, or let him and his cohorts continue without consequence for their actions.

What once might have been an obvious choice turned into a delicate web of decisions owing to the circumstances. He reached out to those who should have been obliged to help him seek justice for his brother, and they had failed him. It was not only the death of Thomas that affected him so deeply, but the threat to the safety of Sara. Ransom not only threatened her, but Noah learned that Violet too had been warned of impending danger if she were to pursue the matter. To allow him to go unchecked and unfettered would render Noah powerless to protect those he loved. He knew that Sara would never feel safe if she constantly faced the prospect of meeting Ransom Cahill on the streets of Dunnigan. That dynamic did not make the grade for Noah.

On the other hand, if he chose to confront him, it would be dangerous. Haynes and the other man were capable of killing, and though he could not be sure, the treatment Ransom gave Sara was enough to convince him that he was also capable of it. He could not help but take thought for his life. It left him with a feeling of guilt and cowardice for even thinking of himself when the safety of his true love was at stake.

  Jenna Cossey

If Noah was to be free of the guilt he felt, he would have to stand up to Ransom. If he did not, the fear and uncertainty that purveyed would result in the eventual destruction of many lives. He weighed all of the options right up until the time came for him to do what he knew he must.

That evening, when he finished his work, he cleaned himself up. He was preparing for an important meeting, and he wanted to look the part. He wore his best change of clothing and neatly combed his hair into place. He carefully arranged his room. He reached under the bed and retrieved the worn-out suitcase that had belonged to Thomas.

After Thomas's death, Noah had gone to the boarding house and packed most of his clothing into the case to empty his room. Among his things, he found a Prince Albert tobacco tin. Inside he discovered $322, Thomas's life savings. Thomas had unknowingly endangered himself to obtain the money, and it ended up costing him his life. Noah had no inclination to spend it. Up until that evening, he continued to keep it stored in the old suitcase. As he readied himself to leave, he reached beneath the crude mattress on his bed and retrieved his own life savings: $349. He always envisioned he and Thomas using their money to buy something together. The old dream was dead. He could only share his new dreams with Sara. He put his money into the tin with the other. If he never returned, he wanted it all to be in one place. He had little else of value.

He drove to Violet's house, and she greeted him at the door, "Come in, Noah."

"Evenin', Mrs. Violet." Sara descended the stairs, more beautiful than ever. "Hi, Sara."

She smiled and said hello. He could tell that she had been crying. It pained him, but he tried not to think about it.

"Sit down for a moment, Noah. Will you?" Violet, too, was visibly nervous.

"Sure."

He took a seat, and Sara sat next to him, holding onto his arm with both hands.

"So it's going to be tonight?"

"Yes'm, tonight." He looked at the floor and then back at her.

"Are you sure you want to do this? You don't have to do this, Noah."

"She's right, Noah. You don't have to do this," Sara chimed in as she choked back tears.

"I'm afraid I've got to. If I don't, I'll never be able to live with myself. I have to do it for Tommy." Noah hesitated. "And I have to do it for myself."

"I don't suppose there's anything I can say to make you change your mind that I haven't already said," Violet said.

"No ma'am, I don't reckon so."

"I hate to see you do it, but I guess I know why you feel that you must." She reached over and gave his shoulder a reassuring touch. "I just wish there was something more I could do to help."

"There's not anything you can do. You've already done enough, and I thank ya for it." He reached up and patted the back of her hand.

He stood up and extended his hand to Violet, but she rejected it in favor of a caring embrace. She hugged him and wished him well.

"You be careful. We expect you for dinner tomorrow night." Violet smiled, but finally lost the battle to keep her tears at bay.

"I'm gonna do my best, Mrs. Violet."

"I'll leave you two." She smiled a sympathetic smile and left Noah and Sara standing there.

 Jenna Cossey

He turned and looked at Sara. His face was solemn, and an intensity she had never seen outlined his soft eyes. "I reckon it's time for me to go, Sara."

"I wish you didn't have to, Noah. I know you feel you have to, but oh how I wish you didn't." She began to cry.

"Don't cry. Please don't cry." He swept the tears away from her cheeks with his hand.

"I'm sorry. I promised myself I wouldn't, but I'm afraid for you."

"It's gonna be alright."

"How do you know?"

"I don't know, but I just think it's gonna be alright. No matter what, I'll always have you, and you'll always have me. No matter what."

"Please come back," Sara pleaded.

"I will, Sara. I'll come back." Noah took her in his arms. "I have to go now."

"Don't."

He pulled himself away from her, and his strong hands grasped her shoulders. "Now you told me to come back, didn't ya?" He smiled at her.

"Yes."

"Well, how can I come back if I don't go?" He grinned, trying so desperately to lessen the weight of the moment.

"Oh, Noah!" She fell into his arms, and her tears freely flowed.

He started toward the front door and stepped onto the small front porch, but before he descended the steps, he turned to her one last time. He thought about the first night he came to the house, not knowing that he would fall so deeply in love with the pretty girl who had answered the door. It seemed so far in the past. So much change had taken place. He looked at Sara, memorizing everything about her: her beautiful blue eyes, the way the careless waves of her soft brown hair tumbled about her face, every freckle, every contour.

"Sara?"

"Yes, Noah."

"That first day we talked down at the meadow, I knew I loved you then. I've loved you ever since. Nothin' could ever stop me from loving you; do you hear me? Nothin' in this world. I'll never stop. I'll always love you, Sara." He took her in his arms once more and kissed her, not knowing if he would ever do so again.

<u>78</u>

"He said he'd be here by six, right? I want this over with, so we can get back to business. I knew he would be looking for trouble. His kind is always that way, loyal to the end."

"Yeah, loyal, but not very smart," Ransom quipped.

"I hope he brings an army. He's gonna need it," Haynes said.

"No, he said he was coming alone. He said he wanted to settle this man to man." Ransom fiddled with his fancy silver lighter, trying to light a cigarette.

"Ha! I guess you were right, not too smart that one." Frank Rackley reached into his pocket and retrieved his lighter to assist. "Here."

Ransom Cahill, Haynes, and Frank Rackley waited for Noah to show at the warehouse in Dunnigan. It was a large building that had once been the headquarters of a patent medicine company. Mr. Messina had purchased the building for Sylvestro Carollo at pennies on the dollar. As far as most in Dunnigan knew, it was still empty, but it was home to an ever-growing accumulation. Throughout it lay the sundry procurement of goods. There were barrels falsely labeled "apples" and "sugar," crates with various deceptive freight descriptions stenciled on the outside, full of bottles nestled securely in beds of straw, and smaller wooden cartons of foreign origin. Some crates had no misleading labels aside from being in Spanish. The only time the building received any visitors was in the dark of the night long after the streets and sidewalks of Dunnigan had fallen into their deserted twilight state.

"I don't know why you had him come here, Cahill. It's a risky thing, us being here at this hour." Haynes was agitated.

"What do you mean, *risk*? What *risk*? If you can't tell by now, we've got things under control in this town. Who cares what hour it is?" Ransom was dauntless.

"Me. I don't like it. This wasn't a good idea," said Haynes.

Ransom had his left thumb hooked in the armhole of his vest, and he snatched the cigarette from his lips with his right hand. "Don't you remember why I'm here? It's because of me that we've bought off everybody within a fifty-mile radius, Haynes. My father's the mayor. He's friends with governors, congressmen, police, treasury agents, the whole lot. They all know him. There's *not* going to be any trouble. We were never even so much as questioned over this ordeal with Maclane. Nobody has the nerve to say anything about what we're doing. Look around, Haynes! Who are they going to tell that's going to give a hang?" He held his arms out wide as if to beg anyone in the world to stop them.

"I don't know, but this just wasn't the right way to do this."

"Well, it's nearly time for him now, and it's getting dark anyway. What's done is done."

"Rack, when you let him in, you make sure he doesn't have a gun. You got me?" Haynes directed.

"Got it."

None of them intended for the balance of power to be equal. Haynes and Ransom had taken up the habit of carrying pistols, and both wore them that evening. Frank Rackley was a bearish man who had worked in the steel mill at Birmingham. He looked to be made of steel himself with his large stature and square frame. He carried no gun and repeatedly claimed, "If they're close enough to kill me, I can stick 'em with a knife quicker than I

Jenna Cossey

can shoot 'em." By all accounts, he meant what he said and possessed a five-inch switchblade, which he was not shy about wielding. Noah had the gift of copious amounts of strength, but the disadvantage would be severe if it were three against one.

Ransom wanted it no other way.

<u>**79**</u>

Noah followed the directive Ransom had given him when they discussed the meeting. Like most everyone else in Dunnigan, he thought the warehouse was empty. He learned otherwise from Archie Duncan.

"I hadn't ought to be telling you all this. It could get me killed."

"I know it, Arch, but we've got to know," Noah pressed him.

"Well, it's not far from town, but it's down by the railroad tracks. When the place was still doing business, they ran freight in and out of there. It's got its own rail spur." Archie was so nervous that he left out the most critical piece of information.

"Alright, so how do I get there?"

"When you leave town out here goin' south, you have to go a few miles. The second crossroads you come to, you turn back toward the tracks, and you'll be right there at it."

"Good. You're doin' the right thing here, Archie. You're gonna be just fine. We're gonna get you on that train to Saint Louis this evenin', and you'll stay on with your cousins there until this blows over."

"I never meant to get tied up in all this, and I never meant to get Tommy—" Archie did not want to speak what had become of Thomas. "I'm real sorry, Noah."

"It weren't your fault, Archie. Don't blame yourself for what happened to him." He understood the sense of liability the young man felt. "We just don't know what we don't know, Arch." He was younger than Archie, but as was so often the case, he was the more discerning of the two.

Whatever guilt Archie had paled in comparison to what Noah felt. He was ready to exact the toll from the men who had murdered Thomas, and Ransom would pay, too.

He pulled down the road to the warehouse. He saw the blocky silhouette of the structure against the pastel and rouge streaks in the evening sky. His heart raced. It was the final moment of decision.

If I do this, there's no going back.

The heavy Ford tow truck trundled to a stop next to a car he recognized. It was Ransom's Chevrolet coupe, the car that had initiated the entire affair. *I'd love to take this truck and plow right over that thing.*

He got out of the truck and went in alone. He had told Ransom he would come alone. He was betting on him being such a loathsome coward that he would surely bring his cadre of hoodlums along. He knocked on the door and found that he wagered well. Frank Rackley opened the door and eyeballed him for a second before nodding his head to invite him through. The opening and closing of the door stirred the ambient smell of the alcohol, and the scent filled his nostrils the moment it shut behind him. His eyes quickly darted around the room. *One, two, three.*

He did not know Rackley, but he recognized him as the other man who had come out of the basement of the hardware store the night he found Thomas. Unlike the three of them, Noah wore no suit coat. Rackley patted his pockets and legs to verify that he did not have anything with which to defend himself. Noah could feel sweat beginning to gather across his forehead and the small of his back. Though the October air was cool, adrenaline deceived his body, making it feel like he was passing through a Birmingham blast furnace. Hardly any daylight remained outside, leaving little light to dwindle through the large windows along the top of the warehouse. Noah could not see into the darkened corners of the room. He waited for one of them to say something.

"Maclane," said Ransom. Noah nodded. "Tell me, Maclane, what is it that I can do for you?" Ransom pretended courtesy.

"I think you know why I'm here."

"Do I?"

"Yep."

"Well, just for the record, why don't you tell us anyways?" Haynes interjected.

Rackley was behind Noah, so he looked first into the eyes of Haynes and then Ransom. "I'm here to settle the score."

"Oh! He's here to settle the score, Cahill," Haynes mocked.

"Listen, Maclane. I don't want trouble with you. The best thing you can do is go back to whatever hamlet you and your brother came from in the first place and leave Dunnigan for good before this gets worse. I think I've already shown you just exactly *how* I can make it worse, haven't I?"

"Yeah, it takes a real big man to lay hands on a lady. Lucky for you, I ain't as quick tempered as Thomas was." Noah wadded up his fists.

"There's nothing you can do that will change anything. I think you learned that when you went to the police, did you not? Furthermore, I think you're forgetting that my father is the mayor of Dunnigan. No one is going to believe anything you say against me. There's nobody you can tell who is going to do anything to help you. They are all on my payroll, friend." He patted the breast of his coat.

"Tommy's dead because of you," Noah said. "You knew how he was. You roped him into this mess to start with. You saw how carried away he was with your fancy things and your fist full of money. You took advantage of him. It's the reason you came to the station that afternoon before he got beat up. You were sendin' him on a special errand, and he was happy to do it 'cause you'd waved so much money at him by that time, he figured on gettin' rich."

"Alright, so I paid him to haul some booze for us. Am I to blame for a silly kid that wants to get rich overnight?" Ransom asked.

"No, but if you'd left him alone like I asked you that day I come out to your place, he never would've ended up there that night."

Noah turned to Haynes. "And you—you knew he was a loose cannon. I shoulda known something wasn't right when you two became bosom buddies all of a sudden after he belted you in the mouth. You thought you could turn him rotten like you, but you couldn't. He was game, and he was apt to find mischief, but not the kind you led him to. When he found out y'all was runnin' booze, he didn't want no part of it, and rather than have him get in your way, you just beat him to a pulp and left him there to die."

"There's no way you can prove that," Ransom said.

"I don't have to prove it. I saw it," Noah rebutted.

"You didn't see anything," Haynes said.

"I seen all I needed to. Y'all didn't know it, but I was there in town that night. I watched you go in," he pointed to Haynes. "then Tommy, then Archie. I never saw Tommy leave, but I saw you." He turned and pointed at Frank Rackley. "You were already there. You were countin' on trouble because you knew Tommy would never be able to keep from askin' too many questions. Y'all had to tell him he was runnin' booze before you sent him off to Garden City to find it out for himself, and he bucked up to ya, so you beat him. Now that he's dead, I reckon that means you two have done murder, don't it?"

"You weren't in the room that night; you don't know *what* happened," Ransom told him.

"You're right. I wasn't in the room, but Tommy was."

"Well, we know *he's* not talking to anybody about it." Haynes grinned at Rackley with an evil look in his eye.

It took every ounce of strength Noah had to hold himself back. "One of the last things he was ever able to tell me was what happened to him that night. I know you don't care what you done, but I do. He was my brother."

"You're right, boy. I don't care. Doesn't make any difference to me, and if I had it to do over, I wouldn't do it any different, except," Haynes walked over and got close to his face, "next time I'd make sure I finished the job."

Noah could smell the breath of Haynes, an amalgamation of liquor and smoke. He had done what he came to do. All of the cards were on the table. He took a deep breath. *This is for you, Tommy.*

He drew back his arm and landed a blow across the jaw of Haynes. His head snapped to the right, turning just enough to render him unconscious. He fell to the floor in a limp heap with his arms flopped out, one beneath his body and one draped over his head. Noah whirled around and fixed his sights on Ransom, whose catlike eyes widened as he watched Noah barrel toward him. *This is for Sara.*

He knew he could level Ransom, but he chose a different method. He thrust his left hand into his slim neck and snatched his collar and necktie with a firm grip. Ransom flailed his arms momentarily before he finally attempted to reach inside of his coat to retrieve his pistol. Suddenly, Noah felt an intense pain in his side. Ransom found the grip of his pistol. Noah flattened his right hand and plastered it to the broad side of Ransom's face

                    Jenna Cossey

with an ear-splitting clap. He followed it with his strong right hook. As Noah drew back his arm again, he felt the pang once more. They glared at one another, each hoping to deploy their respective artillery before the other.

A shot rang out.

"Stop!"

Noah let go of Ransom's neck and watched him fall to the floor, clutching his throat as blood surged from his nose and mouth.

Noah reached for the pain in his side and felt a liquid warmth. *Blood.*

His hand was covered in blood.

He collapsed.

80

Alfio Colucci motored across Dunnigan in the darkness, and kept his eyes fixed on the unfamiliar roads. The flurry of activity over the preceding days had finally begun to catch up with him, yet the success of that afternoon had temporarily renewed his energy. He needed to get back downtown to his office, but he was on an important errand. He tried to remember where to turn when he spotted his landmark from a previous trip. As soon as he made the right turn, he became sure that he had made the correct choice. He began to eye each house, looking for the desired one.

Finally, he saw the correct house number. He shut off the engine and looked toward the porch as he straightened his tie. He strode up to the house, stepped onto the landing, and knocked at the door.

Violet Simpson appeared. "Hello."

"Mrs. Simpson, might I come in for a moment?"

"Certainly." She waved him into the parlor. "Could I get something for you, Mr. Lucas?"

"No, thank you. I haven't much time. I've come to bring news."

Sara emerged from the kitchen and came to Violet's side. Violet composed herself to receive the news. "Yes, please tell me."

"I'm afraid it didn't go quite as we planned, though it rarely ever does." He clutched his hat in his hands and wore an expression of concern.

Violet exhaled, and her shoulders dropped. "It didn't work."

"No, on the contrary, we did achieve our objective this evening. We were able to make the arrests."

 Jenna Cossey

Violet put an arm around Sara. "Oh, thank goodness. Ransom Cahill?"

"Yes, ma'am, and the two who were responsible for Thomas Maclane's death. We were able to get the confessions, and none of our men were injured but . . ."

"What's going on?" Sara did not understand.

"What about Noah?" Violet was anxious to know.

"Well, he acted very courageously. We could not have done it without him . . ."

"Aunt Violet?" Sara became frantic.

"Mrs. Simpson, maybe we should sit down," Alfio suggested.

"I don't want to sit down." Sara's teeth were clenched, her eyes swollen and tired. "I want you to tell me where Noah is. Please. Tell me right now!"

"Sara," Violet tried to calm her.

"Well?" Sara looked at them, pleading for information.

"You didn't tell her?" Alfio asked Violet.

"No."

"What? Tell me what? Aunt Vi?"

"Sara." Violet held her closer.

"Please, if we could just sit down so that I can explain. I don't have a lot of time here," he tried to persuade them.

"Come sit down, Sara. Listen to Mr. Lucas," she urged.

"The meeting that occurred tonight was arranged intentionally. In talking with Mrs. Simpson here about your situation with Mr. Cahill and in speaking with Noah Maclane and Archie Duncan, we had enough to go on, but we needed to set these men up to catch them and have enough evidence to convict them."

"I still don't understand. What about Noah?" Sara asked.

"I'm coming to that. Noah came up with the idea to have the men meet him in the warehouse where they've been storing liquor.

It was a dangerous thing for him to do. Under normal circumstances, we would not have even considered it, but he insisted. Once he arranged the meeting, we breached the warehouse and had a number of officers hide there before the suspects arrived. We watched the building for some time and felt confident in our ability to get some men in there without them knowing it. In short, he was able to initiate a conversation during which two of the three men, Cahill and Haynes, confessed to their crimes. In fact, they confessed to several crimes. The third man signed his confession once the ordeal was over. Thanks to Noah, I think it will be an open and shut case."

"So, where is he now?" Sara asked.

"Well, that's really why I came. I'm sorry to say that he was injured."

"Injured?" Sara asked.

"What is the extent of his injuries?" Violet asked.

"He has multiple knife wounds."

"Knife wounds?" Sara cried.

"It all happened very quickly, but thankfully we were able to intervene before anyone was hurt any worse."

"Is he going to be ok?" Sara asked.

"I believe he is going to be ok. He's being looked after here in town presently. The doctor expects him to make a full recovery."

Sara breathed a sigh of relief and sank against Violet, who hugged her tightly. "See? There now. It's going to be alright."

"I must be going now, ladies. My apologies for the imposition, but I didn't feel that telephoning was appropriate under the circumstances."

"Not at all, Mr. Lucas. Thank you so much for coming over in person."

"It was the least I could do. You've been a great help, Mrs. Simpson. Without you, Mayor Cahill might never have gotten on board."

"I just did what anyone would have done in my position," Violet acquiesced.

"No, Mrs. Simpson. You did what most people would have been afraid to do, and so did Noah. I'm grateful." He extended his hand.

"I suppose we all have plenty to be grateful for, don't we?" Violet shook his hand.

"Yes, ma'am. I must be going now."

81

Charlotte Cahill gritted her teeth and glared at her husband. In only a few sips, she dispensed of the brandy he had supplied from the small crystal decanter he kept in his study. She rotated the snifter in her right hand as she clutched the arm of the chair with her left. "How could you?"

"He left me no choice. I had to put a stop to it before anyone else was hurt or killed." He had suddenly gained a measure of courage in dealing with his wife.

"My son. You would do this to *my son*."

"He did it to himself. He made a deal with the devil, Charlotte. It was only a matter of time."

"So now what do you intend to do about it?"

"Nothing. This was the last straw."

"What do you mean, nothing?"

"I mean exactly that. I've washed my hands of the entire situation."

"Do you understand that I can destroy you?" she threatened.

"Yes, I suppose that's possible, but after giving this some consideration, I've realized that I'm not the one whose reputation is at stake here. For a great many years now, you've made me believe that you have some power over me, but you don't have any more power over me than your father did. If you try to ruin me over this, you're the one who will lose."

"I believe you underestimate me, Edward. You forget that I know things, lots of things, all of your crooked, dirty secrets."

　　　　　Jenna Cossey

"And I believe that you forget the position you are in yourself. How do you think your social circles would receive a woman who conceived a child by a man other than her husband? If it were to become known, you would be a pariah. It is your reputation that stands to be ruined here, not mine. The boy wears my name. I'm already bearing consequences for what he's done, but so help me, Charlotte Cahill, if you make this worse, it's you who'll be destroyed in the end, not me."

"You wouldn't dare," she challenged him.

In trying to discharge Ransom of personal responsibility for his actions, she had finally overextended herself. She knew that she was looking at a man who had been pushed too far.

"Wouldn't I? Are you willing to put me to the test?"

Charlotte glowered at him, unable to answer.

82

"You knew about this all along?" Sara did not fully understand what had transpired.

"Well, not entirely, but I knew that Noah was cooperating with Mr. Lucas to catch those men."

"Why didn't he tell me?"

"I guess he just didn't want to give you any greater cause to worry." Violet patted her arm.

"What did he mean when he said, 'Without you, Mayor Cahill never would have gotten on board.' What was he talking about?"

"Let's just say that I had a promise to keep. I promised Noah I would do what I could, and I guess it worked." Even in heroism, she was modest.

"It's just too much for me to get hold of, Aunt Vi."

"I know, dear, but hopefully, it's all over now."

"But Noah . . ."

"Mr. Lucas said he was going to be alright, thank goodness."

"I have to see him."

"You will, but first, I need to call down the street and see if Easton can stay there for a little while. I don't want him to go with us to the hospital. He was so torn up when Tommy died. The poor little fella has just now stopped talking about it. I don't want to get his mind on it again. Go wash your face a bit. We'll go here shortly."

Sara was desperate to see Noah. That day, for the first time since she had met him, she was forced to contemplate the real possibility of him never returning. She could not accept a picture

Jenna Cossey

of her life without him in it. She wanted to be near him, to know for herself that he was going to be alright. As usual, Violet sensed her angst. They left Easton at the Carson house, and the two of them made the short drive across town to the Dunnigan Hospital.

Sara was nervous. She had little experience with hospitals, and despite wanting to see Noah, she dreaded the unknown. The solemnity of the atmosphere did not improve the feeling. She braced herself as they entered and inquired as to his whereabouts. They negotiated a series of hallways and doors before they arrived at the area where Noah was being treated. Her eyes pitched about the room. She looked and listened for any sign of him. She spotted him.

"There," she said quietly to Violet.

As she approached him, she found his bronzed skin washed of its color. He was pale and still. It disquieted a hidden corner of her mind, the one that reminded her of the horrible night she had lost her mother. She started to cry.

Violet threw an arm around her. "It's okay."

Sara collected herself and moved closer to him. She perched lightly on the edge of his bed and pressed his hand between both of hers. His eyes cracked open, and he squeezed her hand.

"Sara." He smiled.

"Oh, Noah." She cried still.

"Don't cry. I'm alright." His voice was weak.

"I'm so glad you're okay. I was scared to death."

"I know. I'm sorry, Sara."

"Please don't be. Mr. Lucas said you got them. He said you were so brave."

"All I could think about was doing right by Tommy, and—" his voice faltered from the lump in his throat, "and you, Sara. I just wanted to get back to you. I woulda fought through a hundred of them to make it back to you."

She pressed his hand to her cheek. "Noah, I don't ever want to let you go."

Noah smiled, coveting her words. "That's sorta what I was hoping."

83

The last of the leaves dropped from the trees. The crisp fall air receded into the biting frosts of early winter. The year would soon end, and 1929 would become a memory. For locals, the shockwave of scandal in Dunnigan was far more palpable than the death spiral of distant Wall Street.

The misdeeds of Ransom Cahill and his cohorts rocked the political and social circles of Central Alabama. Lives changed forever as the chips fell here and there, none more than his own. His struggle for independence became a type of confinement and kept him from seeing all of the angles. He had been too foolish to understand that the Mr. Messinas and Silver Dollar Sams of the world rarely bore the brunt when the law caught up with some minor player in their intricate schemes. He was only a pawn sacrificed in the ugly, crooked game. Selfishness and greed left the entire Cahill family in ruins. With the hands of Edward and Charlotte tied, Ransom was left to bear the consequences of his actions.

Noah mended quickly after facing off with Ransom and his cadre of hoodlums. He returned to his work with Mr. Haskins as soon as he recovered. Losing Thomas had taught him that sometimes one is forced to choose between something that jeopardizes those they love and the sense of loss that comes with letting go. Motivated by the prospect of his future with Sara, he worked harder than ever. The two of them talked of the life they wished to have together, and he was determined to do his part to build it. His new dreams helped him to leave the pain of the past behind. She was his true love, and his first and last thoughts each day were of her safety and happiness.

The joy that Sara found was beyond her imagination. She was no stranger to trials and trouble, but Noah added something to her life that no one else could have. He gave her real love. It was the kind that asked nothing in return. It was able to bear the weight of all her insecurities and give her strength. Most of all, his love gave her hope. The moments of fear that brought her to her knees had also been opportunities for her to summon the strength she never knew she had. With the knowledge of life's peaks and valleys, Sara determined never to take anything for granted, least of all the people she loved.

Jenna Cossey

Acknowledgments

I first want to thank my mother and father. My childhood was a fantastic one in which I could dream, imagine, and play. It fueled my creative spirit, and they always supported that. They also instilled within me the ability to see a task through which has come in quite handy during this project. Familial bonds are central to this story, and, along that line, I want to express my deep love and appreciation to my immediate family. I thank each of you from the depths of my heart and love you beyond words.

Though the seeds for this novel were planted many years ago as I listened to my grandmother talk about her childhood, the real catalyst for my headlong leap into novel writing came in the fall of 2019 after hearing one of my favorite authors speak. I was so inspired, and I uttered a crazy dream out loud, "One day, I'd like to write a book." A lifelong friend (and coincidentally my cousin) was with me, and she challenged me to get started, do some research, set deadlines, and see where it took me. I accepted that challenge, and life has never been the same! Thank you, June Fann, for encouraging me to push the creative side of my brain.

Listening first hand to stories that occurred almost a century ago is a rare privilege, but I was able to do that during my research. Three special people enriched my research and inspired me immensely during the writing process. Though some are no longer with us, I would like to acknowledge their contributions to this work, Mrs. Mae Reid Hyden, Mr. Eules Cossey, and Mrs. Louella Martin Pyle. This story would have been a very different one without their valuable insight.

I started my research in 2019, and so many people assisted me in that regard. On a whim, and due to a random tidbit I came across, I visited the Blount County Historical Society in Oneonta, Alabama. As I made that drive, I knew my characters would have their homes in that general region. The individuals at the BCHS were most helpful, and I want to offer my sincere thanks to them. I left with my pen on fire. That is the way *Dunnigan* was really born.

Several people answered my seemingly endless questions, endured the reading of early manuscripts, advised me, and encouraged me. I reached out to different people in the writing community, essentially asking for tips and tricks of the trade. My inquiries never returned to me void. I am thankful to the very gifted writers who shared their talents with me. I am grateful for all of the feedback and advice I received from the developmental phase through the very end of the project. I found a marvelous group of people to proofread the final product before going to press. I want to thank them for reading with red pen in hand, dog-earing the necessary pages, and sharing their reading experience with me. Many people helped me bring this book to the finish line.

Lastly, I want to thank all who may take the time to read this story. Without readers, it would never truly have a life of its own. I hope this book touches and teaches the hearts and minds of all who read it.

www.ingramcontent.com/pod-product-compliance
Lightning Source LLC
Chambersburg PA
CBHW050903130726
47900CB00015B/1900